UNFOLDING

PRAISE FOR *UNFOLDING*

'On the surface, Rahul Singh's *Unfolding* is a brilliant portrait of love, desire and overlapping relationships, but at its core, it is an extraordinary depiction of conjugal loneliness and how people hold on to the slimmest of hopes to perennially resuscitate a dead relationship.'

—Aruni Kashyap

'[Here is a novel that] speaks of contraband love, yearning for familial approval, society-sanctioned definitions of relationships, and the chasm between classes. *Unfolding* is brave and heartbreaking in equal measure.'

—Hansda Sowvendra Shekhar

'[Rahul Singh's] *Unfolding* provides a much-needed exploration of contemporary queer relationships in India. Important and timely.'

—Daisy Rockwell

'Deftly, humanely, Rahul Singh portrays love in its universal recognizability, reminding us, too, that love is strange because it's indistinguishable from the foibles of individuality and sexuality. In this enlivening novel, Singh is nothing if not sympathetic to love's unpredictability.'

—Amit Chaudhuri

UNFOLDING

a novel

RAHUL SINGH

HarperCollins *Publishers* India

First published in India by HarperCollins *Publishers* 2026
HarperCollins *Publishers* India, Cyber City,
Building 10-A, Gurugram, Haryana – 122002, India
www.harpercollins.co.in

2 4 6 8 10 9 7 5 3 1

P-ISBN: 978-93-6569-368-3
E-ISBN: 978-93-6569-383-6

Typeset in 11/14.7 Sabon LT Std
by HarperCollins *Publishers* India Pvt. Ltd

Printed and bound at
Nutech Print Services Pvt. Ltd.

This book is printed on FSC® certified paper
which ensures responsible forest management.

HarperCollins *Publishers*, Macken House, 39/40 Mayor Street Upper,
Dublin 1, D01 C9W8, Ireland

'How plotless real life was! In novels, events led up to something.'

—Anne Tyler, *Dinner at the Homesick Restaurant*

'So when I think of autumn, I think of somebody with hands who does not want me to die.'

—Toni Morrison, *The Bluest Eye*

SUMMER

2019

1

The espresso tasted sharp on their lips. The whisk rattled against the sides of the enamel bowl. Drops of vanilla fell like paint. Then the oven swallowed the cake tin.

The year was 2004. Ralph was eighteen. He was awaiting admission to a hotel school. His mother had brewed strong black coffee that had cooled. They discussed the different kinds of beans that would add more flavour to the coffee-almond sponge sitting on the baking rack. Ralph had grown up helping his mother with mixing the batter, lining the tin, preparing butter cream frosting and, finally, pressing a handful of strawberries into the middle of the cake. Empty coffee mugs were scattered in the basin. Ralph's mother placed the sponge on the icing turntable. She was ladling silky beige frosting into a piping bag while Ralph dried the edge of the metal spatula with a cloth. His mother scooped a layer of frosting like a ball of snow and laid it on to the scraped surface of the sponge. The two of them laughed as the cake spun on the turntable.

That was then.

Now, Ojas said, 'We need to go home, come on. It's late.' Ralph trailed behind, dimly aware of the drinks circling in his body. He ignored the bar they had been at. He preferred to avoid alcohol because of its ability to dispossess him of the world he was in—where his mother was dead to cancer and he was a thirty-three-year-old pastry chef at a hotel.

The road turned quiet—a tranquillity disrupted by the cars flashing by. Ojas was tapping his phone, trying to book a cab. Ralph tiptoed forward and leaned against a stump to see an empty Ballygunge Phari—a rare sight. One of the busiest intersections of Kolkata, its crisscrossing roads brimmed over with buses, trams and people all day. At 3 a.m., it stood motionless, unclothed—a streak of vulnerability that the city often hid. A yellow taxi stopped a little ahead of Ralph. Ojas came forward and asked, 'Tangra?'

The driver tilted his head back to invite them in. The cab drove through Park Circus, and they said their goodbyes to the night, holding each other's hand as a fresh summer morning drew closer to the skies.

At home—Ralph's home, where Ojas stayed for a weekend or so—they got into bed, kissing. Ojas fell asleep instantly, but Ralph remained awake thinking about the texts Ojas had been getting when they were at the bar. His mind, soaked with chilled beer, recalled Ojas's grin upon receiving the texts. The excitement he didn't bother hiding made Ralph feel dreadful.

He ran to the washroom. The chicken, the fried rice, the burnt taste of several cigarettes, the yellow beer—they rushed out and drained into the commode, where he often sat and contemplated his relationship with Ojas, besides the youth that was ebbing away, the arduous way into the thirties, and the need for a home—a home in a man. Here, in the bathroom, at the commode, he would go back to Ojas's words and the new form their relationship had assumed.

He scuttled to the kitchen. In this two-bedroom flat, where each room was a step away, he had built a haven, one that was his, where his everyday triumphs and struggles settled and he knew ease. As he drank water out of the fridge, he saw a series of images unfold in the refrigerator light. His mother's giggling. His friend Sujoy's protective scolding when Ralph said something offensive. The compliments on Ralph's Beef Wellington by guests at the hotel. Ojas's soft kissing. He remembered all of this when the present seemed unendurable. The tumult of seeing Ojas choose others over him, and not having Maa by his side.

He finished the whole bottle of water, then released a loud burp, the faint taste of vomit biting the back of his throat. Taking another bottle, he moved to the sink and poured cold water over his face, while ensuring that his T-shirt did not get drenched. He stood there, holding the edges of the sink between his hands, staring at the wall ahead. The refrigerator beeped, disturbing the eerie silence. He let it beep for ten seconds before he shut its door.

On the bed, he watched the rising roundness of Ojas's stomach. Peace began mantling Ralph's body. The speakers outside their home crackled. A man's voice recited the morning prayers in Arabic. He lay down beside Ojas, feeling the same softness of the nipples he had once known. Ralph began tumbling down a hole of memories; of chopping walnuts on a worn-out board, zesting an orange rind into a chipped ceramic bowl, tossing apple slices into a pan of melted sugar, and waiting with his mother over tea to let the brownie, the slab of orange chocolate and the apple pie cool. How he hated waiting for his desserts to cool, especially after his mother died. She wasn't there to offer him tips on how to get the temperature right, inquire after the book Sujoy was reading, or ask Ralph about the boy he was seeing at that time. In his sleep, he held Ojas tighter.

It was his day off. At 10 a.m., the help, Zubina, rang the bell. Ralph rose and walked through the narrow doorway into the living room that was flushed with sunlight pouring in from the balcony. He squeezed his eyes against the blinding light and drew the curtain over the big glass door, almost pulling it off the hook. He used the marble top of the credenza by the wall as support to stand straight as he opened the door.

Zubina slipped inside the flat without a word and marched straight to the kitchen, where she would begin preparations for breakfast. She knew her way around the flat, having worked there for almost two years now. She had got used to Ralph's kitchen after several mistakes and mishaps. In the beginning, she had had a tough time distinguishing between cocoa powder and the exotic instant coffee Ralph would order online. Later, she understood that those tall glass jars filled with wheat-coloured sticks were some form of pasta and not some thicker version of sevai or chow mein. Earlier in January, with the help of both Ralph and his so-called friend, Ojas, she had divided the kitchen pantry in two halves. One side housed the salt, sugar, tea, flour and spices she could toss in without any measuring spoon. The other side contained those ingredients that were still alien to her. She was ready to learn how to use them in her cooking—so, Ralph had taught her that a hint of vanilla could flavour kheer deliciously and that a sprig of fresh basil and dill could elevate the taste of steamed rice when it was cooked. Ralph and his friend Ojas, whom she saw stay over some weekends, loved the gola ruti she'd make for them on Sunday mornings. The rutis were a splendid substitute for Ralph's sweet pancakes. Ojas loved them. He would tell her that he could eat it all day and not be bored of it.

Zubina prepared tea for Ralph, unaware that Ojas was home. She put the cup on a tray with a disc of digestive biscuit and carried it to his room. The door was ajar, so she entered unannounced, but stopped after seeing the bed where the two men were fast asleep. Ralph was sleeping on his side, facing the door. With no space between them, she noticed Ojas's arms coiled around Ralph. Ojas slept with no T-shirt. He was breathing on Ralph's neck. His lips quivering. She was about to leave, when Ralph opened his eyes, swatting Ojas's arm away from him. He sat upright, staring at her wide-eyed, taking a deep breath and gesturing that she keep the tray. She set it down, averting her gaze from Ojas's bare chest, and left without making her presence felt.

Taking the cup in his hand, Ralph thought about the scene Zubina had witnessed. In the mirror, he noticed the sleep still heavy in his eyes. All this time, he had ensured that she had never seen him being intimate with Ojas when he stayed over. Once, she had rung the bell when both of them had just woken up with their morning erections and Ralph had gone down on Ojas's crotch. They had to stop midway. Ojas moved to the other room, the guest room where Ralph's friends or father came to stay every now and then.

Ralph whispered to his reflection in the mirror, 'I won't mention it to her. There's no need to.'

Ojas stirred in the bed, searching for Ralph with his hands.

Ralph sipped his tea, now cold, and put it back on the tray. He moved to Ojas's side of the bed and said, 'We almost got in trouble. You were holding me and sleeping, and Zubina-di walked into the room.'

Ojas drew Ralph's face to his and kissed him. Ralph tore himself away from the kiss. 'Let's brush and have breakfast.'

Ojas murmured, 'Yes, baby.'

'Right,' Ralph said and moved to the bathroom. Ojas joined him at the washbasin in his trunks. They inspected each other in the mirror as they brushed their teeth, and Ojas winked at him with a smile, as though he were reminding him of the love they had built over the last year-and-a-half.

Ralph and Ojas had met at Ralph's workplace when Ojas had gone to taste desserts for a business conference that was to be held there. Ralph had been followed by his juniors, who carried plates of chocolate mousse and other pastries. It was the chocolate mousse garnished with raspberry that had brought them together. Ojas had put the spoon down and said, 'This is the best mousse I have ever tasted.' Ralph had thanked him and offered to pack one for home.

The next day, when the business conference was in full swing, Ojas had stepped out and found Ralph smoking a cigarette. Ralph held one out for him. Ojas asked, lighting it, 'You like working here?'

Ralph shrugged. 'I do. I have always loved being in the kitchen.'

'I wish I had such a love, too, for something ...' Ojas stopped, considering his words, and then he completed his sentence, '... something I was so passionate about that I would want to pursue it as a career.' He released a light chuckle after saying that.

'We all have such interests. I am sure you do as well.' Ralph paused and then asked after a moment's silence passed between them, 'What kind of business do you run?'

'Textiles, it's my father's. I am managing most of it and ... uh ... I think I like it.' Ojas realized he had to continue, so he went on, 'But it's exhausting when everything is on your shoulders ... managing office, organizing such conferences, blah-blah.'

Ralph looked from Ojas to the leafy bushes before which they stood. He was moved by the soft roughness of his face. The beard trimmed and shaped well. The aquiline nose that had a mole on the left side. The thick lashes that quivered when he blinked. Ojas had felt Ralph's eyes on him and he passed him a quizzical glance.

With some courage, Ralph suggested, 'Anytime you wish to take a break and fancy a chocolate mousse or coffee, feel free to drop by. It'll be on the house.'

Ojas was surprised. 'Sure, thanks, Mr ...' His eyes fell on the stitched-in nametag and he completed, '... Mr Ralph.'

'You're welcome, Mr Garg. I hope you have a successful conference.'

With that, they left, stubbing the ends of their cigarettes in the metal dish of the garbage can.

Ojas wore his clothes and headed to the kitchen for a cup of tea, leaving Ralph alone in the washroom. Ralph was repulsed by Ojas's constant dismissal, as though he couldn't see how much he hurt Ralph with every conversation he had with other men. Ralph latched the door and began undressing himself. Under the shower, he let a jet of water rain down on his body. He picked up the loofah and squeezed a blob of body wash on to it. As he lathered his chest, he felt the increasing layers of fat around his stomach. He wondered if this was why Ojas wanted to seek other men. He bent down and scrubbed the back of his thighs, staring at his buttocks in the mirror. They were not as arched or shapely as they had once been. He bent further and cleaned his calves that were matted with hair, his thick ankles, and the space between his toes, until he was scrubbing the tiles on which he stood. Didn't Ojas obsess over his body all day when they were beginning to get fond of each other? The water began washing the suds off his broad and thick shoulders. His chest growing a pair of grizzly pouches on the two sides. His shaven crotch resembling a half-opened walnut. And his legs—they were not tall enough to make up for the weight distributed around his body. He splashed water on his face and scrubbed it hard with a facewash to remove the dark circles, the patches of acne scars across his cheeks, the stubble which he wasn't allowed to grow into a beard because of his job. In his youth, his mother and his friends would tell him about the possibilities he had waiting for him because of his body. People often told him that he had a faint resemblance to a male version of Julia Roberts. He would laugh at that and find it ridiculous—laugh with his wide mouth, pointed nose and playful eyes. What a horror to age, he thought, as he dried his body with the towel. From Julia Roberts's doppelgänger to this ridiculous disproportionately-shaped dolt. He wished Ojas would simply leave him and find someone else. At least that would let him grieve in silence.

'What year is it?' Ojas asked, as they sat down to eat their breakfast.

'Huh? It is 2019. Where are you?' Ralph said, tearing the gola ruti with his knife and fork. He was rather displeased with the morning by now and wanted Ojas gone.

'According to the Bengali calender, I meant. Today is Bengali New Year,' Ojas rolled his eyes at him. 'You should know better, shouldn't you?'

'Hah, right!' Ralph paused, then said, 'Well, Baba said it is 1426.' He chewed his breakfast without meeting Ojas's eyes.

'So weird, isn't it? Living in two different centuries at the same time.'

Ralph wanted to say it wasn't. That they lived in different worlds. There was Ralph's world which comprised Ojas in-and-out, exclusively. And there was Ojas's world which liked the idea of transgressing all that Ralph held sacred. Their worlds had stopped being the same many months ago when Ojas had chosen to want something different.

Before Ralph could reply, Zubina entered offering more rutis. She paused, regarding them as they ate.

Ralph felt a discomfort grow in him and cleared his throat

to send her off, but Zubina said, 'Today is a day to be with your family. Why are both of you here in such gloomy mood?'

'It's not a big day, Zubina-di,' Ralph replied. 'Though my mother, if she had been around, would have been busy making elaborate meals.'

'That's what I mean. Praying to god and eating nice food with family. Why are both of you sitting here all alone?'

Ralph and Ojas did not respond to her. She said, 'Well, I have cooked chicken with your spices from the hotel.'

Ralph nodded. 'Sure, Zubina-di, thank you.'

Her gaze rested on Ojas. 'Paneer is also there for you.'

Ojas thanked her and they resumed eating. Zubina waited, took the empty plate and strode to the kitchen, murmuring to herself.

Ojas observed Ralph's reluctance to continue with their conversation. When they fought, he let Ralph win and ended up apologizing even when he knew Ralph was at fault. Unlike Ralph, he liked the silence of being together and watching a film, visiting a park, eating at a restaurant or buying clothes and shoes. He failed to understand how people could sit and talk for hours, especially to those they had known all their lives or to those they'd meet every day. The last time Ojas had spoken to him at length was four months ago. He had tried to explain to Ralph why he wanted to open their relationship.

'I know we are a little over a year into our relationship, baby,' Ojas began. 'I know it's too soon to ask for this, but I think I want to talk about it.'

Ralph listened to him, helplessness spreading over his face.

Ojas continued, 'We can try opening it, you know. I am not saying this is going to be a forever type of situation for us, but we can give it a shot and see if it works?'

'Why do we have to do it at all? We have a good sex life. We have a steady relationship, don't we?' Ralph asked, holding back his tears.

'Yes, we do. I am not denying that. I feel ...' Ojas stopped to think. He was nervous about saying it aloud. He didn't know how to communicate it to someone other than himself. He said, 'I feel I am ageing. I am already thirty-nine and I see a future with you and I want to be with you. But I don't want to box myself in just yet. Do you understand what I am saying? I know you feel the same way. You know you want this as well ... don't you?'

Ralph expelled a mocking laugh. 'So, this relationship is a box for you? Ojas ... no ... I don't want what you want. And seriously ... you are only fucking thirty-nine, that's barely an age to feel that you are ageing. Age looks better on you than on me.'

'My body is getting old, Ralph! Look at me, I am losing all shape. And I don't have the time to change when I have to manage a goddamn business.'

'But you will have the time to sleep with other men, right?' Ralph retorted. 'And as for your body, it is perfect. I love it as much as I did the first time I set my eyes on you. There is nothing wrong.'

'I don't want to explain things further if you are going to be such an asshole when I am opening up to you.'

'Ojas, for once, stop thinking of ... of getting back at me. We will fucking lose ourselves in this,' Ralph gestured to the air around him with his hands. He rarely felt this helpless.

'Ralph, I want to sleep with other men, but that does not mean I don't want to be with *you*. All I ask is that we give it a try. Please, just once ...' With that, Ojas left the flat.

For a week, they didn't mention the topic. Until Ojas brought it up again and Ralph concurred—he'd give it a shot.

He wanted to scream at Ojas that their path to ruin had begun. But when he tried … what could he say, after all?

Ralph's reserve at the breakfast table unsettled Ojas. As much as he liked silence, this was the kind that Ojas detested—the kind that carried the shadow of closeted anger, unspoken complaints and misgivings.

Ralph and Ojas had begun sharing silences of this kind more often now.

When Zubina left after preparing lunch and cleaning the rooms, Ralph retired to the couch in the living room. He turned on Netflix and waited for Ojas to get done with his call. Ojas said over the phone, 'Today is Bengali New Year, it's a holiday. You don't have to work yourself crazy. It's your festival, Dharu-da.'

Ralph smiled to himself, hearing Ojas speak Bengali. He could sense the effort, the pauses to avert the possibility of a mistake, to appear fluent after having lived in this city since birth. Between themselves, they mostly spoke a mix of Hindi and English. Ojas refused to speak in Bengali to Ralph, even when Ralph had tried a number of times to begin a conversation in the language. Later, when Ralph pointed this out, Ojas blushed and said, 'I can't speak.' And Ralph replied, 'But you do so well with your staff.' Ojas only shook his head and got back to what he was doing.

Ojas disconnected his call and asked Ralph, 'You aren't meeting your father?'

Ralph said a no while fiddling with the remote. 'I called him. He said he'd like to rest.'

'Right. So, what are we watching?'

'We will finish this season of *Schitt's Creek*.'

'Okay, but first … you come here,' Ojas said, extending his hands, inviting Ralph for a hug.

Ralph demurred but finally entered the folds of his arms. Ojas kissed his forehead and said, 'At the bar last night, I got a text from Divya. She's getting married.'

'Why didn't you tell me? I haven't congratulated her,' said Ralph. He smiled with relief.

'You were too drunk. And you were talking to me about the last caramel custard you fed your mother, and then you went back to the year 2004 … when you were making some coffee cake with her.'

'Hm,' Ralph mumbled.

'Shubho Noboborsho, baby,' whispered Ojas.

Ralph chuckled. 'Shubho Noboborsho.'

Ralph was happy to be in this place he had created for himself. There was little to ask of life since his mother had died. He had been lonely and anguished until he moved out of the house in Alipore. In the large, spacious kitchen, her breath still lingered across his face, making cooking impossible. He couldn't face the whisks, the mixing bowls and the padded gloves, where his mother's fingerprints had been etched permanently. Ralph had felt soothed when he had first entered this flat, in a neighbourhood sprawling with Chinese restaurants, temples, small masjids and factories producing all kinds of sauces.

But grief crept in without a warning.

Ojas entered right then. The man who replaced grief with his love, his care; in whose arms Ralph nestled when the world seemed insensitive. The discontentment seemed to disappear when he heard Ojas's reassurances, when he felt he was all that mattered.

When Ojas went to take a piss after an episode of *Schitt's Creek*, Ralph noticed two messages on his WhatsApp. One from the fifth floor-man Ralph had hooked up with when Ojas had decided to open the relationship. The other from Sujoy, who wrote, 'Need to talk about something important. It's urgent, Ralph!'

2

Two shrill voices rose in frenzied unison. Zubina's house in the slum neighbourhood of Topsia had turned into a school where two classes were being held without a partition separating them.

'Tomorrow, all ... all ... of you bring chocolates for Soniya because she has been a good girl,' one said in broken English to an imaginary class of attentive students.

'Children, if you don't do your homework, I will make you stand in the blazing sun outside the principal's office,' the other scolded in Bengali.

Suddenly, the door banged, and Amrin and Soniya heard their mother bellow, 'Open the door, will you?'

The girls stared at each other in horror. They picked up the scrap of cloth, wiped the wall haphazardly and opened the door. Zubina strode inside coughing for breath, 'Why do you keep this house locked? Come on, open that window and let the air come in.'

She sat on the chowki that stood on three layers of brick. She tilted her head up to the fan attached to the dank ceiling and let the fan dry her sweat. The cobwebbed, patchwork corners of the ceiling cried for repair before the rains.

Her elder daughter Amrin, all of eleven, who taught in Bengali, knelt down and scurried under the bed to fetch a bottle of water. As Zubina finished drinking and put the deflated Coke bottle aside, she asked, 'Did you cook rice?'

Amrin replied, 'Even dal, did you get anything to eat them with?'

Her mother passed her the plastic bag she carried and said, 'Here, chicken curry. You start eating and feed your sister too.'

She saw the two sit in front of the door as the curtain rustled against her younger daughter, Soniya. They were watching the television that was perched on top of the almirah. A cartoon of Hindi-speaking cockroaches played as the girls licked their plates clean.

Zubina dozed off.

She startled awake when she heard a steel glass hit the floor. She scanned the house. 'What happened? What fell down?'

Amrin spat at Soniya, 'This idiot kicked my glass of water because her eyes were glued to the TV.'

Seven-year-old Soniya eyed her sister with nostrils flared. 'I didn't see and you had kept the glass too close to me.'

Zubina grabbed the scrap of cloth the girls had used as a duster for their blackboard and wiped the water away. She noticed tiny rivulets of chalk trail down the wall. She turned to the girls. 'Have you two started writing on the wall again?'

The girls sat still and expressionless. Amrin muttered, 'No, we haven't.'

Her mother pointed to the trail of white. 'What could this be then?'

Amrin said, 'Oh, that … that is …'

'Ammi, that's powder, talcum powder. I sprinkled it because the house was smelling awful!' Soniya saved them with a scrunched-up face; it added a dramatic effect to her attempts at hiding their crime. Amrin wanted to pat her sister for that.

Zubina enquired further. 'How is talcum powder going to change the smell?'

'Oh, I don't … well, I thought maybe it could,' whispered Soniya.

Zubina was about to touch the white flakes and sniff at them, when the curtain at the door parted and a cool breeze filled the house. Her husband was home.

'What is going on here?' Aadil came inside, kept a bag of vegetables on the stool wedged between the chowki and the almirah. Soniya tore into the bag and extracted her chocolate and offered Amrin hers. Their father never came home during lunch without a stick of chocolate or wafers for them.

Zubina mopped the floor again and said, 'Wash your hands, I will serve you lunch.'

Aadil splashed a mug of water on his face. The neighbourhood was alive. Children ran around—boys in Kolkata Knight Riders jerseys and girls in ribboned pigtails. Carts filled with trash or goods from the mini shoe factory were being pushed aside. The sun beat down on women who cooked meals outside their houses; beads of sweat dampened their faces. The dogs were asleep under vehicles or anything that offered shade. Aadil poured water on his ankles and cleaned his hands of the grime from the leather factory.

The television screen was now playing Sridevi's *Judaai*, one of Zubina's favourite films. She sat beside her husband on the mat and gazed at the screen. Amrin and Soniya were on the bed, tittering between themselves over TikTok. Despite the heat that made the simple act of sitting and watching the TV screen unbearable, there was joy in this moment, smack in the middle of the day. Her girls were home from school. Food was cooked. Half the day's work was done. And her husband was right next to her. They would talk a little and then perhaps doze off before the evening prayers.

'Do you like the chicken curry?' Zubina asked her husband when the ads began.

'It's tastier and different, yes.'

She collected the fallen grains of rice and answered with pride, 'I used one of those spice-mix powders they use in big hotels.'

'This is from that Christian man's house?' Aadil asked, then clicked his tongue. 'Zubina, he must be eating pigs. Why do you do this? I have told you not to serve me food from his kitchen.'

'Keep quiet and eat. I know what I am doing, and I fear god as well.'

Aadil rolled his eyes and scarfed down his meal. Zubina said, 'Today I saw that friend of his in his bed.'

Her husband moved his head and bit the chicken. She eyed him with anticipation and continued, 'He was not wearing a shirt.'

He stopped eating. 'Do you go there to watch men naked?'

She held his arm. 'Lower your voice, the girls are still awake.'

He pushed her hand away and drank the remaining gravy as though it were water. 'He must have been a friend who was just sleeping. There's nothing wrong. Your brother and his friend used to sleep on the same mat, wearing only lungis.'

'They did that because they didn't have a flat with two AC rooms,' stated Zubina, surly.

She took his empty plate and washed the dishes at the door. Zubina scrubbed the steel plates, as her bangles clanged against them. She muttered to herself and admonished Aadil for crushing every curious thought of hers with idle talk. Zubina had seen enough, she told herself, to know that things weren't as they appeared. Her nails dug into the green dishwash bar. She turned the plastic soap dish upside down to drain the foamy water it held into the bowl from which Aadil had slurped the gravy. Bubbles, water and mushy grains of rice squelched between her fingers.

She had often seen Aadil hold his friend's hand on their way to work when they were newly married. She had never paid close attention to it. They were men, after all, who had known each other since childhood. The lanes of this neighbourhood were their playground, where every nook and cranny had certain markers, drawn on the walls or carved into the metal cart that hadn't moved for more than thirty years. She thought of the Indian flag that Aadil and his friend had tied on a tall bamboo pole on Independence Day—they were fifteen then. Aadil had told her about it when she had first come to the neighbourhood as his bride. Twelve years ago, they had the one-room tenement only to themselves. Aadil had come out of nowhere and claimed her. She didn't know what marriage was or what being a spouse meant. She had moved in and made a home of this house.

Every now and then, she wondered what Aadil meant to her besides being her children's father and her chosen husband.

Still, she had never seen Aadil sleep with his childhood friend the way she had seen Ralph sleep with Ojas. Or perhaps he had slept with his friend, when his siblings would crowd the house and leave no room for him to rest. She was thinking too much; she chastised herself. Maybe Ralph and Ojas were merely close friends.

Her husband and daughters were fast asleep. Without making a noise, she turned off the television and ate her meal. After that, she fixed her husband's shirt, torn at the armpits. Cacophony from the slum slackened at this time of the day. She let the unnecessary thoughts crowding her consciousness slip away. Ralph and Ojas were not her business. What they did and how they lived was not up to her to decide. God was watching and he'd make things right. It didn't matter what Aadil meant or didn't mean to her so long as he was a good husband and a better father. Which he was and always had been, according to Zubina. She hummed a quiet tune and stitched until she couldn't keep her eyes open. She fell asleep on the mat. Oh, how she enjoyed an afternoon siesta!

Aadil got ready to leave for his evening prayers. He hurried toward the masjid on Raicharan Lane. Zubina covered her head and kneeled when the prayers from the speaker filled the neighbourhood. The harsh sun had waned, the squabbles outside were quieter and the call for prayer was gratifying. When she opened her eyes, she saw her daughters were awake.

Amrin stuffed her bag with two notebooks and pencil boxes. She tidied herself, first by parting her hair, then by fixing it with a clip of purple ribbons that dangled across her curls. Soniya tried snatching it off her, but Amrin shoved her hand away with a glare.

'Neha-di was wearing the same one,' she said with pride.

'Neha will scold you if you don't get there quick!' Zubina reminded the girls of their evening tuitions.

'Oh, she loves me,' declared Amrin, as she cleaned her red slippers.

'No, she doesn't,' Soniya retorted and applied a generous amount of her mother's discarded blush across her cheeks. Her face came alive with two round cherry-red discs.

Zubina took the end of her dupatta and scrubbed off the blush until it got faint. Soniya frowned at her mother and toyed with a lipstick she had stashed in her schoolbag. Zubina asked Amrin if she could speak English better.

Amrin stopped focusing on the gaudy slippers.

The memory of Neha-di keeping her phone aside flashed in her mind; she had said, 'Two sentences, Amrin! How long does it take? Haven't I taught you the basics of writing and forming sentences in English? You say you want to learn English, but how will you learn if you work at a snail's pace?'

Amrin recovered from the disappointment of the last class and said, 'Yes, I can. A test will be there soon, and I am studying very hard for it, Ammi.'

'I will not walk from the kabristaan side,' Soniya interjected. Her lips glowed a hot pink shade.

'Why would you take the longer route?' asked Zubina.

'Because of her!' Soniya pointed at Amrin. 'She tells us stories of djinns in the class and then takes me there ... I get so scared.' Soniya looked miffed, then inspected her cheeks in the mirror. She pinched them to get the cherry hue back and dabbed some of the lipstick off her lips and onto her cheeks.

Amrin's face fell. Zubina waited for an explanation. Amrin cleared her throat and told the story she had said to Soniya and her friends at the tutorial some days ago. 'I sleep at night and I feel somebody is calling me from the kabristaan.'

Soniya ran to her mother at the mention of graveyard.

'I ask, "Who is calling me?" And it tells me, "I am Djinn!"' Amrin mimicked in a roaring voice. '"I have come to take you to jannat." And I tell him to take his jannat away. I need to learn English properly to ask god in jannat for all my wishes.'

'And then?' Zubina asked.

'Oh, he goes away,' Amrin motioned with her hand, 'like ... whoosh. And I am back to sleeping on my bed.'

Zubina drew out two five-rupee coins—one for Amrin and the other for Soniya. She said, 'Talking about these things is not a joke. Djinns are real and can cause harm!' Zubina looked pointedly at Amrin. 'Why do you want to scare her?'

Amrin said, 'I ... I don't ...'

Before she could complete her sentence, Zubina said, 'Now hurry, or you will be late. Don't talk about djinns'

As they went off, she saw Amrin scowl at Soniya for speaking over her; she wouldn't give her any money if Soniya didn't learn the art of silence.

Zubina returned to the mirror and dabbed her face with a rose-scented cream. She muttered a prayer to Allah for her girls and sought forgiveness on their behalf.

She combed her hair, wrapped a dupatta over her head, put the empty lunch boxes in a packet and then locked the door behind her.

It was time for her evening shift. She didn't have much work that day as Ralph had wanted to cook for himself. She walked through the maze that was the slum, smiling occasionally at the women whose weddings she had once attended, or whose family drama had entertained the entire neighbourhood, or who were her dearest friends. There, sitting on the steps, was the lady who stitched blouses and salwars, and whose son was once jailed for theft. Zubina smiled at her. In the shop beside her house, she saw Nazma selling bidis to an old man. She tried to catch her attention, but Nazma was far too preoccupied rolling a bidi to notice her. At the stall a few houses away from Nazma, the rich aroma of chicken being deep-fried wafted out. Sona was warding off the stray dogs with her ladle dripping with hot oil. A white cat with grey eyes stood motionless on the tin roof of the stall and observed a line of fat rats crawl.

Zubina adjusted her dupatta, walked on, and greeted the oldest lady in the neighbourhood, whose age nobody knew; she was sitting in the open, wearing a nightie. It seemed as though she was waiting for someone. Zubina rushed past her; she was now tut-tutting at the dogs barking at two mating lizards on a wall beyond their reach.

These were some of the women in whose company Zubina had found succour when she had come to the neighbourhood twelve years ago. She knew so much of the world around her because of them. The evenings when there was no electricity, the scorching afternoons when the children were away at school—these hours brought them together. When someone complained of her drunken husband lolling his big cock at her face when she wanted to sleep, somebody else shut her up and pointed to his tiny stature. Snooty male employers were referred to as 'gandu'. Fair-skinned young girls of the neighbourhood who made repeated trips to the parlour were called 'Kareena Kapoor'. Young boys who danced around in playgrounds making TikTok videos were 'lawandas'. Money was 'maal'. Zubina had grown used to this litany of words. They connoted friendship, or sisterhood, to her.

Yes … friendship.

And then, there was Ralph who slept with a man without clothes and cooked dinner. She had never seen any friend of his other than Ojas. There was no woman who could be his fiancée. Ralph did all the wifely duties—washing, cooking and drying clothes by himself. There are men of such making, for sure, but Ralph couldn't be a wife to that friend Ojas, now, could he? No, no. She sighed and pitied Ralph's sad life. She wouldn't be able to survive with only one friend. All her friends were indispensable. She resolved to be nicer to Ralph the next time she went to his house. She would also observe them closely. Perhaps.

She arrived at the fourteenth floor and rang the bell. This was her husband's employer's apartment. How many times she had been reminded to ring the bell, never to knock. Finally, she had grown used to it.

She left after completing her tasks and headed to the next place of work. She smiled to herself, wondering if Aadil was nothing but her closest friend. The most intimate one.

Issh, she said, as she cleaned the sink of the remains of food, waste and dirty water. Friendship is different. Friends don't become parents.

3

Ralph returned to his station, peering over the long vanilla sponge sheets that were being rubbed with sugar syrup. 'Careful, it's still delicate,' he told one of the young trainees. On the opposite side of the kitchen, almonds and cashew nuts were being tossed into the toffee sauce. Popping a coated almond into his mouth, Ralph studied the hands of the trainee as he stirred the nuts in. The almond split between Ralph's teeth and the taste of the warm toffee filled his mouth. He patted the counter—'Good!'—and walked over to the other side where Sujoy was sprinkling chocolate shavings on layers of sponge cake, glued together with cold whipped cream. Ralph said, 'I will get the cherries.'

'That will be a huge favour,' Sujoy said.

Ralph placed the box of cherries before him. 'Now, tell me what has happened? What was that message about?'

Sujoy scraped the excess whipped cream into a bowl. He paused to consider his response, then asked, 'Umm … how is it for you and Ojas?'

'How is what like?'

'Opening a relationship,' said Sujoy.

Ralph felt as though he had been punched in his stomach; he was unable to breathe or form words.

'Sayantani is asking me to try and open the relationship,' Sujoy said.

'Okay, and?'

Sujoy shrugged. 'And I don't know, Ralph. I don't know if I would be comfortable with the idea of her sleeping with someone else.'

'Right.'

'And I don't want to lose her, you know. Like, I really love her and I want her to be happy.'

'Okay.'

'You and Ojas seem to be having a smooth open relationship, so I wanted to ask you … what's it like?'

Ralph felt violated … but this was Sujoy. He recovered. 'Well, it's not easy. It isn't. But we are trying, you see.'

'Yes.' Sujoy waited.

'It's not always good. You feel hurt … but if it saves a relationship, maybe give it a try?' Ralph couldn't believe the words he was saying.

They had begun placing the cherries on the frosting. Ralph placed one at a time. Sujoy made each sit perfectly with the help of a tweezer.

Sujoy sighed. 'I hope so. I told her I need some time to think this through.'

'Yes, take your time,' Ralph said, searching for something else to offer.

Sujoy changed subjects. 'Anyway, you tell me. What's happening? Sorry I kept talking about myself.'

Ralph replied, 'The other day, Zubina-di saw me sleeping with Ojas.'

'What? And?' Sujoy had a look of surprise on his face; it resembled the excitement Ralph had seen him carrying as a child. Sujoy, his friend since seventh grade, had always been there with him, mostly listening, if not reading. He had dog-eared the page of *Memoirs of a Geisha* when Ralph had told him that he baked with his mother. Ralph believed that Sujoy would be like the boys who bullied him. Instead, Sujoy had asked, 'Will your mother teach me baking too? Can I come to your house?' Ralph still remembered the fear ebbing away as he spoke to Sujoy. Sujoy had added, 'My mother and I watch cooking shows together, but we don't have an oven. I can ask my mother if she will allow me to go to your house to learn.'

Sujoy began dropping by at Ralph's house every Sunday, where they'd wear colourful aprons and bake cookies, muffins and cupcakes with Ralph's mother. Sujoy continued reading his books and nursed the desire to someday write a novel of his own. But he chose to devote his professional life to being a chef. Ralph and Sujoy attended the same hotel school but were separated when they got placed in different cities. After eight years, they were back together, at one place, baking, decorating cakes, garnishing mousse with twigs of mint. Popping fresh blackberries into their mouths when no one was watching.

'Well, I have not broached it … buuuuuuut I think she has some thoughts.' Ralph stretched the sentence, thinking about Zubina's gaze in the bedroom.

'Hilarious. I want to meet her now and see what she thinks of the two gays she works for.'

'Let's get back to the batch of turnovers now, shall we?' said Ralph, pointing to the browned bacon-and-cheddar turnovers, releasing steam.

When his shift got over, Ralph hailed a cab and headed towards Hindustan Park. He kept re-reading the text from Ayub—'Want to meet soon? Come over, or I can come to yours. My flatmate's gone for a week.'

Ralph had slept with Ayub a month after Ojas's request to open their relationship. He hadn't wanted to. Ralph had been enjoying a dinner date with Ojas on a cosy January evening at his flat, when Ojas had admitted, 'I am meeting Raghav tomorrow.'

Ralph knew Raghav lusted after Ojas. He had fought with Ojas over Raghav's flirtatious comments against Ojas's pictures. Raghav was in his early twenties and that unsettled Ralph even more. He had debated asking Ojas if he was into younger men or if Ralph was too old for him. His gaze had fallen upon his belly, and he saw how it had changed since the last time he had considered it in his twenties. Looking at himself had never made him feel this weak before.

Ralph had nodded. 'Use protection.'

'Of course, I will.'

After sex with Raghav, Ojas seemed joyous and more willing to spoil Ralph by buying him clothes, taking him for long drives, and speaking of his desire to make a joint trip someday to the museums of Amsterdam and London. Ralph had the urge to clamp Ojas's mouth shut or cover his ears. Every word reminded him of Raghav's figure—his youthful energy. As Ojas prattled on about cheap planes to London, Ralph muttered to himself, 'Bitch in heat ...'

A week after that, Ralph had written to Ayub. He had asked Ralph out a couple of times whenever they had shared the lift or bumped into each other at the gate. Ayub called him over. They had sex. After sex, Ayub asked him if he liked it.

Ralph wore his clothes and forced a smile. 'I enjoyed it.'

Ayub drew close to kiss him. 'I just love your body. We should do it again.'

Ralph blushed. He was overjoyed; the dread that had beset him post-coitus slipped by when he heard how his body was still enjoyable to other men. That he wasn't too old.

But he moved away, saying, 'I am already with someone, Ayub.'

'Let's see how long that lasts,' Ayub snickered, removing a string of semen off Ralph's chin and forcing it between his lips.

Ralph flinched, pushing his hand away, and left the flat without caring to shut the door. Somewhere along the way, he had swallowed the semen.

The next day, he had mentioned Ayub to Ojas. Ojas said, not taking his eyes off the laptop, 'Okay. Did you use protection?'

Ralph was enraged. 'What does it matter, Ojas? We are now sleeping with other people. Not each other. I hope that makes you happy.'

He had done it to spite him, to make him feel bad, but Ojas showed no signs of discomfort. He kept working. As he lit a cigarette, Ralph wondered if Ojas's response was a curse on his post-hookup joy.

Maybe he deserved it, after all.

After reading Ayub's text one last time, Ralph deleted it and blocked him. He recalled the snicker.

Ojas was already sipping his coffee when Ralph entered the café. The coffee shops in Hindustan Park were teeming with people. Ralph wiped the sweat off his neck with a tissue as he sat down on the fluffy chair. Ojas passed the menu over and waited for him to place an order. Ralph said, catching his breath, 'I will take an iced tea.'

'How was your day?' Ojas asked.

'Usual,' said Ralph, slurping the drink, and then added, 'Sujoy made a delicious panna cotta today. The guests went crazy over it.'

'It's been so long since I have seen him. How has he been?'

'He is okay, I guess. A little distracted these days, is all.'

'Oh, okay,' Ojas said, taking a sip of his coffee. 'What happened?'

'It's Sayantani, this time,' Ralph said, staring at the glass of iced tea.

'Are they breaking up?' Ojas sounded worried. Nothing was more important to Ojas than seeing people around him find a partner and settle down with them. When he came to know that his close friend was marrying, he had jumped with joy in the bar, at ease that she wouldn't grow lonely or filled with rage. Years of loneliness, of being cheated on, of being told that he had to part, that long distance wasn't working anymore, that there was more to life than commitment in the twenties, had left Ojas praying for a partner, for a stable relationship that would outlive every setback.

Ralph tucked his head between his shoulders and said, 'No, she wants to open the relationship, and Sujoy isn't ready for it.'

Ralph was twisting the soiled tissue in his fingers, when Ojas said, 'Hmm.'

A long moment of silence extended between the two men as they waited for the other to say something.

Ojas leafed through the menu to pass time and asked, 'Has Zubina-di said anything?'

Ralph scanned the café as though he had forgotten what this was about, then recovered, 'Oh, that … no. I told Sujoy. He wanted to talk to her about it!'

'Oh, god!'

'Anyway, I'm sure she knows nothing about "gay" men. She is religious. And if she is uncomfortable and wishes to leave, she can.'

'If she asks you about what she witnessed, what will you say?' Ojas asked, jocosely.

'We're friends, what else? I can't be bothered with activism and building awareness.' Ralph was tired but was also glad that this conversation was sparking some excitement. 'Ojas …'

'Yes?'

'When will you tell your parents? Isn't that more important than telling Zubina-di?'

Ojas looked out at the neighbourhood from the glass doors. Evening had sauntered in; the sky was lit by the pink neon lights of the café's board. He considered the city by his side. It seemed to be relaxing after a rather torrid day. Ojas enjoyed the silence, or lyadh, as he learnt to call it in Bengali from Ralph. He was sharing the silence with the city and Ralph, until he realized that Ralph was waiting for an answer. He replied, 'I don't know. Let's walk. The weather is good.'

'Walk? Aren't you tired?'

'I need to be active. I am old, remember?' Ojas winked and sighed in mock embarrassment.

Ralph rolled his eyes and let Ojas pay the bill.

Outside, the scorching heat of the day was replaced by a gentler breeze. It was almost the end of April, time for Kalbaisaki. At 8th Day Café & Bakery, Ralph noticed a group of boys and girls sitting in the open and playing a song; the tunes from the strings of their guitar seemed to brighten the street. It reminded Ralph of his days learning the guitar at the hotel school in the city. Of the breaks he'd spend at the dosa stall outside the college, strumming a tune, talking about his professors and mentors, and voicing those looming concerns about placement—working at a hotel that'd pay well. He saw one of the young boys eye Ojas and him. A suppressed glee flitted across his face and he held Ojas by his arms. Ojas's sturdy frame made Ralph forget the dread that had upset him throughout the day. Here was his protection. This was why he had sought Ojas. He wanted to soak in the feeling for a while.

They had come close to the sombrely lit doors of Byloom Canteen when they heard a loud, rumbling noise. Ralph surveyed the sky through the leaves of the tree above them and saw a dazzling flash of lightning. The people on the street began running towards the cover offered by small buildings. Raindrops began dotting the cemented road. Ralph asked, 'Where's your car?'

Ojas pointed with his chin, 'Right ahead, across this street.'

They darted, Ralph holding on to Ojas's forearm, his hand across Ralph's waist. The April rain had begun in earnest, as Ojas tapped the button on his key fob and the black Corolla blinked. They rushed into the car and slammed the doors; the space inside was filled with the sounds of their bodies gasping for air.

Ralph dried his hair with his handkerchief. The car sputtered as the air conditioner was turned on. Ojas took Ralph's hand in his and held it for a while. Ralph waited in an upright position for something to happen, for Ojas to speak, but he was quiet and the silence rankled. The sky rumbled again and lightning flashed across the windshield.

On the dashboard, Ojas's phone blinked with a text message. He continued to hold Ralph's hand; he read the text to himself, then announced, 'There's a queer party. You want to go?'

'Where?'

'Here, check!' Ojas passed the phone to him. Ralph went through the details—Sunday evening in Park Street, unlimited drinks, a drag performance.

He returned the phone saying, 'I can't do this.'

'What? Okay, we don't have to go,' said Ojas, still holding on to his hand.

'I am fucking tired of this bullshit situation we are in, Ojas.'

'Baby ... Ralph?'

'I mean,' Ralph laughed with a touch of anger in his voice, 'why on earth am I with you if I am available to other men? Doesn't that strike you as being stupid?'

Ojas said, 'You're missing the point.' He motioned with his hand to himself and Ralph. 'This is ours, this relationship is ours only. We are only available to each other. Sex is different, you know it as well as me. The sex bit ...'

'Yes, go on? I am listening. I don't know how sex is different from anything else. What about the sex bit? Explain it to me.' Ralph freed his hand.

'Ralph, please ... I am not leaving you and settling with other men.' Ojas tried to hold his hands again. 'I love you.'

'Don't give me that love crap anymore, Ojas. I will just crush it under my feet and feed it to those young men you sleep with,' Ralph hissed, pushing Ojas's hands away from him.

'Fine, I won't. Frankly, I am quite frustrated with your drama. It's so fucking annoying, Ralph. Your high-handedness is doing us no good. Stop behaving as though you've been a saint all along.' Ojas began scratching his beard.

'I only want to save us. I think of protecting us,' muttered Ralph, watching the city from the windscreen as though it were a large television screen. He wished a kiss could help them sort whatever it was that had made them so hateful to one another. A long, enduring kiss without the taste of alcohol. Only their lips speaking about how much they wanted this over anything else they thought they needed.

It was Ojas who had first said 'I love you'. They were in Ojas's car, on a long drive—going through the Kona Expressway. It had been three months since they had started talking to each other. They were used to taking long drives when they'd meet after work.

On that drive, they spoke about Ojas's family. His mother, who was hell-bent on getting him married to a woman; his father, who had gradually stopped going to the office and preferred sitting around at home; his younger brother, who was aspiring to be a scientist. Someday.

After paying the toll fare and rolling the windows up, Ralph had asked why he hadn't come out to his folks. Ojas scrunched the receipt in his hand, saying, 'I don't want to … I mean, you know, I had almost tried once, but it didn't work.'

It was the winter of 2017. The conservative Hindu Gargs were at the dining table, ready to have their lunch, when his father muted the newsreader's voice about the Pride march in Kolkata. He scoffed, 'Ridiculous, plain ridiculous. Soon, we will see two boys in a mandap taking the pheras.' Ojas stopped eating; an awkwardness came creeping over him. His mother added, 'Modiji is going to foreign lands and bringing their weird culture here.' She clicked her tongue and asked Ojas if he wanted more daal. He didn't know what to say; the strangeness of the situation stared him in the face. He was the 'weird culture' in the room, at the table where his parents were 'normal' with a straight and sacred marriage. His brother was heading towards that. The horror of knowing he was the weirdo, a creature of ridicule, someone transported from another land and another time, made him recoil. He couldn't bring himself to say what he wished to, to his parents. He thrust his plate forward for daal. He knew he had to keep matters to himself for a few more months, years maybe—until he didn't feel the need to say anything at all. He didn't care what his parents thought of him. He detested repeating those words of evasion each time the possibility of marriage was discussed. At thirty-seven, he was tired of it. He wanted it to stop.

Ojas had told his friend Divya how futile revealing his true self was, but he had promised her that he would try. He did try. Now, here he was—convinced that he didn't need to come out at all. Not to his parents, not to anybody. Life went on just as well without the unnecessary task of informing his family who he wanted to sleep with.

Ojas, over that road trip, spoke in tiny fragments, across many stops and cups of tea in make-shift stalls along the highway. The sun was setting when they had changed lanes; they were headed back to the city from the inner parts of Howrah. Fields of paddy spread on either side; a poster on a billboard waved in the wind. Ralph pointed, 'The sky is pink and purple.'

Ojas stole a glance at him and said, 'I love you.'

The smile on Ralph's face faded as he kept admiring the sky. Ojas continued driving, wondering if Ralph had heard him; thinking, perhaps, that he had to say it again; worried that it wasn't mutual, that this man he had been talking to and meeting for the past three months detested commitment. The car came to a standstill at a traffic signal, somewhere near Santragachi. Ralph lowered the volume of the music and said, 'I love you, too.'

Ojas burst into laughter. It conveyed the relief he felt inside. He ran a hand across the steering wheel, almost honking on a clear road. As the sun set, they entered Kolkata. They praised the vastness of the river under the bridge; praised, too, the prospect of the relationship that lay ahead.

What had everything come to? Ojas and Ralph thought, as their car sped through the downpour and past the blinding lights of the cars ahead.

I will get old with him, Ralph had once promised his mother at her grave. You won't be there to see me through that, but I have found someone, Maa. I won't feel bad about getting old anymore. Like you had Baba and me when you were weak with that terrible illness, I have a man who will look after me.

He had teared up while saying that.

Now, Ralph regarded Ojas with a sidelong glance and wondered if he ought to control the tears welling up in his eyes or let it all cascade down. He had ceased being at ease when he was with Ojas.

4

The unusual heat of the city took a toll on Zubina. She scrubbed expensive tiles and cooked four dishes on four burners in the houses of her employers. It made her throat parched. The last drop of water and the last bite of food she had had had was at sehri. But it was at this hour when she worked the hardest—in the early afternoons.

Once she was done with her work at Firdaus-bhai's house, Aadil's employer, she padded out. She bumped into her husband. His white shirt was clinging to his skin against a film of sweat. He looked tired. He wanted to reach home and sit.

'What are you doing here?' she asked.

'I was done early, so I came to take you,' he said. His gaze loitered and regarded his employer's apartment. He had seen it alter since the day he had begun working at the factory. The ornate doorknobs, gilded windows, marble-topped tables and carved wooden couches had been replaced by plastic, glass, leather and sunmica. Still, his adoration for the apartment lingered. It spoke to him of the change his life had undergone from when he was fifteen to now—he was a thirty-eight-year-old man, a father and a husband.

Zubina handed him a packet that contained some old clothes Firdaus-bhai's wife had given her and strode towards the lift. She watched her husband walk ahead, his back straight and rigid. It filled her with desire; she wanted to touch it.

Zubina fanned herself with the dupatta and complained, 'This heat is getting unbearable, don't you think? Gone are the summers of our childhood in Kolkata.'

Aadil held his phone in his hand; he squinted his eyes. He ignored the need to comment that the city had never been kind to him; he had been left alone to fend for his family. Instead he said, 'Why is your brother calling me again? Is he in trouble?'

Zubina told him that her brother was hunting for a job at the leather factory as his current employer was being troublesome.

Aadil puffed up and responded, 'Zubina, why don't you talk a little sense into him? People need to stick to their job and work. There's nothing at the leather factory. Ask him to leave the city. He always wanted to.'

Zubina sighed and the lift doors opened at the ground floor. Aadil strode ahead. He questioned the validity of his statement. He stuck to his job because that was all he had been bequeathed by his father. He didn't know what else to do with his life than to wake up and head to the factory every morning. Money was important, he had come to believe. Not words. Not aspirations for another life. The sight of his mother's somnolent stare and his sisters' worn-out, sweating bodies was enough to make him put his head down and get to work. And now he had to look after his wife and daughters. Woman and girls again, whose lives couldn't be compromised.

Zubina matched pace and said, 'I will speak to him. You don't get worked up about it now.'

He nodded, feeling grateful. She carried the burden of running the house, and never pushed him to do more than he did.

As they walked past the neighbourhood, Zubina greeted her friends and Aadil felt obliged to say salaam as well. An urge to recede into his home had begun to grow in him over the years. Friends and families from his childhood were kind.

They were warm to him. But the neighbourhood and its people still bore the imprints of his past; they reminded Aadil of what a hardworking man he has been; the backbone of his family. Every young boy needed to be told about him; he had become an example. His life a fable for kids to claim.

Nonsense, he would much prefer them leaving him out of such stories. The only thing he enjoyed was spending time with his girls and his wife. Nothing was more pleasing to Aadil than watching Zubina frown over fickle matters, ask questions, look settled within herself, and unwind after an exhausting day with Amrin and Soniya.

When they reached their house, they found the door unlocked. Amrin and Soniya were sitting on the tattered mat on the floor, watching a cartoon. Aadil kept the bag of clothes and kicked it under the bed. Zubina watched him sit under the fan with his eyes shut and mouth agape. She stood at the threshold and recalled her conversation with Ralph on love the previous day.

Zubina was sweeping the floor; Ralph was sipping his tea. He offered, 'Why don't you sit for a while and drink tea as well?'

Wearily, she had declined. 'I am fasting.'

'Oh, yes. It is Ramzan. I am sorry I asked.'

Zubina talked about the mangoes she had put in water and the watermelon she had brought the previous day for iftaar. The watermelon resisted the knife. She had to stick the knife in and hop on it. She added that if her husband hadn't come right then, she'd have broken her wrists.

When he put the empty cup back on the saucer, Ralph had asked her, 'Do you love your husband, Zubina-di?'

She widened her eyes in alarm. 'Love? What are you talking? We are not kids.'

'Yes … but why not? Don't you love him? He is your husband, after all.'

Her shock settled on her face as a blush, 'Yes, he is my husband and I have the utmost respect for him.'

She hadn't considered the word 'love' ever since her sister had mentioned it all those years ago.

'So, you love him.'

'Then you must have someone you love too?' She shot back with determination.

There was a quiver of hesitation on his face, which meant he had. He was hiding something from her, Zubina understood.

'Are you … are you and Ojas bhai each other's support because he isn't married either?' she asked, largely to change the topic.

'Uh …' Ralph, it seemed, was not expecting this. He mouthed some inanity which flew right past her as she resumed her work. In her mind, she kept tossing the word 'love' towards Aadil.

Ralph's question hadn't left Zubina. She stood there and wondered: Did she love Aadil? She wiped her sweat and combined the words 'love' and 'Aadil'. They unfolded into twelve years of marriage and two beautiful girls, going about their business in the hot afternoon.

She saw Aadil open his eyes and stand up.

She saw the empty stool he had been sitting on and felt as though something was amiss. He had been there. He was *always* there, like light in front of her eyes, or like her shadow; her reflection. And that vacant space seemed to suggest a life when he wouldn't be there. It made her sad. Was that love? Surely, she would ask Ralph someday if presence meant love, if the idea of someone always being there was love.

But love couldn't be just that. Her memories associated with the word love were unpleasant. She shoved them away.

She knew Ralph was in love with someone. She wanted that fierceness, a power that seemed to heal all wounds. That's what she saw in Ralph's eyes every moment—be it while talking to her about domestic things or sharing a cup of tea with Ojas over a smoke. She saw the ferocity of his love volley forth to the other.

She was startled when Aadil called out her name and asked her to rest. What lurid thoughts the hunger stirred in her mind.

Zubina finished her evening shift at Ralph's house. She had cooked beef curry, butter paneer and pulao, and had made kulchas. It was not seven yet; Aadil wouldn't be home. Amrin would have broken her fast and eaten an elaborate meal comprising wedges of fleshy watermelon, sizzling kebabs, nimbu sherbet, crispy spring rolls, and chow mein from Sona's stall. Soniya would've joined her. Zubina forbade her younger daughter from fasting because of her coughing bouts. They must have gone to Neha's place for their tutorials.

As she walked towards her home, Zubina stopped at the old woman's house, where her friend, Nazma and the old woman's daughter-in-law sat and talked. They told her about a lady who would visit them soon to talk about opening some kind of bank account. Their money would be safe and would also earn interest. Zubina showed active interest in the matter and said she would be there for the meeting. They complained of work, they spoke of Eid, and then parted ways.

Secure more money than what she deposited—well, that sounded like a great opportunity, Zubina thought to herself. When she was young, she had grown up with few things; few new clothes, not enough dolls to play with, none of the food that she saw advertised on billboards. She hadn't realized that she had missed out on these things—not until she had had her daughters. Her girls, who got to wear a new tunic every Eid, enjoy the pastry or pizza she occasionally got from Ralph's or when their father took them out for a treat, and buy phones which had made the plastic dolls useless ...

Once, Zubina saw Amrin push Soniya and kick the doll with her leg. She gasped—the audacity! Her girls not only reminded her of the childhood she had never had, but of her inability to ask for or expect a better one. Earlier, the helplessness untethered her, enraged her, made her feel like a fool. But she had come to accept the futility of envisioning a life that was not meant for her, that had even escaped her. She made silent promises to herself, to never let her past come between herself and motherhood. This was more important—*this*—being Ammi to her girls.

And her childhood wasn't all that bad, Zubina consoled herself. She thought of her mother mollycoddling her with sour tamarind sticks every Sunday; her younger brother protecting her from the neighbour's truant boy, who always wanted to walk around and ask her uncomfortable questions; her elder sister, who was the pillar of strength in their family when their father died in a road accident.

Her sister had started to work at a young age, she had taught her to work too, and both of them often slept close to each other, breathing the same air.

How, then, could she regret the childhood she had had—even if she were to compare it to the one she gave her daughters? Surely she had been happy as a child ... and wasn't that what mattered?

And now there was her own family that needed her ...

She recalled Amrin's fascination with Neha's lipstick in a video.

'Ammi, see this colour,' Amrin had said the previous evening at iftar, thrusting Aadil's phone in front of her face. Neha twirled with a rose between her lips. A boy walked past her with another girl. Neha broke down in ugly tears.

Zubina frowned. 'What is she doing? Why did she start crying?'

Her daughters chorused in excitement, 'It's TikTok! She makes many videos!' Amrin added, 'Someday, I will be in one of her videos too.'

Aadil burst into peals of laughter. 'Doesn't she go to college?'

It softened Zubina's heart when he put his glass aside and placed Soniya on his lap. Zubina found her cheeks grow warm as she watched him listen to Soniya. She complained about Amrin, who scared her with tales of djinns and the kabristaan after Neha-di would go away.

Zubina would have liked to stop the talk of djinns. But to see Aadil listen to them with such avid interest—it broke her heart to disturb the scene. He was a shy man who never spoke much. With his daughters, however, he knew the right words to say. Amrin was never bored when she conversed with him. He never tired of indulging her fancies. Soniya, well, she wanted to be the apple of her father's eyes. And he never made her feel otherwise.

Amrin said, 'It's just silly talk. She's scared as a mouse, just like her friends.'

Aadil patted Soniya and said to Amrin, 'Don't start doing those Neha di-type videos now.'

'Oh, Papa! She is my idol. She was very angry that I didn't follow her immediately or like all her videos,' explained Amrin. She started liking all the videos with a fervent tapping of her finger. 'I want her to know how devoted I am.'

The excitement with which Amrin expressed her admiration for Neha and her desire to be like her moved Zubina. She wondered if she had someone like Neha in her life when she had been a girl. An elder to admire. A person whose life would be hers to work towards.

As she reached home, her eyes looked through the open window, with a lazily fluttering curtain. She squinted and watched. The scene unfolding inside her house froze her. It took her back to when she was seventeen, no more a child, standing outside a room, bent over a crack in the door, seeing something she should never have seen.

That evening, Amrin and Soniya had returned home after their classes with two girls, Yasmin and Rina, whom Soniya liked best. The four girls ran to Zubina's house and quickly threw their bags and notebooks. In a huge box with pieces of scrap that Zubina had managed to ferret out of the tailor's rubbish heap, Soniya found dolls and distributed them amongst the girls. The girls sat in a circle and started playing 'Home'.

Soniya was the mother, who was perpetually irritated by her daughter's stubbornness. Her daughter would not eat the right food and would not go to school. The other two girls were mothers of their own daughters who had similar issues; they also had to deal with their husbands, who complained every day and threatened to beat them up. Amrin was the girls' tutor initially, moaning about all the trouble the girls gave her by not studying and only gossiping. The mothers apologized and slapped their girls when they were home.

In a while, Amrin assumed the role of Soniya's husband. The other girls prepared dinner on miniature plastic pans. Once Amrin and Soniya had their dinner, they climbed on to the bed and put their daughters to sleep. Yasmin and Rina climbed on to the bed, too, and occupied the left-hand side corner. The lights were switched off. An emergency light—used when there was load-shedding—was switched on. When everything lay silent, Soniya whispered, 'I think they are asleep.'

After that, Amrin placed her body atop Soniya's lean figure. Soniya watched Amrin over her, the way she moved up and down over her body, slow, then increasing her pace.

Amrin whispered to Yasmin and Rina, 'Be ready, the djinn will come to you now.'

It was at this moment that the door flung open. The four girls screamed, seeing an apparition with a dupatta over her head, scrambled closer to each other, yelling at the top of their voices.

Zubina stood at the entrance and stared at the scene on her side of the bed. She switched on the lights and glared. Yasmin and Rina got down from the bed, their howls subsiding. Zubina collected herself and said, 'Come on, go home, both of you. It's late.'

Once they were gone, she locked the door and interrogated her daughters.

'What was all that going on?'

Amrin murmured, 'We were playing "Home".'

'What part of "Home" was that on the bed? What were you trying to do?'

Amrin and Soniya looked at each other.

Zubina poured water for herself and drank it. She said, 'From today, you will never ever do that in your life. That is wrong. It is no part of any game. It is garbage, do you understand?'

They nodded.

'You will simply never think of it again. Do you get that?'

They mumbled a yes.

'If this happens again, I will tell your father.'

Their heads bobbed without a word.

Amrin crouched on the floor and gathered the bits of cloth strewn from the plastic bag. She swallowed her thoughts indignantly. Her mother didn't probe further. Had her mother been a little more insistent, she would have said that the scene she had witnessed was also a part of 'Home'. She would tell her that, on nights, when she wasn't able to sleep, she would hear her parents fidget for a while and then—as she'd make a hole in her bedsheet with her finger—she'd see her father atop her mother, their waists covered by his lungi. She would see her father push forward and backward. She'd hear a voice calling from somewhere far. The djinn.

It lured her with seductive promises of jannat.

Amrin hit Soniya's hand impetuously, when she tried grabbing the dolls from her.

Zubina made a moat in the bowl of flour and stared at it. She couldn't face her daughters. She felt the burn of public humiliation. If she told Aadil, he would be ashamed of himself and their life together. She knew that had she persisted, her daughter would have spoken truths she may not have wanted to hear. She kneaded the dough with renewed strength in her arms.

No, she couldn't let Aadil into this.

Besides, it wasn't her daughters that set her off; it was the past that smouldered her present consciousness.

5

Following repeated entreaties, Ralph ceded to Ojas's request to attend the party at Park Street. Ojas's car was waiting downstairs as Ralph doused himself in Calvin Klein from head to toe. The loose yellow T-shirt hid the tummy, making him look youthful. He had on a pair of brown chinos and black loafers to complete the look. He plumped his lips with tinted gloss and admired himself in the mirror. Ralph did not like complete make-up. As he reached the car, he hoped Ojas would sniff out the panic in his gait and avoid other men.

In the car, Ojas told Ralph about the friends who would be there at the party. Ralph detested those friends. Single assholes, good-for-nothing gay sluts, who had tasted every cock that was available. From the party a year ago, Ralph had made detailed notes about their character profiles—all of which got used as ammunition when he and Ojas fought.

At the venue, they waltzed in, greeted by a cheer. Ralph demurred at Ojas's body being felt through, as sundry men hugged him and kissed his cheek. Ralph froze at the hugs coming his way. He kept an eye on Ojas while he asked for a Gin & Tonic. When he couldn't follow him around, he sat at the bar on a high-rise chair and played with the stirrer in his drink.

The DJ opened the dance floor with Britney Spears and the group charged dizzyingly at it. Ojas moved around but left the stage when he could. Ralph pouted as he took a sip of his drink and observed the goings-on. Ojas was a towering man for his friends, his family and the world; he was at their beck and call and always promised attendance. Yet, in a party, he was no more than the decor light fixture, tall and ungainly, if not dazzling. Ralph had a hard time putting together the two sides of him. In the past, he'd wince at Ojas's need to cater to everyone, even when Ojas confessed to him that he was simply doing it out of love and respect, not because he wanted to. Over time, Ralph came to believe that everything Ojas did was for himself. Ojas *wanted* to be around. He wanted to be in the presence of others. He wanted to be acknowledged. Ralph wondered if Ojas sought recognition; if he searched for crowds simply to remind himself that he mattered, even if the interaction felt awkward to him.

Ralph was now joined by a stranger to his left, who asked for a beer. He wore suspenders over a white shirt, tight-fitting grey pants, and a pair of large rectangular spectacles—they gave him a nerdy cosplay vibe. He was both tempting to Ralph and a creature to envy. He wanted him. He yearned to be as young and fit as him.

The stranger began speaking over the music, closer to Ralph's ear, 'First time here?'

'No, second time,' Ralph yelled back.

'It's my first. I don't know anyone!' He had an accent which Ralph couldn't pin-point.

'Have fun. Make friends.'

'I am trying with you,' he said, making Ralph blush.

Ralph covered his face with his glass and scanned the crowd. The drink burnt his throat. Ojas was at the other end of the bar. He doubled over with laughter; someone's hand went over his torso. Ralph felt his stomach tighten as he called for a refill and faced the stranger.

'Nice to know. Are you from the city?'

'I shifted recently,' he answered and rubbed his thumb on the rim of Ralph's glass that was smeared with his pink gloss. Ralph's finger held the glass from the bottom, as he saw the stranger's finger caress the print of his lips.

Then the stranger asked, 'Hey, do you want to go dance?'

Ralph's glance flitted over to Ojas, who was offering his drink to somebody. He said, 'Sure, let's go.'

They were on the dance floor. Moving back and forth, in circles. Their feet were tapping to the song. They held each other by the waist, then the shoulders, as they danced in the crowd. Suddenly, Ojas joined them, sharing the stranger, while staring into Ralph's eyes. Ralph held Ojas by his gaze. The stranger let himself get squeezed between them, as Ralph and Ojas's hands grazed his torso and curved buttocks. The stranger then left Ralph and threw himself at Ojas. Ralph's dancing quieted as the stranger swivelled, lunged and raised his rump, pushing into Ojas's crotch. Ojas held him from behind and tried dancing. He cast a mischievous gaze at Ralph, whose erection dropped instantly.

Ralph left the bar ablaze with anger and lit a cigarette. It trembled between his fingers as he recalled Ojas's lips. They had touched the stranger's neck. His hands had caressed the stranger's waist. Ralph had witnessed it while being ignored.

He muttered 'Christ' to stop the trembling. That's what his mother had told him to do. 'Ask Christ to see you through your troubles.'

He said it again and again to get past the anguish that Ojas had caused him. The man who led a life of such extravagance, ran a sizeable business, catered to his parents while hiding himself—that man, Ojas, would do nothing to prove his love to him. Ojas wanted to chase a fantasy, it seemed. A botched-up fantasy that had destroyed them as a couple. Ojas would find the latest source of excitement and go trundling there.

'Christ, Christ, Christ, save me.'

He was about to call for Maa, when Ojas came up and took him inside without a question. In a group, they drank and ate, while two drag queens sang and danced on the stage. The stranger was a part of the group now. A slut in the making, Ralph thought, as he watched them guzzle drinks.

After too many drinks to make him think straight anymore, Ralph told Ojas that he wished to leave. Ojas considered the statement. He wanted to stay. He wished to have one night to make merry. Work, Ralph and his family would take over anyway the next day onwards. This one evening of unrestrained freedom from the clutches of responsibility is what he had been waiting for.

Ralph sensed Ojas's reluctance and left the pub. He booked a cab. Ojas followed him. 'I am calling my driver.'

'No, you stay. I don't want to spoil it for you.'

Ojas did not reply and asked his driver to be there.

In the car, they were quiet. When Ralph got off at his home, Ojas said, 'I hope you have a good night.'

'You aren't coming in?'

'Why? To hear you taunt me?' Ojas shut the door of the car.

Ralph wanted to break down right there on the road. He was riven with guilt for spoiling his night. However, he also found himself calming the rage and the grief that bubbled inside him. Where had he gone wrong? What more could he do to end this? He had loved Ojas. Loved him sincerely from the day he had begun to know him. And Ojas...

He fell asleep.

The next morning, Ralph spent his day nursing a hangover. He scrolled through Facebook. A post reminded him of the general elections, which were to be held in Kolkata in a few days. He made a face; politics and elections held no meaning in his life. Not anymore. What mattered was this—Ojas had not written to him through the day.

At 11 p.m., Ralph rushed to the washroom, half-asleep. He held his knees and whimpered. His shorts were already soiled. He managed to drink two glassfuls of ORS but the diarrhoeic rumble would not cease. Finally, when he saw the sun rise, he fell on his bed. He slept.

When the doorbell rang, he picked up the room freshener from the credenza and sprayed everywhere. Zubina entered, crinkling her nose. 'Such a strong smell of the spray,' she said. He stuttered towards his room, moaning, 'My stomach isn't ok. Don't make tea or coffee.' She nodded and started to work.

Ralph wished his mother were there. He wished she hadn't lost her life to cancer. Despite her illness, she had attempted to sit up when Ralph had once complained of a headache. Ralph had wanted to scream at her, ask her to stop being so caring when she didn't have to, demand that she recover from the illness and not leave him in a state of permanent pain. Instead, he had forced a smile, held back his tears and said he was okay.

Now, he held his stomach and prayed to recover. He yearned for his mother as he picked up the phone and dialled his father's number. He wanted his parents, the comfort of their presence at this hour.

Ojas came an hour later.

He touched Ralph's forehead with the back of his hand. Ralph felt a jolt of current pass through his body. Ojas asked, 'What did you eat last night?'

Ralph blinked and said, 'It's the alcohol and junk I ate at the party, maybe.'

Ojas ignored talk of the party. 'How are you feeling?'

'Miserable.'

'Did you have enough water? You must be dehydrated.'

The door opened and Zubina walked inside with a cup of coffee for Ojas. She placed it on the table and studied Ralph, asking if she could get a banana. Ojas assented.

Ralph wanted Ojas gone. He did not want see this show of care and concern that felt like a pack of lies.

Ojas edged forward, bent over to Ralph's face and kissed him. Ralph moved closer. He liked this—the silence and the smell of morning coffee on Ojas's lips, despite the bitterness crawling at the back of his own throat. He needed such physical proximity. Ojas was the shield each time he was embittered by the world or tossed asunder by circumstances. Perhaps, this had something to do with Ojas being older and Ralph needing to be taken care of. It made it impossible for Ralph to imagine a husband better than Ojas. A mournful indignation gnawed at him.

Zubina came in with a banana the moment Ojas had taken his lips off Ralph. Not paying any heed to her curiosity, Ojas peeled the fruit and held it to Ralph's mouth. Ralph ate it in small bites.

Zubina watched the scene unfold; she held on to the thoughts swarming in her mind. Ojas could see the questions surfacing. Did you kiss him? Why would two men kiss each other? Which friend did that to another?

It irked him, the comments and unsolicited opinions from people not from his world. It seemed as though the two could not inhabit a common life; a realm where his ways of expressing love were not at odds with theirs.

The doctor had arrived. He took Ralph's temperature, checked his pulse and wrote out a prescription. He advised convalescent meals. 'He has to drink a lot of water. If his condition worsens, we'll have to put him on a saline drip.'

Once the doctor left, Ojas ran his eyes through his illegible scrawl. He handed the prescription to Zubina, with some money. 'Get these medicines please.'

She took it while rambling on about the chemicals and toxins in food these days. At the door, she said, 'You are such a good friend. You are taking care of him like a husband or a father would of his sick child.' She organized the notes and the prescription in her hands and continued, 'I am glad he has you as a friend. Few people are this fortunate. I don't think any of my husband's friends would ...'

His gaze met hers, dumbfounded.

Sensing the silence, she opened the door and left.

Ralph avoided Ojas's attempts at making conversation, as memories of the other night crowded in. Ojas brought up the topic of his parents and their search for a bride from a businessman's household ... because how could Ojas marry into a salaried family? He laughed to himself. Ralph tossed around in bed, saying, 'Hmm.' When Ojas talked of Divya's wedding preparation, Ralph said, 'Good for her.'

When it was clear that Ralph was not going to indulge him at all, Ojas said, 'I will go to the office. Get some urgent work done and come back to stay the night.'

Ralph shrugged but said nothing—no goodbye, no thank you. Ojas had been waiting for a moment when he would be able to smile. He loved Ralph. There was hurt. But the love remained. Ralph could have responded to his declarations of care, or asked him to be with him until he was fine. But no ... there was nothing here for Ojas.

Ojas kissed his forehead and carried Ralph's silence with him.

Ralph gnashed his teeth when Ojas left. He wanted to believe that things could change; that Ojas could throw away the world and choose Ralph for himself. That they could build themselves into a unit of love and care. Wasn't that how two people stayed close?

The deprivation of the preceding night stung him harsher than the pain of illness. At some point, Sujoy called him and decided to come over.

Zubina left early for iftaar. She had prepared boiled rice and mashed plantain for him. Ralph was restless in bed. He wanted to go to the kitchen and make pistachio mendiants. But the thought of shelling pistachios and tempering chocolate made him inert.

It was nearing dusk when Sujoy showed up, not in his usual sprightly avatar.

He quizzed Ralph regarding his health and Ralph answered his questions half-heartedly. To Ralph, Sujoy's moroseness was more disconcerting than his own disquiet. Sujoy could never conceal the fact that he was having a tough time, or that he wished to talk. His focus, the seriousness with which he spoke and his lack of eye contact made it obvious to anyone who knew him even remotely that he was in the middle of personal struggles. Sujoy's face warned the world when he was slipping into melancholia.

'What happened this time?' asked Ralph.

Sujoy lowered his head and visibly struggled to express himself. It had never been easy, not then, not now. Ralph put a hand on his and asked in a gentle voice, 'Is it her? And the whole open relationship?'

With both a head shake and a nod, Sujoy said, 'I slept with someone else yesterday.'

The hand Ralph had placed on Sujoy slipped. 'Umm … what?'

Sujoy shrugged, his back hunched, and said, 'First, she acted okay, but I could tell that she was stopping herself from asking more questions.'

Sujoy continued, 'I told her I wouldn't have done this if she hadn't insisted on opening our relationship, and she ... well, she lashed out at me and said that I couldn't sleep randomly with anyone. That I had to tell her about the person first; that we had to inform each other before making any move.'

Ralph waited for him to speak further. Sujoy covered his face with his hands and said, 'I made a huge mistake, Ralph. She is angry with me and I don't know what to do. I was at my cousin's, drinking, and my cousin had friends over, one thing led to another ... and I was in the room with one of the friends, locked in, tipsy ... and it was all done when I realized I was the one who took the first real step in the open relationship. I ... I hadn't even said yes,' Sujoy confessed. Then, he asserted, 'This. Is. So. Fucked. Up.'

'Oh, Sujoy, why?'

'I wasn't thinking.'

'Why couldn't you simply get out of that place?'

'I don't want to lose her, Ralph. I ...' He wanted to continue, but couldn't muster the words.

Ralph's phone buzzed. It was Ojas. He excused himself from the room and took the call. 'How are you?' Ojas asked, as though he were asking a child; there was the sound of papers rustling in the background.

'I am okay ... why?'

'Well, you were sick, so I called to ask if you are feeling fine.' The rustling of the papers stopped. 'So?'

'Nothing!' Ralph was exhausted.

'Well,' paused Ojas, swallowing his hurt. 'I'll drop by later.'

'No, you don't have to. Sujoy is here,' Ralph said, taking in a deep breath.

'Oh, great. I hope he will look after you well!' There was a plangent edge to his voice.

'He will. Thank you.' Ralph's gaze moved to Sujoy, who was distractedly walking around now. Suddenly, he realized he had much to say to Sujoy. He wished to hear him speak, rather than waste his time fighting with Ojas. He hung up.

'Any problem?' asked Sujoy, perceiving Ralph's discomfiture.

'No, it's Ojas. He wanted to come. I said he didn't have to. You were here.'

'Ralph, are things okay between the two of you?'

Ralph paused mid-way and assessed the answer. This seemed like the ideal opportunity to confess the truth about his own relationship and save Sujoy from whatever the future would bring. But he did not want to further complicate Sujoy's life by giving his ruinous example. 'Yes, yes, why wouldn't it be? Ojas had already come during the day, so I asked him to go home.'

Sujoy's face conveyed doubt at his reply, as though he could get a whiff of Ralph's secret. Nevertheless, he went to the kitchen to get water for himself.

Sujoy tended to come in the way of Ralph's relationships, one way or the other. From his first boyfriend back in second year of college (who got attracted to Sujoy within a month of being with Ralph); to the colleague he had been with during his internship; and now, Ojas—each of them had to make space for Sujoy. Sujoy had fixed himself firmly into Ralph's life and demanded the attention he think he deserved over others—not directly, never in words, but Ralph always sensed it, having known him for so long.

With a glass of iced water in his hand, Sujoy sat beside him, 'I am sorry, I came and unburdened my own problems on you when you are so sick.'

'Please don't say that. I'm glad you spoke to me.'

'Ralph, I'm asking again, are things fine with Ojas? I'm not convinced with your answer. I think you are sad.'

This was another thing about Sujoy that Ralph disliked. Sujoy probed far too much into his relationships when he was done sharing details from his own existence. It felt like an obligation, to come clean to Sujoy; to reveal to him the goings-on in his romantic or sexual life.

'Look, I can leave if that's what you want for now. But if Ojas is uncomfortable with my presence then, isn't it … I mean, isn't it weird?'

Ralph didn't know what to say. He fixed his pillow, and replied, 'Sujoy, no, that's not true. I asked him not to come. He has no problem with you. And as for your previous question, trust me, we are fine. We have our fights.'

'How can he fight when you're sick?'

'I was the one fighting, not him,' Ralph said. 'I was rude to him, horrible over some random thing.'

'If that's what you say, I guess, I will have to trust it …' Sujoy knew something was not right. And that irritated Ralph. This probing was doing him no good. He had spoken as much of the truth as he could. What he didn't say was something he wanted to keep to himself for now.

It was clear from Ralph's evasiveness, and the fact that he was now scrolling through his phone, that the conversation was over. Sujoy chit-chatted about their workplace, about the days in Delhi they had spent together during an internship, and about Zubina-di—had she said anything about him and Ojas? Ralph said that he had been too sick to know. His walls refused to break. Sujoy realized the futility of asking, and left.

Ralph lay on his bed, relieved. He slept for an hour and then got up, his sleep broken by Ojas's call, asking if he had eaten his dinner. The care in his voice made Ralph want to weep; he wanted to ask him to come home and care for him; he wanted to say that without him, he would die alone in the flat. He needed him more than a return to health. The thoughts were reduced to a monosyllable: 'Yes.' He disconnected the call.

Ralph yanked out a bag of pistachios and shelled them on his bed. In a saucepan, he boiled water. He placed a glass pot in it, into which he tossed two thick slabs of white chocolate. Tears streamed down his cheeks as the chocolate melted—a silky white ribbon. He turned off the stove and threw the shelled pistachios into the folds of the chocolate. Fuck, fuck, fuck. He was furious that the mendiants looked nothing like they were meant to. He pushed the hot chocolate away. He couldn't stand the sight of it. 'Maa,' he said, 'please return.'

He had his dinner cold.

6

It thrilled Zubina to see her neighbourhood come alive during Ramzan, with the evening extravaganza. Wherever her eyes went, they feasted on pyramids of blossoming yellow mangoes, blood-red apples, ripened papayas, trays of pulpy khajoor, quarters of watermelon that disappeared into black polythene bags. Or dried ladders of sevai shining in the golden light. Her nose sniffed out the aroma of beef haleem, now confused with the mild tang of channa from Mustafa's cart.

Her family had finished their iftari of apples, samosas and tikkis, with rose sherbet. A burp erupted to remind her of the meal, as she entered the maidan where a mela was on in full swing. People pedalled goods, thrusting their hands out. With no change to spare, she ignored them. She found Amrin and Soniya trying their hand at coiled rings, where they aimed at a pencil case. Aadil was at the masjid to perform the tarawih prayers. He would meet them here soon. She had some time to kill. She went and sat on one of the concrete benches and fanned herself with her dupatta under the glaring white lights.

Two young boys passed by her, holding hands. She frowned, shoving thoughts of Ralph and Ojas aside. She focused on Soniya clutching the pencil case to her chest as Amrin threw more rings, but the scene from Ralph's room still disturbed her. *This wasn't friendship. This was something else … but what?* Zubina wondered.

In their twelve years together, Aadil had never held her that way, not even when she was sick. She fanned herself harder to shake away such inane comparisons. Maybe such friendships were common among Christians. She tucked her tongue by her corner tooth, searching for a morsel from the iftar meal, spitting it out. However unseemly or alien that friendship may have been, at least she had been witness to the care Ojas had showered on Ralph.

But why didn't Ralph's lover turn up when he was sick?

This wouldn't do, she scolded herself.

She focused on Eid, which was around the corner now. She needed to ensure her bonus came in soon to buy her daughters their clothes. And then, somehow, she had to save some money to repair the ceiling. She peered at the evening sky. She moaned. The bed sheet spread across the ceiling would be soaked with water. It would drip mercilessly when the monsoons would arrive. She had to discuss the matter of the ceiling with her husband. The sooner the better. She rose and began to walk about the maidan.

Aadil joined her at some point. They followed Amrin and Soniya across the stalls. The girls were with their friends. They showed off their prizes. Both Zubina and Aadil walked together with a slight awkwardness at the mela. Eyes always darting at something or the other. Aadil moved away to buy khajoor and ice apple for sehri. Zubina greeted Sona at her stall; she was dipping chicken in a velvety besan batter.

On the way, Amrin instructed Soniya not to disturb her the next day as she had to study. The impending test would be an important milestone for her. 'Neha-di will never let me be a part of her videos, or speak to me of things beyond studies, if I don't do well.'

'What things?' Soniya asked, opening the pencil case and pouting at the little mirror inside.

'Her boyfriend ... duh ...' whispered Amrin and broke into a tiny giggle, as the warmth of such remembrance filled her body.

As they walked past the tailor's shop, they saw a man talking seriously into the microphone to a group of boys and men. He spoke about the rising problems Muslims faced in India. He pleaded that Allah's children come together in this hour of need and pray sincerely to restore lost harmony. At the mention of the word 'ibadat', Zubina saw Amrin ball her sweaty palm and fingers into a fist and whisper, '*Bismillah Ar-Rahman Ar-Rahim*'. Zubina sighed. She could not forget what Amrin and Soniya had done on her bed. Now, as Aadil walked next to her, she looked away. The girls' indecency still shamed her. She went across to the other side and held Soniya. Soniya was intent on holding her father's hand, but Zubina fixed her with a glare. They marched ahead despite Soniya's repeated refusal to hold hands with her mother.

At home, the girls sat down to watch the serial they always caught, whilst mimicking the actors during breaks. Zubina picked out items they had shopped for from the bag. Aadil took off his shirt and searched for a vest; he bent close to her face. She took in his scent—a mix of lemon, antiseptic soap and sweat. She resisted the urge to hold him near. She felt his hands press her back as he extracted the item of clothing he sought and winked mischievously at her. Zubina's face flushed with sweat; she felt desire for Aadil build within her.

The first time they had shared a bed, Zubina had been scared. The thought of a man climbing on top of her body, taking off his clothes and her own, and fusing parts of himself with her made her anxious. There was no love that made anticipation a possibility. Before her stared duty—the duty of being a responsible wife, of baring her body for the husband. Her elder sister told her that she shouldn't resist, she should give in ... and maybe find it enjoyable.

When Aadil made love to her four months after their wedding, he stroked her back, asked her to breathe and reassured her that it wouldn't hurt. But it did hurt and she held back her tears with a smile because her sister's face flashed before her eyes—*don't resist*.

Yet, Aadil's gentle hold over her body, especially her back, ensured that she found a nugget of enjoyment even in the pain.

Zubina, in due course, started waiting for the nights when they would make love. The earlier tremors of uncertainty died, and she relished being with Aadil—the way he held and caressed her body with his hands. These were her moments of ecstasy.

Zubina was brought back to the present by music outside—it did not seem to stop. Amrin and Soniya complained about not getting to watch their serials in peace. But they also enjoyed sitting at the door and singing along loudly, until Zubina asked them to sleep.

In bed, Zubina nudged Aadil, pointed towards the ceiling and said, 'We have to get it repaired.'

Aadil agreed. 'Yes, I have been talking to some men about it.'

Abruptly, Zubina turned to him and asked softly, 'Do you think I am beautiful?'

He caught sight of her eyes in the dark and chuckled, 'What is this question?'

'No questions, just answer me. Do you think so?' She could imagine his face going crimson. She had never dared being this audacious before.

He whispered, 'Zubina, have Sona and Nazma been filling your ears about their husbands spoiling them?'

'No, I want to know.'

He put his hand on her and explained, 'Their husbands drink daaru and go home. They speak whatever.'

'I …' Zubina wanted to tell him that she wanted to know for herself. But he stroked her arm and said, 'Go to sleep. We have work tomorrow.'

In less than a minute, he was dead to the world.

Zubina closed her eyes and let her arms brush against his, recalling his touch earlier that evening. She knew he had more worries than he let on. The house was his. He owned it. It was one of the few houses in the neighbourhood that had been bought by the one living in it.

Yet an umbra of melancholy accompanied him; he was followed by the ghosts of his family's strange decisions. Love or beauty remained alien to his world. He was a man designated to protect a house from falling over and a father who ensured his children were never disappointed in him. He had become a pillar over the years.

A pillar. Standing upright, without a sigh.

Zubina slept and dreamt of a life when Aadil would feed her and hold her hand when she was unwell or tired to the bones after a day's work. She found herself inhabiting a fantasy where he was kissing her on the lips as he left for work and told her that she was the most beautiful woman he had ever seen. She dreamed of love coursing through her body, even as images of Ralph and Ojas smiling appeared in snatches. They held hands, and now Ojas was kissing Ralph and saying something into his ear. Zubina was witness to this with a blank look on her face. They were speaking of her, weren't they? Then, she felt nauseated. The nightmarish quality this love possessed churned her insides. The next moment, in that dream, Aadil was kissing her while he held her by the waist. He said that he loved her more than his own breath. She could hear it in his kisses—that he didn't want to be the pillar she had seen him become over the years.

A few days later, on an intensely sunny afternoon, Zubina finished her work and lay flat on the chowki in her house. Amrin was jubilant. There was a jounce to her steps as she fed Soniya, washed the dishes, folded their dried clothes, lit a citronella incense cone to ward off mosquitoes and opened her notebook to solve questions about tenses. Soniya sniffed the curling citronella and said, 'Ammi, you should have got more of this from their house. I could eat it.'

'Ammi, someday if I move out of this house and begin living at Neha-di's, you won't mind, will you?' Amrin asked, dismissing her sister.

'Huh? Why would you live with her?' Zubina tossed this way and that on the chowki, sleep heavy in her eyes.

'I did quite well in the test,' Amrin declared. 'Neha-di wouldn't stop looking at me with admiration.'

'Lies,' Soniya butted in. 'She said you made mistakes too.'

'Yes, but that was nothing. Stop interfering, jealous witch,' Amrin glared at her sister.

Soniya dodged her with a worn-out badminton racquet's end. She resumed putting her face through the racquet's gaping hole, with a tongue stuck out at Amrin. She wanted to lick the air thick with incense.

Amrin ignored her. 'Ammi, I think Neha-di will soon ask me to go out with her friends. You have to say yes and give me some money for the outing. Please don't say no.'

Before Zubina could reply, Nazma, her friend, dropped by to inform her that the meeting regarding the opening of bank accounts was about to begin; it had been organized by an NGO. Nazma added, 'I will talk to you about something after the meeting. Stay there, okay?'

'Okay, I will.'

Zubina rearranged her clothes. She mumbled about how her sleep was ruined and wondered at the problem Nazma could be facing. She held her hair tight in a fist and combed the ends with some struggle. Nazma's husband was a drunkard—this was a known fact in the neighbourhood. She hated to see the constant suffering on Nazma's face whenever she took leave from work. She prayed that nothing too bad had transpired.

After rolling her hair into a coiffed bun, Zubina covered her head with the dupatta and dragged herself to Sona's stall. Her thoughts ran on as though on loop—Eid-shopping, a broken ceiling and bonuses. It dawned on her that only nine days were left for Eid.

The meeting had already started when she reached; details were being taken to open the accounts. Once the details were noted, the supervisor said, 'I will come tomorrow, since it will soon be time to break your fast. I will get your signatures and I need ten rupees to open the account tomorrow. Is that understood?' The group agreed and the circle opened.

Right then Nazma walked towards Zubina with worry written over her mousy face.

'Listen, my husband lost his job. I really need your help.'

Zubina asked, 'How did that happen?'

Nazma spoke as quietly as she could, 'He got into a fight with one of the other men at work and the boss threw him out. You know how these garment factories can get somedays.'

Zubina pressed her lips together. 'Well, I don't know how to help him, Nazma.'

Nazma spoke, her voice pleading, 'Why, Aadil-bhai has a job in that leather factory. Can't you talk to him?'

'I don't know. Last time I asked him if the factory had a vacancy for my brother and he said, "No, it doesn't."'

Nazma clicked her tongue, then said, 'Okay. At least try once, won't you?'

Zubina held Nazma's hands. 'Yes, I will try, of course. But I don't want to make any promises.'

Nazma smiled. 'Yes, that's all I wanted to hear. You know how things are difficult at this time, with Eid around. They didn't even give him the bonus and he wanted to go to the boss and fight for it. I somehow managed to stop him.'

Zubina assured her that things would get better. Then, she remembered the time. 'Okay, it's getting late for iftari, Nazma. Amrin's father will be home. I will mention your request to him.'

Zubina thought about Nazma's worries on her way back. She didn't like seeing Nazma being reduced to such a vulnerable state; she understood how intolerable her husband could get. Nazma worked tirelessly at her small shop, where she sold lozenges and bidis all day—this, after her early morning cleaning duties in a couple of houses. Zubina had known Nazma since the day she had come to stay in the neighbourhood after her marriage. Nazma was the one who walked into her house and assured Aadil that she would help Zubina get work. She didn't want Nazma's Eid to be sad.

The next day, after finishing work at Firdaus-bhai's house, Zubina asked his wife for her bonus.

The wife gritted her teeth. 'Yes, yes, Zubina. Tell me about it!' She threw her hands in the air and continued, 'I am running helter-skelter, as you can see!'

Zubina bowed her head weakly to convey that she understood her situation.

The wife went on, 'I will talk to Firdaus and ask him to pay it to Aadil, does that sound all right? I don't have money in my purse at the moment.'

Zubina looked at her hands and said, 'Okay, whatever suits you.'

She picked her plastic bags and left the house. On her way to Ralph's, she laughed sardonically, imitating the lady's reply, 'I don't have money in my purse.' She walked with an umbrella in the plastic bag. She felt horrible asking for a bonus, and wished her employers understood her plight and gave her the money at the stipulated time. She dreaded the thought of what she'd hear at Ralph's.

Ralph opened the door and she hurried inside, asking, 'Is someone around?'

He shot her a suspicious glance and asked, 'No, why?'

She locked the door. She dispelled the thought of asking for money right then; the moment wasn't right.

Ralph went into the kitchen. Suddenly, the light in the flat faded and a shadow was cast over the living room, where she stood. She kept her plastic bag and tied the ends of her dupatta around her waist as thunder rolled across the sky. She stepped into the balcony to remove the clothes that had been put to dry and surveyed the flotilla of clouds. They were slit open by flashes of lightning.

In the kitchen, Ralph was caramelizing sugar in a pan. He was humming to himself as the sugar released golden bubbles. Zubina said breathlessly, 'I need my salary and bonus for Eid early this month. I have a lot of household expenses coming up.'

Ralph didn't look at her. His focus was on not spilling the scalding hot liquid as he poured it into a tin. 'All right.'

After putting the caramel custard in the pressure cooker, he gave Zubina her salary with the bonus. He said, 'Sorry for making you wait. I am following the recipe exactly how Maa had asked me to.'

She carefully counted the notes and said, 'It's okay ... and I will taste it tomorrow.'

In the living room, she drew the purse from her bra—a small, faded, zipped pouch made of red velvet that one gets in jewellery shops. She meticulously placed the folded money in it. She put her purse back, patting her kameez to ensure it was held firmly inside her bra. Then she returned to the kitchen.

She exhaled with relief at not having to listen to an excuse again. She began preparing tea.

The money and then the sight of milk and sugar took her back to the days when Zeenat, her elder sister, got the weekly provisions. Once, they had to go to their cousin's house for tea because Zeenat had drunk all the milk with heaps of sugar in the morning. Their mother would be cross with Zeenat, but none of them said a word because they knew it was Zeenat who ran the house. When the mother found out and tried to quiz Zeenat about the missing sugar, Zeenat lost her temper and left the house. She did not return until it was quite late. Zubina's only pair of rubber slippers fell apart as she ran with her brother, Tausiq, to the houses Zeenat worked in and the tiny school run by the government where she cleaned the floors. She was nowhere to be found. At eleven at night, they retraced their way back home, crying. Their mother promised them that Zeenat would return, that nothing would happen. While cleansing her bloodied heels, Zubina told her mother, 'I will go to work from tomorrow.'

'What did you say?' her mother scolded. 'What about school?'

'School? Really? And who will run this house? What will you do with your broken leg?' Zubina retorted.

'But …'

Someone knocked at the door. As young Tausiq was asleep, the mother dragged herself forward to open it. Zeenat lumbered in, her breath reeking of alcohol and bidis. They did not say anything to each other. Zeenat went to her corner and fell asleep. Zubina moved towards her, then lurched back; she slept some distance away from her sister.

In the morning, when Zeenat was brushing her teeth, Zubina went to her and brazenly said, 'Take me to work. I want to work.' Her sister weighed her words for a minute and spat red paste from her mouth. 'Get ready,' she said, 'and wear my old slippers.' Zeenat celebrated Zubina's first earnings by gifting her a lipstick that she had wanted for a long time. It was the happiest moment in young Zubina's life—seeing the money she had earned in her hands. Life, and all the possibilities it held, opened out before her.

Now, Zubina thought of Nazma. Penniless, helplessly pining for money to run her house and being curtailed by her husband. She couldn't bear the idea of it. She had asked Aadil the previous night about the possibility of helping her—but the conversation had yielded very little.

Zubina served tea to Ralph by the couch next to the balcony. He seemed lost, his legs curled. She swept the floor. She tried to make small talk about work and his father, but Ralph's answers were clipped. It seemed as though he were holding back; that he had a lot to say but she wasn't the person he could talk to. When she mentioned how Ojas had not come lately, he got up from the couch and stared hard at the phone screen. The pressure cooker whistled in the kitchen.

She remembered the kiss in her dreams. The bearded face of Ojas and the clean-shaven face of Ralph meeting in odd harmony, with a kind of hunger that she had never encountered. They were leaning into each other, mocking her.

It upset her that she was calling forth the image again. The bedroom door seemed to stare at her. What games was her mind playing on her? The word 'love' returned to her and it made her shift uncomfortably on her haunches.

Her phone rang. Amrin was on the line, she was in tears, screaming that she return home immediately. *Astaghfirullah!* Zubina rushed out.

7

Back at work, Ralph immersed himself in the kitchen. He tried recovering the strength he had lost from the previous week of ill health. A big luncheon for diplomats from various countries had to be organized. Ralph leafed through the menu that had been prepared and suggested last-minute changes—replace bruschetta with canapés to go with the welcome drink; fresh berries on the tart instead of a jam. While issuing commands, he forgot to season the loaves with rosemary, and now they looked much too sad and naked for focaccia. Immediately, he replaced the plan for focaccia with schiacciata, which he had recently mastered when a couple from Tuscany had asked for it from the hotel's bakery. The kitchen turned busy, as bowls and serving plates rattled, got filled with food items and, wrapped in cellophane, were carried up to the hall.

Ralph noticed Sujoy at the counter where the brownies were being cooled and cut into squares. All around: discarded butter paper. Ralph went over to clean the mess, but Sujoy was too distracted to notice him. Ralph understood that something was troubling him again.

Suddenly, Ralph remembered a winter morning in Delhi during their internship.

It was in Delhi that Ralph had confronted Sujoy: 'Sujoy, I get it. I am sorry I kissed him.' Sujoy, half-asleep, opened his eyes. He was stunned to find Ralph at his bedside. 'What?' he asked.

For Sujoy, this had been his first trip beyond West Bengal. His family didn't travel because his father never earned enough to pay for a vacation.

At the hotel where they interned, Ralph was excited seeing people from Mumbai, Chandigarh, Imphal, Indore, Chennai, all in one place. In fits and starts, he interacted with most of them and often hung out with the lot after work. Sujoy took a liking to them, too. But unlike Ralph, who wanted to explore the city in company, Sujoy wished to return to their one-room flat in Dwarka and read Joanne Harris's novels. When Ralph would insist, he would accompany them to Connaught Place, where Ralph would often spot other gay men and act untrammelled, even as his group teased him about the guys he happened to woo.

Once, when they returned drunkenly to their flat at midnight, Sujoy did not join Ralph on the mattress. He changed into his pyjamas, sat on the plastic chair and read *Chocolat* by the window. When Ralph woke up in the middle of the night, he was surprised to find him there.

'Won't you sleep?' Ralph asked.

Without looking away from the page, Sujoy replied, 'Do you care?'

For days, they ate and slept in separate corners. Ralph was frustrated with Sujoy's unexplained silence. Finally, he confronted Sujoy when he was asleep.

'It's okay. I know what it is. You don't have to tell me.' Ralph apologized to Sujoy for kissing the man at a bar who flirted with him.

Sujoy looked stunned. 'What?' he managed to ask.

Ralph bent forward and pressed his mouth tightly on Sujoy's. It was like two dry stones being rubbed against each other for a spark. He could sense Sujoy trying to say something but he had kept kissing him; a shiver ran through his spine.

At last, after failing to say what he wished to, Sujoy pushed Ralph away. Ralph jerked back, knocking his head against the wall. 'I love you too,' he managed to gasp.

'What's wrong with you, Ralph?' demanded Sujoy, wiping his mouth with the back of his hand.

'Fine … I understand it. It's difficult for me to imagine you as a lover, but if that's the way I can keep you in my life, I will do what I have to,' blurted Ralph.

'Are you crazy? From where on earth did you get that?' Sujoy asked, unable to get over the shock of what had happened and the discomfort he felt at the back of his throat.

'Sujoy, I … okay, listen, I understand you find it difficult to admit to some things.'

Sujoy went to get water. 'Ralph, I don't understand what you're getting at. I want you to know this … I am not gay or bisexual, okay?'

'Sujoy, you want me. I know that. You are possessive about me, and you didn't like it when I kissed that guy in the washroom at the bar, did you?'

'Wait a second! So all this while, you thought I was angry because you kissed someone?'

Ralph nodded.

Sujoy placed the bottle of water down with a thud and said, 'No, Ralph … it's sad that you don't see why I'm disappointed in you.'

Ralph's brows knit together. He looked pale. He saw Sujoy's face soften as he spoke. 'I didn't want to go to those bars or socialize with a bunch of people. First of all, it's beyond my budget. And also, I don't like such things. Even in Calcutta,

I'd always return home. I'd get busy reading a book or experimenting with a new recipe. You've seen that. I was angry with you because it seemed like you didn't care. You forgot who I was. You forced me to tag along—sometimes, by emotionally manipulating me—disregarding what I wanted. And …'

'What?' Ralph was dumbfounded.

'Yes, you'd tell me that you weren't happy when I was unavailable, that you needed me as a crutch, that I was the only life support you had in a sea of strangers. And … and I didn't want to say no to you because … well, I wanted you to be happy, to enjoy this city. I mean, unlike me, you don't read, and you have nothing to entertain yourself with in this flat. So, I joined you.'

'Is it manipulative to say that you are my only support? Can I not expect presence from a friend?'

'No, what was wrong was this—that you wished to *gain* something by saying that. You wanted to make me accompany you.'

'Wow, okay. Sorry … for *manipulating* you?' Ralph did not sound apologetic at all.

'Keep your sarcasm to yourself, and next time can you try being sensitive? That is, if you are my friend.'

After that conversation, Ralph and Sujoy weren't on talking terms for days. They kept to their corners, went to work separately and Ralph made lame excuses for Sujoy's absence when he hung out with his colleagues.

Finally, Ralph, unhappy about the possibility of losing Sujoy, went over to him. It was late at night. He sat on the floor, next to Sujoy's mattress. He ran his fingers over the cover of *Gentlemen & Players*. He knew Sujoy wasn't asleep. He whispered, 'I am sorry.'

Sujoy said, 'It's okay.'

Ralph curled up near Sujoy and held him by the forearm.

'Don't kiss me,' said Sujoy.

They both began laughing. They returned to being the friends they once had been. But something had changed after that argument. Both of them felt it in the air that floated between them. Physically, they were awkward hugging one another. There was also discomfort in the fact that when they had to hang out, Ralph felt compelled to choose places that were cheap—a concession that didn't escape Sujoy. He hated it.

The moment Sujoy got placed in Odisha, he left. He couldn't withstand a soured friendship anymore.

In the kitchen, Ralph realized that, once more, it had come to this—he had to get Sujoy out of his shell.

He took him to their usual smoking corner and asked him about Sayantani.

Sujoy was startled by the directness of the question. He hesitated, then muttered, 'We are talking.'

Ralph didn't speak for a while. He hoped Sujoy would go on, but Sujoy seemed determined to let the conversation lapse. He asked if he could leave.

Ralph held him by his arm. 'Why don't you want to speak?'

Sujoy shut him up. 'I will when you talk about what's going on between you and Ojas, okay?'

Ralph was aghast. It felt to him as though Sujoy was being petty. He wanted to say it out loud, but he remembered what Ojas had once told him about Sujoy. They had had a fight after that, but the comment never seemed to leave his mind: 'You know, I think he keeps wanting more because he has always felt deprived—money, attention … status? His family background … you know, the whole low caste bit … it goes against him.'

Ralph yelled at Ojas—how he couldn't say such a thing about his friend, *his* friend, the one he had known since childhood?

The damage, however, had been done. Whenever Ralph felt overwhelmed by Sujoy's demands and requests—for hanging out, for sharing the more intimate details of his existence—Ojas's words rang loud in his ears.

Do I pity Sujoy? he found himself wondering. *Do I?*

No, no, no, this can't be happening.

Sujoy left Ralph to his thoughts.

A text flashed on Ojas's screen as he made his way towards his home at Lake Town. It was from Piyush, an ex—a hook-up from some years ago. Ojas read the message over and over; his lips ran over its casual wording: 'Hey, Ojas! How's u? In Calcutta for a week ... work. Wanna grab dinner soon? So much to tell you and hear from you. Long time.'

He forwarded the text to Ralph with a message: 'I agreed to see him.'

Ralph replied with a thumbs-up emoticon: 'Need to get back to my caramel custard.'

Ojas abused Ralph in his mind; a desire to throttle him took over as he messaged Piyush: 'Hey, yesssss, see you soon. Let me know the date, time and place.'

A puja was being conducted in the drawing room of the Garg's spacious apartment. Ojas was in no mood to be part of his family's rites; they seemed more interested in the beige and white decor of the flat than the puja—the cushions were not unlike square candies dipped in caramel. Sandalwood sticks were lit to create an air of luxurious piousness. Ojas's mother's peacock crewelwork had been displayed on the accent wall. Its riot of colours—all shades of blue and green—always made Ojas stop in his step. He greeted his relatives, admired the peacock's metallic blue crests, and resisted the temptation to touch it as he had done when he was a child. His mother remained busy getting thaalis of ghee ladoos, which she laid on the expansive dining table. Ojas promised to join in; then, he went to his room and locked the door. In the long mirror, he saw a tall, bearded man stare at him with disgust.

He changed into a pastel green kurta and white pyjama after a shower and participated in the aarti. He had believed in the idea of god; he participated in all rituals that involved worship with his family. With age, however, he had come to believe that he—or men like him—weren't in god's scheme of things. None of the stories he could recollect seemed to reflect the struggles of his life. There were tales of Ram and Sita, Krishna and Radha, Shiva and Parvati—two beings tied together by sacred forces. But what about Ojas and Ralph?

While serving food to his aunts and uncles, Ojas wondered if they knew who he truly was—a gay man struggling to keep his life together.

The guests at the dinner table under the chandelier were preoccupied with questions about his marriage. The way his parents kept their heads bowed and shrugged and delayed their responses or attempted changing the subject irked Ojas further.

'When are you going to marry?' A voice intruded.

Ojas remained silent.

'There are young girls from our community, fresh out of college … surely, you wouldn't want a working woman?'

Silence again.

'I know this girl who is a CA, but her father was telling me she'd leave her job if she was married into a business family.'

Ojas said nothing.

'Ojas, boys do get married at an older age … but you seem to be crossing all limits. Thirty-nine! You want to be a father at forty-two or what? Bringing up a young child at that age is challenging.'

Ojas refused to offer a response.

For the sake of his mother and father, he sat still and let the invasive questions pass over him. His parents' Marwari pride was central to their personalities. It had gained in strength following years of struggle—after leaving a home in Rajasthan and earning a reputation away from family. The relatives recounted stories from the 1970s, when Yash-bhaiyya, Ojas's father, had come to Calcutta and worked in a shop that sold inner garments at Bara Bazar. From there, to buying a godown in the vicinity, and having a business that his son ran so well—his was a success story, and all that was left was one matter. Ojas was told: 'This marriage is the only thing you need to do to keep that father of yours smiling ... well, your mother too ... ah, look at her cry, dear Madhu ...'

Ojas wanted to run away from the house when he saw his mother sob and his father's eyes well up with tears. His brother, Sarvesh, observed him from a corner. Ojas tried keeping a straight face; he swallowed his guilt.

The pain on their faces was too much to withstand. He felt churlish. Soon after the guests left, Sarvesh attempted talking to Ojas, but Ojas simply slammed the door on his face and left the house.

It was 11 p.m. He checked his messages. Ralph had sent him a picture of the dessert he had attempted making: 'Custard failed. Overcooked. What a shame!'

The ex-hookup had sent a text saying he was excited about dinner.

Ralph's father was making his way through sumptuous Himsagar mango segments when Ojas rang the bell.

Ralph was taken by surprise at the visit. He was on the verge of shutting the door, but his father welcomed Ojas in and encouraged him to share the cold mangoes. Ojas sat at the dining table with them. He ate the mangoes with relish as he exchanged pleasantries with Ralph's father. Ralph washed and peeled two more mangoes, sliced and served it to them, drawing a chair between the two.

The mood had been tense prior to Ojas's visit—but, now, that dissipated. Ralph's father had paid a visit out of concern. He had requested his son to leave the flat and live with him in their house in Alipore. Mike, their dog, was difficult to manage singlehandedly, he had said. Ralph himself would have someone who'd take care of him if he was sick.

Ralph had reassured his father that he was okay.

His father looked unhappy.

Then Ojas had unexpectedly arrived.

Ojas entertained his father like they were friends catching up, as though they hadn't once been caterwauling at each other.

'The heat is unbearable, yes. Today, one of the workers fainted in the godown,' said Ojas.

Ralph's father had complained about the changing weather.

'The AC which his mother got in 2013 still works. So, I keep Mike there throughout the day,' his father informed both of them.

'Ojas,' his father said after a pause, 'I don't have any problem if you come and stay in our house with Ralph. I hope you know that.'

'Uncle …' Ojas was waiting for Ralph to intervene; he hadn't been privy to the earlier discussion. He felt unable to understand what was going on.

'What happened at that time … forget it, please.'

'I have,' Ojas said, his voice reassuring.

'Good …'

'Baba, please don't,' Ralph said. 'I am fine.'

The subject changed. Ralph served the payesh he had prepared. His heart made rapid thumps in his chest as he watched the most important men in his life enjoy his cooking.

Always cook with and for love, he remembered his mother once saying to him.

Ojas licked the back of his spoon and said to his father, 'Your son's hands are blessed.'

'His Maa always said that,' his father added, placing his empty bowl on the table.

'It was she who made it back then,' said Ralph, looking away.

When it was time for his father to leave, Ralph suggested he stay over. His father expressed concern for Mike; Ralph informed him that he had already called Anita, the cook, and asked her to stay the night with him.

Ralph heard the door to his room click and asked Ojas, 'You didn't go to your dinner with Piyush?'

Ojas shrugged his shoulders. 'Not tonight.'

'Baba was asking me to move in with him. I said no,' Ralph said, taking off his clothes.

'Why can't you?' Ojas asked.

Ralph slip into a pair of boxers. 'I told you … it's not easy for me there. Sujoy also thinks it's not a great idea.'

'Why is Sujoy deciding things for you? Why can't you make a decision for yourself?'

'He knows me well.' Ralph folded the garments he had tossed away, avoiding Ojas's gaze. 'And certainly better than you do.'

'Sad that he isn't gay, no?' said Ojas, sardonically.

'Fuck off, Ojas!' Ralph glowered, almost yelling. 'Don't you dare open your mouth about him.'

Ojas reached out to place his hand on Ralph's mouth. Ralph flinched, thinking Ojas was about to slap him.

'Stop shouting,' Ojas said in a low, scolding voice, holding Ralph by his shoulders.

Ralph released himself.

Ojas stepped back and studied Ralph. 'Are you okay?' he asked.

'Sleep ... or leave,' replied Ralph.

'Ralph ...'

Ralph opened the bathroom door. He began washing his face. Ojas tried reaching for Ralph's ass. Ralph pushed him aside. 'I haven't douched.'

Ralph wanted to throw himself at Ojas. To be fucked unclean and moan hysterically. He wanted to tell him about his day, the conversation with Sujoy, the failed custard, his father's disappointment that he wouldn't move back and the fact that Ojas's ex's text suffocated him.

He was done adulting.

As a young boy, in his twenties, he had envisaged the thirties offering a sense of being settled. He imagined the scenes of his life fitting together—a job, a partner, a kinship unlike any other.

What he saw before him now was not a seamless panorama, but wreckage. It got worse with every passing day.

Ojas let his displeasure known by fidgeting with his phone and hair. He tapped at the screen with force, ignoring his brother's texts urging him to speak up. He wanted to talk about his day with Ralph; communicate the drama that had unfolded within the family gathering; tell him of his inability to shut them up by announcing that he was not going to marry a woman and that he had a man in his life—Ralph. They'd frown upon a Christian name. They'd say, 'These Christians are all outsiders, part of a weird culture.' He wanted to announce that he was part of the weird culture, and he wanted to share that culture with Ralph. He wanted to laugh about all of it with him. Or pat him on the ass and tell Ralph that he was only his.

But Ralph's dead stare at the ceiling warned him against any kind of disclosure.

Finally, Ralph slept.

Ojas thought of Ralph's confession that his mother's presence lulled him to sleep. It was a confession that made Ojas want to protect his family—even while their insistence that he marry a woman, their persistent forwarding of CVs and photographs on WhatsApp, their refusal to pay heed to his excuses, made him deeply uneasy. *What perseverance*, Ojas thought, recalling the tears in his mother's eyes.

He pushed his crotch between the plump cheeks of Ralph's ass and clutched him with all his strength.

He dreamt of a peacock shaking its crest violently with desire.

8

Zubina ran to Amrin after her call.

Soniya wailed at the top of her voice, her palm covering her forehead. Her fingers were sticky with blood.

Amrin exclaimed, 'She fell off the bed when I was speaking to Yasmin and Rina outside!'

Zubina found the two girls; they were nodding their heads.

'What were you all doing? Those games again?' Zubina asked.

'No, no. Soniya was playing with her dolls,' Amrin clarified.

Zubina dabbed Soniya's forehead with cotton soaked in the iodine solution, offered to her by her neighbour. Then she grabbed her daughter and rushed her to the clinic. The rain dripped down the ribs of an umbrella that had snapped at several corners. Water wet Zubina's hair and ran down in rivulets along her neck as she ran to the doctor.

Zubina did not trust Amrin and Soniya with those girls. She was surrounded by the odour of sweat; not even the rain could wash it away. She struggled to get rid of it as the doctor cleaned Soniya's wound, applied an ointment and then gauze to cover it.

Amrin was in the house arranging buckets with the help of her friends. The rain leaked through the roof. The sky thundered. They spread a large plastic sheet over the bed and arranged steel bowls all across to keep it in place.

In the neighbourhood, the drains had filled; they reeked of rotten eggs and carcasses. Kids stood on furniture, and adults screamed at them—'Don't drop things into the water!'

Zubina returned with Soniya. Amrin was in the middle of taking a bowl brimming over with water and emptying it with a splash outside. Everyone changed into dry clothes. Soniya was asked to remain seated in the corner of the bed that was as yet untouched by water. Zubina tried to help Amrin with work but left it midway. She was restive. She started discussing everything to do with the shopping that was due, the ceiling that needed urgent repair, and the food she wished to eat for the evening's meal. She was breathless with chatter. She wanted to continue without losing her daughters' attention.

Finally, she paused, then cleared her throat and croaked her question. 'What were you talking about with those girls?'

Amrin bit her lips—her mother's hoarse voice terrified her and she couldn't lie. She said, 'They were planning to tell more girls about our secret game. They said if others joined in, it would be fun. I was telling them that if they did, Neha-di would get to know too, and then, she'd never look at me.'

Zubina watched Amrin cover her mouth with her fingers and continue, 'I don't know who I will be without Neha-di. I made them promise never to say it to anyone ... that's when Soniya fell.'

Zubina left Amrin and emptied pails of water. The rain was abating. She saw the waterlogged neighbourhood. The heat was back with a vengeance, ending the respite that the showers had offered from summer's intensity. She asked Amrin to get Yasmin and Rina. Amrin was about to question her, but Zubina had already wrapped her slippers in polythene bags and was pushing her out of the house.

The girls were shaking with fear when Zubina ushered Rina and Yasmin inside. When all the girls were seated at the edge of the chowki, Zubina began speaking.

'You see, last time Amrin mentioned the djinn, I entered to stop you. I was sent by the djinn to prevent you from committing a sin. This time, you talked of that thing again, and Soniya fell down. The djinn is listening and watching you all,' she paused and held them with her pointed gaze. 'The moment you talk about what you did with other people, or even think of doing it again, it *will* strike.'

Eyes were wide in horror. The girls clutched each other's hands and shook their heads. 'We will never talk about it. I won't tell my family even.'

Amrin and Soniya joined them. 'Yes, Ammi, we will never speak of it or do it again. We promise. Please ask the djinn to go away.'

'Yes, don't talk of it or think of it. The djinn will let you be happy. Djinns can be nice when you are good girls,' Zubina concluded. Her hands trembled with nervousness. She wondered if the djinn could hear her tell these lies. She was anxious about the djinn hunting her down.

That evening, she invoked Allah in earnest. Her face contorted with self-loathing as she mouthed the prayers and recited '*Ayatul Kursi*'—'To Him belongs whatever is in the heavens and whatever is on the earth. Who could possibly intercede with Him without His permission?'

Once Aadil received Zubina's pay from Firdaus and his own, Zubina took her share with effervescent glee. She did not let Aadil keep a penny for miscellaneous expenses.

Aadil asked, 'What happened? Such a bright smile!'

Zubina replied, 'You don't know what a relief it is to see this money. Amrin and Soniya have driven me crazy about their clothes. I will take them shopping tomorrow itself.'

Aadil unbuttoned his trousers and asked, 'What will you get for me?'

Her gaze spun towards him, as his trousers fell to his feet—'Oh'—and then lingered, taking in his bare thighs. 'For you … uh, I'll see.'

He stretched out his hand and held her chin between his thumb and index finger. 'Shop well.' He let his thumb run over her lips. 'Buy a pair of shoes for yourself, take money from me for it.'

Her cheeks brightened; she removed his hand reluctantly. 'Don't do this when everyone is awake. The girls can be home from their classes anytime.'

He laughed and hung his faded trousers from the almirah door.

Zubina pored over her face and his firm, muscular back in the mirror as he wrapped a lungi around his waist. She did not tell Aadil what she had seen their daughters do. Nor could she tell him of the ecstasies of desire she felt in the middle of the day when he touched her.

Zubina cleaned the smudges on the mirror with the side of her fist. Was Aadil seeing her turn beautiful? She could still feel the heat radiating from him; it seemed to reach her mouth. She could imagine his rough, calloused hands on her powdered face. Her body tensed with longing.

Twelve years of wait. She swallowed the thirst that rose in her mouth.

Love coursed through her blood with speed and not with the gentleness she had always accorded it. It was as though the ferocity of love she had seen in Ralph now rushed between Aadil and her, as he flashed a smile in the mirror.

She looked away when she heard two girls squabbling at the window. Then, she left for her evening shift.

Ojas's restive smoking in the living room and balcony, and Ralph's refusal to allow him close, told Zubina of a major turn in their friendship. A disagreement. An ugly fight. In the past, she had heard them bicker, but things had never come to this pass. There was a strained silence now. At the breakfast table, in the bedroom, in the balcony over tea, in all the spaces they shared, there seemed to be a repressed scream.

Zubina's heart felt heavy with what she saw. Ojas managed to cast a smile in her direction.

What could have caused this? she wondered.

She tried to connect the dots. Often, Ralph and Ojas would talk in hushed tones; they'd turn quiet when she'd enter their room.

Some evenings, when Ojas wasn't around, she'd hear Ralph talk on the phone to someone endearingly. He'd bloom like a flower, burst into peals of echoing laughter and, once, she heard the sound of a kiss being pressed against the phone before he disconnected.

She had waited for the girl to come home ... but she never did.

Some days, when Ralph was not yet home and Ojas was there before him, he'd be on a similar call. He'd ask questions like a protective husband regarding work and health, tease the person on the phone intermittently, whisper things about the chocolate mousse he craved ever since the person at the other end had fed it to him. He'd disconnect minutes before the bell rang and Ralph entered.

They never talked to these people on the phone when they were around each other. Zubina found it curious. But she had never cared to mull over the fact until this moment. Now, her mind buzzed with questions.

When Ojas had smoked the third cigarette that evening, she asked, 'Do you have a brother or sister?'

Ojas nodded as he sipped the tea she had served. 'A brother, yes.'

'Is he married?'

He laughed. 'No, no, Zubina-di. He's too young to be married.'

'Oh, well, and how can he marry when the elder brother hasn't ...'

Ojas unlocked his phone. He showed her pictures of his family.

She said, 'Ah, your brother looks just like you. And, oh, your mother, so beautiful!'

'As are you, Zubina-di. I am sure you have a beautiful husband and beautiful daughters, too.'

'Hah ...' She rose quietly, then added, 'By Allah's grace, I have a family and children ... it does one good. You will know when you have your own.'

She noticed the look of dismissal on his face. The images of him kissing Ralph returned to her mind. She hurried towards the kitchen before he could say anything. She washed her hands and face vigorously, and then poured herself a glass of cold water. She stared at the rows of jars that contained the many spices she used to cook meals for the two men.

The next day, Zubina took leave from work for Eid shopping. Only four days were left for Eid. Zubina rose at seven—rising for sehri made her want to sleep even more—after being reminded by Amrin, 'Everyone has got their clothes, Ammi!' Her sister repeated the statement, seeking additional sympathy by pointing to her forehead that was still healing.

Zubina gathered the clean dishes that had dried and said, 'Yes, we will go today. Come on, go and stand in that line. Fill up bottles and buckets with water ... we won't be there later to do it.'

Amrin and Soniya collected the empty Dalda and Saffola containers and bottles of Thums Up, and put them into two bags; each carried one. Zubina used the leftover water that Amrin had collected into one of her small, red plastic tubs and sprinkled in some detergent from a sachet. When the water developed a thin layer of foam, she plonked in the unwashed clothes. While they soaked, she swept the house. When she was on her haunches, mopping the floor, she heard some distant commotion. She peered through the curtains and asked a neighbour, 'What happened?' The neighbour, in turn, stopped a boy coming from the direction of all that noise and made a few inquiries. He said, 'That Prakash and Hamid are fighting over the washroom and water again!'

Zubina left her mopping cloth in the bucket of brown water. She locked the door behind her and marched towards Amrin and Soniya. She saw them sandwiched between Nazma and the tailor's daughter, holding their bags. Their eyes were fixed on the two men who were quarrelling. Zubina stood beside her friend and asked, 'Nazma, what is this?' Her girls swivelled, startled to see her. Nazma stared at the men and answered, 'The daily drama. These stupid boys. Always fighting about who gets to enter the toilet first because one has to go to mandir and the other has his work.'

One of the older women intervened and asked them to stop their gunda-gardi. The argument fizzled out. Zubina waited in the queue with her daughters. Nazma pulled her closer and whispered, 'Did you talk to Aadil-bhai?'

Zubina looked away, while squeezing Nazma's hand. 'I did. But … I don't know, Nazma …' She scanned the crowds and tried to find words that conveyed her inability to be of use to her friend.

Nazma sighed. 'I don't know what I will do. I have managed to get money from the houses I work in for Eid … but it won't last long.'

Zubina patted her, 'Don't worry, by Allah's grace, all good things will happen. Amrin's father will keep an eye out for any vacancy and I will also ask my brother to do so.'

Nazma moved forward in the line and said, her voice low, 'Yesterday, he came home drunk. My son was scared because he began abusing him. I had to send my children off to my sister-in-law's. The whole night he didn't sleep and kept hurling filthy words at me. I was ashamed to show my face in the morning. Everyone … Zubina … all the families were looking at me … what does one do when the person who heads the family makes you fall so low?'

Before Zubina could react, it was Nazma's turn to fill the buckets she was carrying. The conversation fell through. Zubina waited for Amrin and Soniya's bottles to fill. Once they were done, they loaded their bags and carried some bottles in the crook of their arms.

Her daughters went past her with the keys.

Zubina was aware of something troubling her. The fog that seemed to envelop her thoughts eased a little when she took a sharp breath. Nazma's voice echoed in her mind.

It took her back to another time.

Zubina remembered being all of seventeen—young and docile. She was washing clothes at the house where Zeenat, who was twenty-one then, did the cleaning and cooking. Zubina heard her enter the bathroom, where she sat on a little plastic stool and scrubbed the shirts, trousers, undergarments, salwar kameezes and bedsheets of the couple who employed them. Zeenat dumped a new shirt into the bucket and asked, 'How long will this take you?'

Zubina tucked a strand of hair behind her ear and said, 'I will be done in another twenty minutes.'

'Okay, I will go and clean the other rooms by then. You wait for me.'

Zubina scrubbed the collar of the shirt and said, 'Okay, be quick.'

Once she was done washing, Zubina took the stairs to the terrace of the two-storey house, where she clipped the clothes on a wire with thick black pegs, before making her way back down the stairs. From a corner of the terrace, one of rooms on the second floor was visible. Her eyes, suddenly, fell upon her sister in that room. She squinted and looked closer; something was not right about what she saw.

Stealthily, she tiptoed down the stairs and past the corridor that led to the room in question. It was locked from the inside. She examined the corridor to check that no one was around, then peeked through a crack in the door. She saw her sister naked, her pink salwar kameez lying on the floor. She was holding Daanish-bhai's face to her bosom and was letting him kiss her breasts as though he were her child. Zubina was about to cry for help, but stopped herself when she saw Zeenat pick up a glass brimming over with liquid gold. She pressed it to her lips and let the drink pour down her throat. Daanish-bhai peeled his face off her bosom and poured more liquid into the glass from a bottle—Zubina understood that it was alcohol. He took a sip and got on his knees and put his mouth between Zeenat's legs, releasing a jet of gold into it. A slurping sound from between her sister's legs reached Zubina.

Zubina closed her eyes and crawled on all fours down the corridor as noiselessly as she could. Half an hour later, her sister came down and found her waiting at the doorstep. She took her home.

Zubina did not mention what she had witnessed to Zeenat or to her mother. She didn't know what to say, how to phrase it or what would come of the revelation.

Two days later, after Zubina had put her mother to sleep, Zeenat came home reeking of alcohol. Tausiq, her brother, had gone to Howrah for the weekend, to their grandfather's home. Zeenat entered the house and began dancing. Zubina hissed at her and pointed to the mother who was asleep. Zeenat twirled her thick waist in circles and winked at Zubina. She hummed a tune and invited Zubina to dance with her. To stop her, Zubina got up and swayed her hands. But memories of Daanish-bhai flooded her mind. She said, 'You awful creature.'

Zeenat was taken aback. 'What?' she whispered.

'I saw you with that man!' Zubina said under her breath and spat at her sister, 'Randi.'

The dancing ceased.

Zeenat grabbed Zubina by the hair and slapped her. She fell to the floor. The house seemed to shake. The mother woke up with a start. 'What happened?'

Zeenat bent low, offering Zubina her hand. Zubina flinched. Zeenat drew close and whispered, 'Don't you dare say anything. And you won't go to that house anymore.'

That night, Zubina slept on her brother's side of the mattress and avoided Zeenat.

Nazma shouldn't have mentioned alcohol, or the fact that her husband had stooped low—especially not on a day she had planned to go shopping.

Zubina reached home, finished her work and cooked a frugal meal for Soniya. Amrin was fasting. After Soniya ate and complained, and Zubina finished washing the dishes, she asked both of them to get ready. Zubina wore the salwar kameez she had bought the previous Eid—a bright mix of lavender and pink hydrangeas against white. She wore leather chappals and moved the cash from her daily-use pouch to her blue wallet. She lined her eyes with a kohl and dabbed her lips with a hint of lipstick. Amrin wore a blue tunic lined with gold lace, a pair of black pants and a big hairpin to the right of her head. Both the girls smothered their cheeks with pink blush and resembled ripe tomatoes. Lips—a thick smear of red. Zubina was about to admonish them, but then she let it be because they were going shopping. It was a joyful day! Amrin made Soniya wear her favourite pink Barbie top and blue denims.

'Let's go,' Zubina said.

They held each other's hand, with Soniya in between, and left the lane. Zubina asked, 'You have got water for Soniya, right?' Amrin swung her free hand out and said, 'Yes, I have.' Zubina walked while Amrin spoke of Neha-di. The sun beat down harshly.

They reached the auto stand and waited in the line. After fifteen minutes, they sat at the back; another lady and her son were in the front. Throughout the journey, they travelled quietly—only to be interrupted by Soniya's questions about the cars passing by, what her mother would buy, if she would get her a doctor set, and if Amrin would be given the shoes she had longed for last Eid. Zubina replied to her questions as patiently as she could; exhaustion had already taken hold of her mind. When they reached the next auto stand near the Park Circus bridge, Zubina paid the fare and listlessly followed her daughters to the next auto. She was growing restless. Amrin swung her head and hummed a tune Zubina failed to recognize.

When the passengers ahead of them were ready to get into an auto, Amrin suddenly said, 'Ammi, you know, I wrote a full answer in English without a mistake. Neha-di liked it. She said I am a bright girl.'

Zubina put her hand on Amrin's head and tried to sound happy. 'How nice is that! What else did she say? Please show her remarks to your schoolteachers as well.'

Amrin replied, 'I will tell them … but they don't care.'

Zubina clicked her tongue. She felt the heat crawl through her skin.

Soniya chimed in, 'It's our turn. Let's go quickly.'

Zubina robotically shepherded her girls into the auto; she wanted nothing more than to drop the plan and run far away. She wasn't able to match their enthusiasm anymore.

In the auto, Zubina's thoughts went back to Zeenat.

Zeenat and Zubina continued working at Daanish-bhai's house, despite Zeenat's threat that Zubina was no longer welcome.

Zubina remained anxious between noon and 2 p.m., when she had to be there. She toyed with the idea of telling her mother of the goings-on in the house, but she knew that her sister—ever since she had started earning for the family—had ceased listening to Ammi. She resisted the urge to confess to Riya-apa and tell her that her hired help slept with her husband. But she couldn't muster the courage. So, she let disgust and apathy consume her each day, or every time Zeenat returned home drunk and, sometimes, dishevelled.

One evening, Tausiq, who was fourteen, entered home angrily. He bellowed at Zubina. 'What does she do? Today my friends were laughing at her when they saw her stumble by the steps of this house. They called her a mad woman.'

Zubina gathered that they had seen Zeenat inebriated. She asked Tausiq to keep matters quiet. She told him everything she had seen, while the mother snored in the background.

Tausiq looked aghast. 'What do we do?' he asked.

Zubina shrugged, 'Nothing. She won't listen to us.'

'She should have died instead of our father,' said young Tausiq.

Zubina squeezed his hand. 'No, don't say such things, please.'

Just then, the door opened. Zeenat walked in and threw her bag on the floor. She wasn't drunk this time. She poured water from the claypot into a steel glass, drank it and asked, 'So, what are you two talking about in secret?'

'Nothing ...' Zubina said.

But Tausiq interjected, 'That you drink alcohol and you have no shame and we suffer because of you.'

She put the glass down and said, 'How does that affect you? Do I ask for *your* money to buy my alcohol?' She carried on, 'I work day and night and earn. I pay for this house too. And still I have to hear such taunts.'

Tausiq glowered. 'People laugh at us when you come home the way you do ... and Daanish-bhai? Have you lost your mind, Apa?'

'Listen, both of you,' Zeenat said disdainfully, 'it is not my problem what people think of me. Next time, if I'm drunk, I will be careful about how I enter this house ... but I will not stop sleeping with the man I love.'

'Love?' Zubina was shaken. 'You call that love?'

'Yes, Zubina, it is love. He loves me and I love him.'

'And?' Zubina asked. 'What will you do? Keep sleeping with him whenever Riya-apa goes to the market?'

'That's for me and him to decide,' replied Zeenat.

The conversation was over. She got up to prepare tea for

everyone. Zubina stared at her unbelievingly. She wanted to scream and rescue her sister.

She desperately tried clutching on to the happy times she had spent with Zeenat to make up for this instance when she felt the full brokenness of her household.

Her interactions with her sister stained Zubina's future. She resisted the urge to think of the love she felt for Aadil. The word had destroyed Zeenat, after all, and it would destroy her, too.

Zubina instructed Amrin not to leave Soniya's hand even for a second once they got off the auto and entered New Market. They walked past crowds swarming like bees around the phuchkawalla, who only spoke Bhojpuri; past an old couple who sold posters on the sidewalk in fluent English; past a line of young boys who pulled pedestrians towards their stalls, peddling phone covers, deodorants and sunglasses for one hundred rupees. The KMC building at Hogg Market stood undisturbed, immune to the madness around the cigarette shops, Nizam's roll counter and the biryani kitchen at Aminia—the aroma made Soniya lick her lips.

Amrin eyed the balloon-seller who had released a string of bubbles from the wand in his free hand. But her mother's deliberate footsteps forced her to concentrate on their immediate mission.

They reached Nusrat Garments, where women of all ages were leaning against the counter and fondling the pile of clothes shown to them by the salesmen. Wearily, Zubina moved towards the kids' section. She waited by the counter and said, 'Show me some nice clothes for little girls.'

The salesman said, 'Yes, yes, tell me, what colour? What design?'

Amrin inched towards the high glass counter. 'Uncle, do you have a white kurta with green leaves on the sides?'

The man bent down and presented a white kurta ensemble with wild leaves printed all over. Amrin rejected it. Zubina started feeling troubled by the sight of Amrin's glistening pink cheeks.

To quash that feeling, Zubina said, 'What about my younger daughter?'

Soniya moved forward excitedly. 'I want a yellow colour dress.'

The man bent down again and rose with four bright yellow-coloured kurtas that were styled as gowns. He said, 'These Indo-Western kurtas arrived only a week ago. Do you like them?'

Soniya beamed at them and pointed to the second one in the pile. The man opened the packet it was in and called her to the other side of the counter. He stretched the kurta across her shoulders and said, 'Careful ... we don't want all your make-up on the dress, Madhuri Dixit.' To Zubina, he asked, 'See how beautiful she looks?'

Amrin agreed and Zubina considered the garment with critical eyes. Soniya dashed out and jumped beside her mother, 'Ammi, I want this. I want this. Please buy me that one only.'

'How much are you going to charge me for that?' Zubina held her daughter, supressing the panic rising in her throat. Soniya's face seemed inflamed with all that make-up.

The salesman said, 'This is one thousand five hundred rupees, but for you and your daughter, I will sell it for twelve hundred.'

Zubina widened her eyes, 'No, no. This is too expensive.'

The man assured her, 'I have reduced the price, madam, you won't get it at this rate elsewhere.'

Zubina shook her head, 'I won't pay a rupee more than eight hundred rupees for this.'

The salesman laughed, 'What are you talking about, madam? Eight hundred? I will lose my job if I sell it at that price.'

Zubina couldn't stand the laughter. She wanted to sit down and hand the purse to her daughters, so they could buy whatever they wanted. Eid shopping was a mistake. Her knees were crying for rest. She wanted the day to end and for her body to be delivered to her house right then.

She said, resting her elbows on the glass, 'I buy from you always ... almost all the older girl's clothes, I have taken from you ... and we have had to throw the clothes away after two or three washes because they can't be mended.'

'Madam, this is festive wear! Look at the work! I am sorry, I can't offer a bigger discount.'

Zubina held her daughters's hands, 'All right, don't! I will buy what I need from that other shop. He was giving me the same dress to me at *my* rate.'

Soniya almost began to wail, but Zubina gave a piercing glare and told her to follow her. Amrin knew what was going to happen. She was well-versed with her mother's tactics, although she didn't know why her mother was extra surly today. She was usually cheerful while bargaining, and laughing with her daughters, as though she was not their mother but a friend. No sooner did they take a step away than the man called out, 'Okay, madam, nine hundred? Neither mine nor yours, what say?'

Zubina put the money in his hands. 'Eight hundred and fifty. That is the last offer. Not a rupee more.'

The salesman gave up. He threw his hands up in the air. 'Okay, fine, only for that little Madhuri Dixit and because you are an old customer.'

The salesman packed the dress and wrote out a bill. Zubina tightly held on to the plastic bag in which he had put the dress and marched into the crowds. Her daughters hung around and admired the dresses on display outside. She waited. She breathed in and out; she wanted to enjoy her time with her girls.

The three shuffled between a couple of shops and finally found the kind of kurta-set Amrin liked. Again, Zubina succeeded in her attempts at bargaining.

Next, she bought her daughters bejewelled shoes outside the New Market Complex; their feet got stomped on by the women in the vicinity who shouted out the money they were willing to offer. Zubina also got one pair of shoes for herself.

Amrin asked, 'Ammi, you won't get clothes?'

Zubina replied, dabbing at her temple with a handkerchief, 'I have asked the tailor to stitch the fabric I had got as a gift last year. I will wear that with these shoes.'

Soniya drank her bottle of water whilst her mother and sister checked to see they had everything they needed. When Soniya got the ice cream cone that Zubina had promised, they went towards Esplanade and waited for their bus, near a convoy of white-and-yellow cabs that had stopped. Young boys and girls checked number plates and stepped into the taxis, until a traffic policeman came striding in to ward off the growing traffic. From the metro station to the right, a flurry of passengers trickled into New Market every five minutes. Zubina monitored her daughters while her thoughts assailed her.

As Bus 24A zoomed in, she ushered her daughters inside and followed them, holding plastic bags tightly in her hand. She and her daughters got seats easily.

Zubina stared out of the window, sweating and parched. Suddenly, she had the urge to cry, to break down and let tears run down her face. Her daughters talked between themselves next to her. They had arranged themselves on a single seat.

Zubina tried focusing on their conversation—they were trying to decide whose house they'd visit first on Eid, and when they'd greet Neha-di, and the kind of doctor's set they'd ask their father to buy. More passengers boarded at Maidan. Her daughters continued prattling.

Zubina thought of the family she had left behind—a sister she couldn't rescue from the web of trouble she had entangled herself in; a mother, confined to a corner of the house, who had become increasingly lonely; and Tausiq, who displayed an uncontrollable kind of anger when Zeenat's name was mentioned. She had left them all behind and moved in with Aadil. She had two girls and was 'happily settled'. She held the reins of her homestead. She knew she could fully protect this household, unlike the one she had lost. For all these reasons, Zubina had, over time, become content with her lot, her married life.

So, when *that* day came, it destroyed her. It made her furious that she had forgotten what she had to first protect.

She held the plastic bags tighter in her hands. Amrin exclaimed with joy, 'Eid shopping is done, Ammi!'

Suddenly, her daughters looked like two rubies—their cheeks pink and their lips red. Zubina breathed a sigh of relief. She thanked Allah and whispered a prayer, 'Please take care of Nazma.'

9

Lately, Ralph had started hating his slip-ups at the hotel. He had promised the executive chef that he'd prepare a list of ingredients for the pastry section; he forgot the moment the meeting was over. He mixed up names and hours while assigning duties to the new batch of interns. Now, he had nearly burnt his hand against a large tray of baklava that had been cooling unattended. Sujoy came in at the right time and grabbed him, 'What the hell!'

'I am sorry,' whispered Ralph, moving back.

'You're a fucking mess, Ralph. You need to speak to me,' Sujoy said and took him aside.

'It's nothing, Sujoy. Baba wanted me to move back with him, as you know, and you've been so distant ...'

'Yes … because you don't open up to me!' Sujoy held Ralph by his shoulders. 'I am here for you …'

'Ojas is meeting with an ex hook-up. I can't … I just can't deal with it, Sujoy,' moaned Ralph, leaning against the wall.

'I'm sorry … what?'

'I am so exhausted and am nagged by so much guilt. I can't stop feeling this … this strange thing …'

Sujoy prodded, 'What is it, Ralph? Tell me.'

'It's complica … I want to go and work. I can't talk now.'

Sujoy was taken aback.

Ralph poured the cardamom-infused syrup over the flaky

baklavas. Ralph inhaled the overpowering scent of the nutty syrup as he watched it disappear into the neat folds of pastry.

'It is Eid tomorrow,' Zubina said, as she helped Ralph in the kitchen, where he was beating egg whites.

'Yes, there is an Eid party being thrown by someone at the hotel. Today, there was a lot of preparation for that,' he said. The beater splashed foam along the sides of the bowl.

Zubina got Ralph the jar of castor sugar he had asked for, then said, 'Ah, we meet family, friends and relatives. My friends are thinking of taking our girls for ice cream after lunch. It is Chaand Raat tonight. We women will put mehendi.'

Ralph added sugar every twenty seconds to the mixture in the bowl. He felt Zubina's gaze upon him as he measured the sugar.

When the eggs had formed a peak, she asked, 'Why is your friend not coming these days?'

He flipped the bowl to check, 'He's a little busy with work.'

'Why don't you get married?'

The beaten cloud of egg whites fell softly on the counter. Ralph gaped, 'What?' *Was Zubina-di asking him to marry Ojas?*

Offering him a dishcloth, Zubina continued, 'Wouldn't this house be beautiful if there was a woman to take care of it? She would look after you and this space ... look at what you have done! Who flips a bowl full of eggs? Move, I have to clean it up now.'

Ralph scraped what remained of the bowl of beaten egg whites into the bin and said, 'What if the woman doesn't want to take care of the house and me?'

Zubina parted her lips as though she were about to say something; then she seemed to think better of it. She resumed peeling lychees; she had left that task mid-way. Ralph deseeded a bulb of ripe jackfruit and popped it into his mouth. He enjoyed the cool wetness of the fruit. Zubina placed the fruits in boxes and put them in the refrigerator.

Ralph went into his room and lay down. There were messages from Ojas that appeared on his phone screen. He read them and put the phone away. Of course, he was with Piyush, that ex. Ralph clenched his fists and heard his knuckles crack; violent images lurched in his mind. He kept fidgeting in bed as if to get as far away from Ojas's messages as possible. He imagined Ojas's happy face as he shared a meal with that friend; as he chose to visit his residence; as he shared touches and caresses with him on the homeward journey. A soft resistance. Gentle assent. Foreplay at the back of the cab. And then, as the vehicle pushed home, a jubilant sprint towards the door. The quick clasp of the lock. Finally, tingling, unhurried sex.

Ralph booked a cab to the bar.

He asked Zubina to put the food in the refrigerator, take the Eidi he had kept on the credenza, and lock the flat. Then, he left.

The bar's music was loud; it disturbed his insides. He surveyed the place; it was sprawling, with table after table. Spirals of smoke rose from hookahs. Ralph had to cleave his way through these fumes. He halted at every table, only to find groups of girls or boys swaying in high chairs, or couples partying. The glare of the lights did nothing to help Ralph find Ojas and the ex. Ralph's legs grew tired and he sat at an empty table for two. He ordered coke with bowl of garlic peanuts on the side.

His eyes halted at the smoking room; the glass door opened to reveal Ojas with a man by his side. Ralph ducked to hide. He hit against the legs of the table and the glass of coke trembled. He didn't want to be caught spying. It was shameful, Ralph knew it. He reasoned that he was here only to have a glimpse of the ex, and maybe—only maybe—to know if Ojas was happier with other men than he was with Ralph. He would be on his way home once his drink was done.

Ojas had returned to the main bar. He sat with his back to Ralph. The ex was partly visible. Ralph emerged from his hiding spot. Ojas and the ex were drinking beer over fries and onion rings. Ralph's stomach churned with hunger as rice bowls were placed on their table. He sipped his drink and chewed peanuts.

He was bored of what he could hear of their talk and their sluttish giggles. He ordered a whiskey this time and noticed the ex's hand going over Ojas's. He waited; the hand refused to leave. Ralph fumed over his drink. Gay men can be touchy without insinuating any kind of sexual desire, he said to himself. He knew this to be true for himself. But Ojas seemed to like the company of this man. It was evident by the glow on his face. Ojas would kiss him anytime now, and in the bar. To avoid witnessing that, Ralph scurried to the smoking room.

The room was empty when he entered. His phone rang the moment he lit a cigarette.

It was Sujoy.

What did he want now? Couldn't he leave him be?

'Where are you?' Sujoy asked with authority.

Ralph wanted to shut him up, tell him it didn't matter. Instead, he said, 'At a bar.'

'With Ojas?'

'No, alone. Ojas is here, though, with …'

'What shit is this?'

'I just came …'

'To stalk him,' Sujoy completed his sentence for him.

Ralph finished smoking the cigarette; he had no more to say. He had got down to it. To stalking his partner. He hated to see his reflection on the glass door, holding the stub of a crushed cigarette.

Sujoy continued, 'Text me the location. I am coming.'

'Sujoy, there's no need, please.'

'There is every fucking need. And you will talk to me. You will listen to me for once. I may be in a shipwreck kind of situation with my own shit, but that doesn't mean I don't see what you're going through.'

Ralph felt tears prick his eyes as he sent him the location of the bar. He smoked two more cigarettes and left when rejoicing crowds began to gather in the room.

Sujoy arrived in no time. Ralph was afraid that Ojas would notice him, but the people who danced next to their table ensured that Sujoy went unnoticed.

Sujoy ordered beer and fixed himself at the table; he waited for Ralph to continue the conversation, that seemed never to have ended, on the call.

Ralph spoke, 'The whole open-thing isn't working well for us. I mean, I don't want it.'

'Does Ojas know?'

'Yes, he does. He keeps saying, "let's try, try, try," and it's been what ... six months?'

'Leave him,' said Sujoy, firmly.

'Has Sayantani left you?' Ralph asked.

'Huh?'

'After what happened, have you broken up?'

'Why are we talking about me?'

'Well, Sujoy, the way you asked me to leave, I thought...'—Ralph was keeping an eye on the ex who was feeding a spoonful of rice to Ojas—'...maybe you were dumped, and that's why you were asking this of me.'

'No, I have not been dumped. Sayantani is super angry, yes, but we are talking,' replied Sujoy, swivelling to steal a quick glance at Ojas.

'It's the same on our side,' Ralph said. He felt protective of his lot.

Ojas and the ex rose to dance. Ojas simply watched while the ex swirled and drew his hand close. Ralph saw Ojas's cheeks go crimson and it reminded him of the first time they had kissed in his flat.

They were at Ojas's house; his parents and brother were away for a relative's wedding in another city. Ralph had visited for the first time. After eating, both of them changed into pyjamas—Ojas's fit well on Ralph's body. They went to the balcony that was linked to Ojas's room. At midnight, the other windows to the houses in Lake Town were dark. The air was still. The silence was broken by the howling of the dogs; they could be spotted under the glare of streetlights.

Far ahead, the sky started changing. It brought in a soft, rolling noise. A breeze flicked the hair off their faces. Ojas pulled Ralph to his side. Ralph flushed, not knowing what to do. Ojas turned his back to the world; Ralph stood closer to Ojas. Ojas put his lips on Ralph's. They didn't move. They stood there, their lips touching, until the sky roared above them and they broke away from the kiss. It had been two months since they had met at the hotel. So … this was their first kiss, Ralph mused, as Ojas touched his chest, stroked the unevenly shaved stomach, caressed the area between his legs and let the tip of his finger reach the depths of his ass.

It was beautiful, Ralph thought.

Ojas and the ex danced a little more and then called for the check. They were ready to leave. Ralph followed, pleading with Sujoy to pay.

When Ralph was on the road, he found Ojas alone. The ex had hailed a cab.

Ralph hesitated. The sky thundered as though preparing for a summer downpour. Ojas was busy on his phone, unaware that Ralph was behind him, a few metres away.

Ralph's phone pinged.

Ojas had texted, 'I miss you. The meeting was okay. I only kept thinking of you throughout. May I come over? I need to bitch about him and the Delhi Grindr scene. Felt good we don't have to be on that app. Miss you tons.'

Ralph took a step back; he was mad at himself. Sujoy held him and asked if he was fine. He nodded and was about to book a cab, when he caught Ojas staring at both of them in surprise.

It was as though the clouds were slamming against each other. A film of sweat gathered on Ralph's neck as Ojas marched forward. A strong wind blew.

'What are you two doing here?' asked Ojas.

'We … we had come to grab a drink,' Ralph said, as the huge tree behind them began swaying more violently.

'Oh, strange,' Ojas replied, eyeing them with suspicion.

'I have booked a cab,' Sujoy said to Ralph.

'You were stalking me with him, weren't you?' Ojas said to Ralph, dismissing Sujoy's presence.

'No … no, I …'

'He was, yes,' answered Sujoy, 'and he is hurting, Ojas.'

'Is he? And you are his balm? The one with wisdom from all those books you pretend to read?'

'Excuse me?' Sujoy retorted and put his phone away.

It had begun to drizzle. Ojas's car was close and they decided to go together to Ralph's flat. The journey was one of strained silence. As though they were strangers forced to share a ride back home.

At the flat, Ojas began, 'I can't believe you'd stoop to this level, Ralph.'

'Ojas, please,' pleaded Ralph. He rubbed his forehead.

'He is unhappy with the whole open situation, Ojas,' Sujoy butted in.

'Stop interfering in our lives,' Ojas said, then turned to Ralph. 'This was all his doing, wasn't it? Him and his filthy mind?'

'What do you mean, Ojas?' Ralph glared.

'How dare you go and talk about us to other people … and then do this?' Ojas was infuriated.

'I will talk to "other people", because it's impossible to talk to you. I wanted to share my struggles with someone while you went for a fucking dinner and had sex with other men,' Ralph replied, trying to match Ojas's fury.

'Really? Listen, I went to dinner and all I did was miss you. I *missed* you. You asked me to leave that day, and after that you've barely made an effort to talk to me.'

'Listen, Ojas,' Sujoy said, trying to be the calm one in the drawing room. 'Ralph wants you, he does. All I want to suggest is, maybe both of you can end it …'

Ojas turned to him, '*All* I am asking is to give my idea of an open relationship a shot! It's been close to six months and this has been a nightmare because of him!' He pointed at Ralph. 'Okay, wait, how many people do you think I have slept with until now?'

Ralph and Sujoy exchanged a glance. Sujoy shrugged, saying he didn't know.

'One! In six months, only one … just like him!'

'You, too?' Sujoy turned to Ralph.

'Yes, with that man on the fifth floor,' responded Ojas.

'I did it to spite you. So, you would feel bad and end this mess. But now … I am tired of it,' Ralph sighed.

'I am fucking tired of catering to your needs … and, to top it all, you dared to spy on me today!' Ojas roared and shoved Ralph away from him.

'Ojas what are you …' Sujoy tried to interject.

'You shut the fuck up and go back to the hellhole you're from!' Ojas said. 'I have had enough of you being some kind of counsellor here … saala, chu ...'

'Ojas!' Ralph was afraid he would say something offensive.

'What the fuck!' exclaimed Sujoy. 'Did you just talk about where I come from?'

An uncomfortable silence stretched itself between the three of them. Finally, Sujoy wore his shoes and left, slamming the door. 'Fuck you and your problems,' he yelled.

The lock clicked.

Ralph's phone vibrated.

It was his father. Assuming it was an emergency, he took the call.

His father said, 'I was calling to invite you, Ojas and Sujoy for a lunch this Sunday.'

'Oh, Baba,' Ralph moved into the balcony and cried. The rain had eased; it was now a light patter, caressing trees and concrete slabs. The early monsoonal breeze brushed against his skin, making him shiver.

'Ralph? What happened? Are you okay?'

'Yes, I am. I …' he sobbed. 'Baba, I …'

'Ralph, should I come over?' The father sounded concerned.

'No, Baba. I am okay,' he cried into the phone.

Ojas walked towards him and put a hand around his waist.

'Tell me, what happened! I will call the driver and get there right now,' Ralph's father said.

'No, no. I … mm …' He was gasping for breath, 'I miss you and Maa, a lot. I wish she were still alive and we were together like before.' He cried louder.

Ojas leaned into him.

'Come home, I have asked you to come home, son,' said his father.

'I will come over to meet you and Mike tomorrow,' Ralph managed to enunciate.

He disconnected the call and went inside.

Ojas sat on the sofa opposite him, 'Ralph, baby, listen ...'

'What do you want me to listen to? About how horrible I have been? About how I haven't allowed you to sleep with other people?'

Ojas begged, 'Let's put this behind us for the moment. Go and take some rest.'

'Don't treat me like some sick child,' Ralph said, glaring at him. 'I am completely fine. Stop eating into me like a bloody parasite. The punishment you have subjected me to has gone too far.'

'Ra ...' Ojas tried to speak.

Ralph cut him short, 'You know what, I have made up my mind. I don't want you any more. This is it. I am done. I think we should both choose people who aren't so toxic for us.'

'What?'

'Yes. I don't want to bear this pain in the name of a long, stable relationship.' Ralph laughed drily. 'Anyway, who said this was stable? Also, you will apologize to Sujoy for the thing you said ... it was horrible, I can't ... *I* can't forgive you for that.'

'You are being impulsive,' said Ojas in an authoritative tone.

'I know exactly what I am being,' Ralph asserted and lit a cigarette. He took two puffs and said, holding back his tears, 'You can sleep in the guest room.'

The next day, Ralph and Sujoy supervised the preparation of tarts and kunafa. Neither worked efficiently. Both missed each other's cues at various points, and spoke in unison when a task had to be completed—'I will add the honey!'

Sujoy took the ladle from a confused intern and drizzled a ribbon of honey, not taking his eyes off the syrup. Ralph checked the nozzle of the piping bag stuffed with the rose and cardamom filling he had prepared. Then, he placed a petal over each piped tart with a pair of tweezers; the golden-brown empty shells on the counter started displaying pink florets. He helped the juniors arrange the tarts on a tray.

Ralph took early leave from work that day, despite the fact that Eid festivities in the hotel were on in full swing.

He entered the gates of the Bhowanipore cemetery carrying a bouquet of roses. The guard greeted him, 'After so many days!'

He nodded and marched forward, leaving footprints on the moist ground. His mother's grave was at the farthest end. Two men scattered soil to his right, as a family of five cried, holding on to each other.

He reached his Maa's grave, dusted it with his white handkerchief and kept the two vases he was carrying. He divided the roses into two bunches, and placed each into the vases on both sides. At the centre, he arranged a peony nosegay.

'Hi, Maa,' he said, caressing her name with his fingers—

In Loving Memory of
ROSEMARY GOMES
Born: 2 December 1963
Died: 29 November 2016
Loved and Missed

'I am sorry I have disappointed you and Baba so much.'

He saw two dogs jog past him. They tucked themselves by the wall under the shade of a banyan tree.

He took in the moss that covered the graves nearby; the water from last night's rain that had nearly dried under the sun; and an old, misshapen brick wall covered with large green leaves. He remembered early 2017, when he'd visit this place every second day of the month before work. He would sit and tell Maa that he had found someone. He would place the bouquet of roses by her grave and reassure her that this relationship wasn't going to be a disappointment, that this would be permanent, that he'd now know the happiness she had wanted him to experience.

'It makes me hate myself to see what I have done since you left me. I have chosen a man who barely wants me anymore. I did not stand up for Sujoy—the boy you loved so much. I am failing at my job. *The* job! You taught me how to do it.'

He adjusted his Wayfarers, wiped the sweat from his forehead and went on, 'Baba is asking me to move in with him. He says he can't see the house fall to pieces ... no one can look after it the way you did.'

A group of mynahs flew across the sky, creating a triangle. A family was burying a loved one in the distance, and they began singing a hymn Ralph could not recognize. The weight of their mournful humming reached him and he put his hand over his mouth to stifle a sob.

'Maa, talk to me. Tell me what I should do!' Tears ran down his cheeks. 'Are you listening to me? Do you see what has become of me? Sujoy is right, I am a mess. A mess, Maa. That is what your son has become. Baba asked me to get Sujoy and Ojas home this Sunday for lunch. How am I supposed to tell Baba that Sujoy won't speak to me and I have asked Ojas to leave?'

The sun burned his skin.

The family in the far distance had begun to leave. Men were patting the earth back in place with a shovel.

'*Aar bhaal lagche na, Maa*,' he said loudly.

The two napping dogs woke up. They came close to him.

I don't feel good anymore, Maa.

Ralph hugged the slab of stone under which his mother had been buried more than two years ago. The nosegay blew further away as he breathed out.

Come to me.

The sun drew back and sent a waft of air to cool the child crying for his mother's return. The roses shook in the vase.

10

The rain hadn't been all that harsh the previous night. Zubina rose with relief; the shower had come and disappeared in no time. The air in the house still carried the scent of citronella she had lit in the middle of the night because mosquitoes weren't deterred by the nets.

At four, she found Aadil already awake, though the girls were still asleep. She leaned in and lay her hand across his chest. Aadil said in his deep voice, 'It's Eid.'

Zubina yawned, 'Yes, it is.'

'Let's sleep a little more,' Aadil said and held her hand. He commented on the henna in her palm, 'The colour is coming up.'

She watched the big dot on her palm growing darker; the henna on her fingertips had browned. 'Yes, Nazma put it yesterday.'

Aadil brought the palm to his nose and inhaled the freshness of the dot. It was like entering a garden covered with fresh leaves and wet mud.

Her fingers traced his nose, then stopped at his lips.

He pressed her two fingers to his lips and slept.

At five, everyone was awake. It was a glee-speckled day in the neighbourhood, replete with anticipation. In the house, Amrin and Soniya pranced about as the henna on their palms grew in radiance. They lathered it with layers of mustard oil.

Amrin served tea to everyone. Soniya drank a little, too, from a tiny plate which they used as saucer. Her wound had healed and had left a faint diagonal mark on her forehead. Over tea, Zubina said, 'Both of you, go and get the water as soon as you finish. You will come straight home and not stop at the shop or talk to a friend. It is a festive day, don't make me angry and come chasing after you.'

Zubina continued, 'Your father will take his bath first since he has to go to pray. Once he is done, you two will go in together.'

Amrin butted in, 'There will be a long line at the bath today. Remember last time? Papa was late.'

'Yes, that's why he will go for his bath right this minute. Won't you?' Zubina looked at Aadil.

Aadil obediently nodded as though he were her third child.

Amrin put her empty glass down and fixed her hair in the mirror. 'Come, come, Soniya, let's go, or we'll be late.'

In a second, the chatter of the girls had vanished; Aadil, too, had left. Zubina considered the day before her—so many things were left to be done. Nonetheless, she welcomed it with renewed strength and enthusiasm.

After Zubina offered her prayers and locked the door, as Amrin and Soniya left to gather their friends.

She removed her freshly stitched suit set from the newspaper wrapping and put it on. She combed her moist hair that had just moments earlier been wrapped in a gamcha to dry. While applying rose-scented moisturizer to her face, she hummed a random tune she had made up in her mind. It reminded her of how much she loved Eid. She then dusted her face with compact powder that she had recently bought. She had hidden it from her daughters, lest they break it like the last one. She painted her lips a shade of pink. The four strokes of kohl were dark enough to offer her eyes definition. She wore a pair of silver earrings that she had bought on a whim for herself from New Market, before she had boarded the bus back home. Now, she was grateful for that impulsive decision.

She braided her hair into neat plaits and pinned her dupatta to her shoulders. She checked to see if she missed any spot on her face. She wished she had a bigger mirror. She looked down and straightened her clothes with her hand. She approached the box that contained the shoes she had bought, for which Aadil had paid; she threw the paper balls and wrappers away.

She practised a blush, imagining Aadil's gaze upon her. She grinned self-consciously as she slipped into the shoes adorned with crystals and red stones.

Someone was coming. She briskly kicked the box aside and unlatched the door. Aadil, in his thin white kurta-pyjama, entered. He paused. The door shut behind him. His eyes took in everything—his wife's new shoes; the kurta embroidered with sequins and stones that shone; her face. He inched forward and tried closing his mouth that had dropped open.

Zubina glowed nervously, feeling his eyes rest on her.

He held her hands, placed a note on her palm and closed her fingers around it with his. Her Eidi. He kept holding on to her fist, unable to make the next move. She realized how shy he was feeling.

More than a decade of marriage and two girls born; they had never known such a moment of marital harmony. Her heart was beating rapidly in her chest, as though she were back to being young and experiencing first love—like they did in the movies.

His eyes drank in her face. He said, 'Eid Mubarak.'

Her face grew hot. She tried saying, 'Eid Mubarak,' but all that emerged was a faint whistle.

He ran a finger across her cheek, unable to conceal his smile. Zubina's heart wandered from his face and his hand to her own toes. He whispered inaudibly, his eyes glued to the shimmer on her cheeks. She moved forward to hear him and he took a step back.

He looked around the house, and then he tried saying something again.

Finally, he said loudly, 'Mashallah, you look … beautiful.'

He added, 'Most beautiful woman in the … in … the world.'

He held her gaze to make her believe what he had said.

She wanted to throw her arms around him. She wanted to feel the solidity of his body, his chest, but she controlled herself. She let go of her unspoken urges.

This was the second time that tears had filled her eyes on the day of Eid.

Eid at Zubina's natal home would be a day of endless joy and feasting. Zeenat would give Eidi to both her siblings. Zubina and Zeenat would give money to their mother, which she would then divide among the three children.

On Eid of 2005, Zubina was eighteen. She didn't know it was to be her last Eid with her family. Aadil was nowhere in the picture. Zubina had worn a yellow salwar kameez that one of her employers had gifted her after hearing that she didn't have anything new to wear. Her sister had been given a blue garment. For the mother, Zubina had purchased a red kurti with a white salwar, and they had got their brother a white kurta with golden embroidery. For the first time, for Eid, the family had worn new clothes. When Zubina was ready and her sister was done mocking a cousin's horrendous attire, her mother's eyes began to water. Fifteen-year-old Tausiq asked her what happened. The two sisters left what they had been doing and went to their mother and waited for her to speak. Their mother's sobs grew louder when she saw the children by her side. She asked for water, had it and fell asleep. While she rested, Zeenat said to her siblings, 'I think she's happy to see all three of us wear something new for a festival.' Tears had gathered in her eyes as well.

Zubina wanted to share her thoughts with her mother, but somehow the moment to speak never presented itself. She sat beside her mother and chopped guavas into wedges to feed her when she woke up. Tausiq cleared his throat and told them that he was going to visit his friends. Zeenat patted him and said, 'Get home soon. We will have mutton biryani today.'

When Tausiq was gone, Zubina asked, as she sprinkled salt and chilli over the guava, 'Mutton biryani? From where will you get it?'

'Do you want to eat it or not?' Zeenat retorted, and peering into a mirror, wiped away some lipstick that stained her teeth.

'I do,' she said.

'Then keep quiet and eat when you get it,' hissed Zeenat, and fastened the loose strands of her hair with a bobby pin. 'Okay, then, I will be back soon.'

In the evening, when they had gathered to eat their dinner, Zeenat served everyone and said, 'I have good news.'

The rice Ammi had picked up between her fingers fell back into the plate. 'What is it?'

Zeenat arched her chiselled eyebrows and said, 'I have found a man for our Zubina.'

'Who is he?' inquired the mother.

'I know him through a friend. Stays in Topsia. Has his own house. Works at a leather factory.'

The mother patted her chest lightly and took Allah's name. Zubina couldn't eat. Suddenly, she felt she was being propelled in an unwanted direction. Her life was being taken away from her. She was deeply uncomfortable with the news.

In the middle of the night, she woke Zeenat and asked, 'Why is this happening? I don't want to be married.'

'Why not?' said Zeenat, stifling a yawn.

'Well,' she stuttered, 'you ... you aren't married.'

'I won't marry. I have to be there for the family. *You* have to marry, Zubina. I promise you, he is a good man. I saw him yesterday. No alcohol, nothing. He is so pure. Just for you, bachcha.'

Zubina refused to listen further.

What had Eid brought her?

She didn't want marriage, she didn't want a man. She wanted to be here. She cried herself to sleep that Eid.

In a week's time, both the families had met (his family comprised a mother and two sisters, who were already married). Small gifts like fruits and clothes were exchanged. The discussion shifted to a potential wedding date.

Zubina didn't meet the man herself. She didn't know what he looked like.

She spent her days working more fiercely. She avoided any conversation with her family. This went on until, one evening, the man came to their house with a box of fruits and introduced himself as Aadil.

Zubina's sister nudged her. Zubina covered her head and took the box from him. She noted the veins that formed an elongated web along his forearms, his sharp features, the smooth skin against which his perspiration shone, and the soft, heavy drawl of his voice when he mentioned his name.

The chance encounter didn't lessen her anxiety or the powerlessness Zubina had felt since Eid. But it made her curious, in a way she had never felt before.

Zubina folded the clothes and cleaned the mess in the house.

Aadil had complimented her and run back outside—his face as inflamed as Amrin's and Soniya's after they had applied make-up.

Zubina wished she could tell the world what it felt like to be in love. She yearned to speak of the joys of belonging somewhere, knowing that someone would always admire you—their jaw dropping at your mere sight.

She thought of Ralph leaving the flat the previous evening in a dazed state and of Ojas's helpless expression when she tried talking to him. She wished she could tell them that, like life had opened out for her, good days awaited them. That Allah was looking after everyone, both on happy and sad days. He gave pain to make people stronger, so they could appreciate the happier days life had in store.

The image of Ralph and Ojas kissing came to Zubina's mind, but she gently pushed it away and busied herself with household chores. *No, no, no day was appropriate to think such awful thoughts.* She prayed for a mind that would stop traipsing off in such directions.

Ojas and Ralph were friends. Two men. Two good, hurting men. Not a man and woman. Not like her and Aadil. A man and a woman were meant for coupledom, for marriage, a family; for fulfilling god's wishes. Nobody else.

When her sister's proclamation of love came to her mind, she brushed that away too—this was another example of improper love.

What Zubina was felling so deeply and profoundly—*that* was proper love. It was clean, blessed and sacred.

Zubina felt gratitude that Allah had answered her prayers with unexpected benediction. She wanted to make everyone sit around her and tell them how god listened to what the heart desired. That on this holy day, on Eid, she had seen and been seen by the person who had been with her all these years, in this little house. Allah shone its light on her and on her family with this love ...

Her phone rang; Zubina was startled out of her thoughts.

'Eid Mubarak,' a voice said. It was her brother. 'What are you doing today?' He then revealed that he was getting a job in another factory. He asked if she was enjoying a feast.

'Aadil's sister has sent enough food. Don't worry,' Zubina reassured Tausiq and peered at the tiffin boxes that she still had to unpack.

She fought the urge to mention Zeenat. She wondered if he would venture to talk about her. She wanted to mention Nazma's predicament, that she needed a job for her drunkard husband, but couldn't bring herself to.

She ended the call abruptly saying that her husband had come in for lunch.

She prayed for Zeenat and Nazma. More for Nazma, who was braving the day with a victorious smile, as though the world around her wasn't falling apart.

In the days preceding Zubina's wedding, Zeenat would sometimes come home excitedly, poke Zubina and tell her that she had seen Aadil with his friends walking towards the factory, or at a wedding she had been to the previous night. Zubina would ignore her sister's babble.

Every morning, when Zubina would make the tea, Zeenat and her mother would be engaged in a deep conversation about wedding preparations. They'd speak about the things they had to gift, the clothes that had to be bought.

Once, Zeenat forced Zubina to come to Bara Bazaar to buy some clothes—a couple of shirts, two trousers for the groom; a few kurtas and some jewellery for the bride. Zeenat placed a pair of earrings against Zubina's ears, a gold necklace around her neck and looked at her reflection in the mirror. 'Mashallah, Zubina, my beautiful bachcha,' she said.

When Zeenat paid for the trip, the chicken rolls over lunch and the glasses of chilled fresh lime soda, Zubina hesitated. She knew that the money came from Daanish-bhai, who Zeenat believed loved her. Zubina wanted to plead with her sister to stop seeing him. But she couldn't bring herself to say the words. She felt guilty that she was enjoying herself at Bara Bazaar because of Daanish-bhai's money. It was pure evil.

She spent the night going over all the prayers she knew to absolve herself of this sin, so her wrong-doings wouldn't seep into the life that awaited her. Many times, she broke down but her cheeks remained dry. She knew she was crying but there were no tears to show.

She grieved in silence and prayed for her family.

Aadil was unable to ignore the mirth that rose within him. As he visited various aunts and uncles to greet them, he realized he hadn't been this happy in a long time.

Zubina looked striking to him. He could barely stop himself from touching her and telling her how beautiful she looked.

Love was not something Aadil thought about often. In fact, he never had. He didn't have the opportunity to spend time on it. The friends he had grown up with, who had lost themselves in love in their twenties, made him abandon the idea that love could be a worthy pursuit. It's not that he didn't want to fall in love—he had even considered the possibility of it—but he had never found a free hour to pursue it. He married Zubina and quashed any thought that was even vaguely romantic.

He was a husband and that was all.

One of his father's sisters offered him Eidi as he entered the house. She exclaimed, 'My son, come here, come, come help this old woman!'

Aadil helped her stand up. His cousin rearranged her dupatta and the aunt extracted a hundred rupee note and offered it to Aadil. He was touched. The last time she had given him Eidi was when he was sixteen. He had stopped seeing his father's family after that. But the news of a relative's death made him want to visit them now. He kissed her hands.

She said, 'Those years when you had stopped coming, I felt I had lost a son of mine ... Aadil, promise me today, you will be by my side when I am dying.'

'Arrey, Shallo-phupi, you still have years to live,' he said and helped her sit down.

'No,' she said with tears in her eyes, 'what a terrible man my brother had been! I have never been able to forgive myself about your mother's last years!' She took a sip of the water her daughter offered her. 'I wouldn't wish that on an enemy.'

Aadil rubbed her hands and said, 'I am always here. Let's talk about your back today. Does it ache?'

Aadil was gutted at the mention of his family. They had left him lonely and trapped. Families were meant to be havens for boys, so they could forge forward. This was something he had heard from his sisters—that he was lucky to have been born male, that he could do anything, really. Years passed and he waited for that luck to strike. His family had made him stick to a set pattern that he had begun to resent. At some level, he himself had made the choice to remain stuck. Either way, he had got married because that was the only thing left for him to do after buying a house.

An awful mess, he had thought to himself, when he had married and got Zubina to live with him and his mother. To share *his* house with a girl he knew nothing about.

Goodness! Aadil chided himself at some point later in life. For a man, he did complain a lot. He owned his house, all said and done. He had a wife who let him be and was ready to take control when he felt unable to. He had bright and studious daughters. Allah had given him so much to be grateful for… yet he complained even on this auspicious day.

Now, Aadil walked towards his house. He saw Amrin dart past him and saw a hint of Zubina in her. He was filled with an urge to be with his wife. To speak to his daughters.

Why did his past keep coming in the way?

Before lunch, Amrin and Soniya came home and gasped for breath. They sat down in their new clothes and waited for Zubina to fill their plates with the food.

They had trooped down Raicharan Lane with their friends. They had peeked through the drawn curtains of the houses they had passed and wished 'Eid Mubarak' to their aunts. If a friend of theirs happened to be around, they'd enter and help them dress, dab powder on their faces, or tightly pin their clothes to the point of making them gasp for breath.

By lunchtime, they were exhausted.

Amrin had now grown wary of Yasmin and Rina. She tried to ignore their existence because they reminded her of the djinn, who could destroy her. When she had met them the preceding day, they had asked her if they could tell Neha-di about their game. Amrin had avoided offering a response. They had followed her, claiming that misfortune would strike if they didn't seek her opinion. Neha-di had a solution to everything.

Amrin was persuaded for a second. Yes, Neha-di could help. But the thought of reporting her doings made her uncomfortable. She said, 'No, Ammi said that what we did was wrong. We should not talk about it. Bad things will happen.'

Amrin plaited her hair like Neha-di's in neat crosses. Her salwar shone like the glossy lipstick on her lips. Exactly the shade Neha-di wore. She wanted to show herself to Neha-di.

Earlier that day, Yasmin and Rina had joined in at Soniya's insistence. Amrin had gone ahead, saying that she'd like to wish Neha-di and that she'd meet them later. Instead of taking the clue, the entire group proceeded towards Neha-di's. This annoyed Amrin. But there was nothing to do—Soniya insisted that she wanted to wish Neha-di as well.

Zubina, while arranging the plates, regarded Amrin's pout at the mention of Neha.

Soniya said with sadness, 'But she wasn't there!' She sniffed the henna on her palms and added, 'Her Ammi said she went with her friends to Dum Dum.'

'That's okay. We will also go out with our friends after lunch and then get some sleep,' Zubina said.

'I don't think I will go,' exclaimed Amrin, her eyes welling up with tears. She was reminded of her dismay at Neha-di's absence. The two girls had stared at her with discomfort, when Neha-di's mother had sent them off. Amrin's jaw had tightened. She had run towards her home ignoring Soniya's requests to slow down.

'Well, we are going for ice cream. You can stay with Papa,' Zubina said. She did not pay attention to her daughter's sulks.

'I think nobody wants me or likes me. I should just die!' Amrin declared.

'Don't say stupid things on a festive day, Amrin,' Zubina said and passed her plate full with food.

'I don't want to eat this.'

'Why?'

'It reminds me of that old woman outside. She was vomiting brown liquid, it looked like potty, when we were returning. Why can't I die instead of her?'

Zubina paused. 'She's sick. Not dying. I have had enough of your mood swings. Eat or I will ...'

Amrin interrupted, 'You will what? Call the djinn? Go ahead. I want the djinn to take me away from this world. Everybody thinks I am wrong. That I am bad-bad-bad. Maybe Neha-di does too, that's why she left me.'

Soniya slithered behind her mother at the mention of the djinn. Zubina wanted to scream at Amrin for spoiling a promising day with her tantrums. She wished Aadil to come back sooner. He knew the right things to say to console her, reassure her and attend to disputes without fury.

Zubina saw her younger self in Amrin. The uncertain present, the ambiguous future—these provoked in her anxieties, much like they used to rattle her.

She was about to feed Amrin with her own hands, when Aadil entered. Amrin and Soniya both flew into his arms. Soniya accused Amrin of scaring her again, but Amrin held her father and said nothing. Zubina sat there, relieved. The presence of a father would have solved many things in her own family, she thought. She organized a plate of food for her husband.

There was mutton biryani, dahi kebab and chicken chaap that swam in a river of oil. They ate and commented on the food. Zubina appreciated the kebab, it was tender. She thought that the biryani needed more time to soak in all the spices. Aadil ate the mutton. He showed her how perfectly it was cooked and said that she had no reason to complain.

Amrin shoved aside some slices of cucumber and said, 'We should go to Phuphi's house soon. It's been so long.'

Soniya drank water and added, 'And go for ice cream!'

Zubina and Aadil smiled at each other.

'Yes, but is Amrin coming?' Zubina asked.

Amrin asked her father, 'Why won't you go, Papa?'

'With the ladies?' Her father shook his head while swallowing his food.

'Yes, why not? I will give you company. We can sit separately and talk about the friends you miss. Those who have left you all alone on such a special day. Oh … it hurts so much, doesn't it?'

Aadil said, 'We can talk about it here when they are gone.'

'No,' said Amrin and turned to her mother. 'In that case, I would choose the ice cream over being at home.'

After a quick nap, Zubina tidied her daughters, re-plaited their hair and then took them for their ice cream treat with her friends. She shut the door and left Aadil asleep inside.

As Zubina watched her daughters sit with their ice creams, she laughed at a joke Sona cracked and smiled as Nazma's son stuck out his tongue after spilling ice cream on his pants.

The most glorious Eid. Zubina thanked Allah, before she took a bite of her guava scoop.

AUTUMN
2019

1

Ralph had barely slept since June.

At dusk, the minor disturbances of the day would echo in his ears. He'd feel unable to sit with his thoughts. Anger and frustration seemed to steal any possibility of rest.

He considered seeing a therapist. He made his way through several cigarettes, creating a mountain of butts in the tiny ashtray. He routinely consumed a glass or two of red wine after dinner.

From midnight to 3 a.m., his mind would spin, oscillating from his family to Ojas. This was the worst time of the day. Death, a break-up and loneliness. All his relationships had boiled down to this. Unable to distinguish between his many sorrows, he wanted to rid himself of all feeling.

Tossing from one side to another, he'd return to an old childhood trick. When he was little, he believed that the best way to get rid of an unwanted thought was by spitting it out—drops of saliva would skim through the air. He forgot how he had come to learn this, but it used to help him. Now, he spat out thoughts of his mother, Ojas, his father.

The respite was only ever temporary. Old thoughts would swim back the next minute.

He had begun hating mirrors. He'd see himself and believe there was an inevitability to his loneliness. Fat, lumpen, good-for-nothing. And ageing. That's what he was. Where was the doppelgänger of Julia Roberts?

Many nights, he'd put on music to lull himself to sleep, but songs only reminded him of the guitar stashed under the bed, covered with motes of dust. He had forgotten how to play. He'd think about the moments in the past when he'd believe his body was an extension of that guitar. *Touch here and you'll discover a tune.*

Sujoy would remind him, 'Ralph, there was a time you played the guitar beautifully. Do it again.'

But Ralph could not stomach Sujoy's advice. His straight-people-problems repelled him. Sujoy and his girlfriend had decided to drop the idea of an open relationship. Sujoy was planning a marriage proposal; he had not spoken to him for days post-Eid, until Ralph took him out one evening and apologized to him over drinks. Sujoy had not forgotten Ojas's unforgivable comments, however. He snubbed Ralph when he brooded over his lot. 'There are better things to feel bad over than that asshole, Ralph,' he said.

'I know,' Ralph mumbled. But deep down, he was angry. He was displeased that everything in Sujoy's life seemed fine. The two friends had been sailing in the same boat, they had been grappling with their open relationships. But only he—Ralph—had had to suffer a breakup. *How did Sujoy get it easy?*

What also perturbed Ralph was that he had started making mistakes at work. When he had to prepare a batch of eggless macaroons, he beat the aquafaba far too much. The batter deflated into a runny mixture. A fortnight prior, he had been tempering chocolate shipped from Switzerland to make pralines infused with liquor for an international conference. To stir the melted chocolate, he had used a wooden spatula that was still damp. The entire pot of chocolate had to be discarded. Sujoy did not say a word, but the executive chef had expressed sharp disapproval at Ralph's growing inefficiency.

'Maa, why can't you help me?' Ralph cried one night. He walked into his kitchen and stayed there till dawn broke. He poured himself a glass of wine and polished it off in one swig. If wine could not still his agony, he'd pull out vodka and drink it neat. He wanted to let his throat singe.

Alcohol was becoming a silent audience to his pain.

At 5:30 a.m., when the light was starting to assert itself and the birds were twittering, his body shut down. He drifted off to sleep—a sleep that didn't feel at all like rest. It was a kind of unconsciousness.

When he got ready for work, the sinking feeling from the previous night returned. There was a hammering in his head, but he knew he had to steady himself to get past another day of other people's needs and complaints. He did what he could, without mentioning a word to Sujoy or his father.

'Ojas, come back!' he whispered at some point, running his finger across their photo.

In his home in Lake Town, Ojas too lived with a sensation of prickly exhaustion.

Nights of sleeplessness had made him groggy through the day. He'd wash his face but his mood would not alter; everything felt stale. The warmth of tea seemed to vanish between the time he lifted his cup and the time he took a sip. He'd keep checking his phone, only to lock the screen again because he'd forget his reasons for picking the phone up in the first place.

This morning, by the time he had to leave for his workplace, Ojas realized he was fuming. Other people had become intolerable to him.

Ojas wasn't like this. He liked being with people. He found himself within a crowd. Now, without Ralph, he had lost the desire go out.

In the mirror of his car, he saw the lines on his forehead. His hair clumped together with gel. How ugly. He wondered: *Will I grow bald?* Oh god, he had started hating the day even more now.

He jabbed at his phone, searching for a specific contact … then thought better of it and locked the screen.

He reached his workplace and was greeted by employees, who had seen him grow from a little boy to a man. He forced a smile. He went towards the glass cabin from where he handled all business. The blinds were drawn, thankfully, and the air conditioner had already cooled the space. He walked towards a corner where a miniature wooden temple was. It held the Goddess Lakshmi and her companion Ganesha. He lit incense sticks and folded his hands in prayer. He placed yellow marigolds at their feet. He had nothing to ask. He chanted their names and pressed his head against the wooden edge of the temple. He returned to his desk, and deleted emailed files of prospective girls for marriage; his parents had scouted hard.

Three square panels were placed on his desk—indigo, aquamarine and cerulean. These new dyes were being tested on polyester. Ojas ran his fingers along the colours. He looked clueless as two men knocked and entered his cabin. He had to communicate his decision—which of the colours appealed to him? Which one was safe to ship? Ojas cleared his throat and said, 'I will let you know before lunch.' They left.

He wanted to push the panels away and crouch under the desk. He wanted to release a cry of horror and pain at what was becoming of him. He had stopped replying to the texts of men showing interest. Every time a man or a young boy, fresh out of university, commented on how handsome he looked, or how they would love to 'be of service' to his 'tall, bulky, Zeus-like figure', he recoiled with grief instead of the usual joy. After

Ralph, fleeting pleasures from these conversations had vanished too. Ojas felt as helpless as he had when he was twenty.

It must have been the turn of the millennium. Ojas and Divya were about to complete their undergraduate courses.

Everything felt right. The 2000s had begun with Ojas's dating life taking on a renewed vigour; he met guys over walks or for sex. Dates, hook-ups and hopes of having a relationship where he felt cared for, filled his youthful fancies. There was no space for a career or for ambition. Such dreams were for Divya, who got into a business school.

At a college fest, Ojas came across the handsomest man he had ever set his eyes on—Prithvi.

Both of them hit it off right from Ojas's 'hey'.

After a month and a half of texting, Prithvi called Ojas to his flat and they made love. Ojas was mad with desire for him. He let Prithvi take control of his body and do as he wanted. The pain as the muscles of his ass were parted was more intense than he had imagined. Extra oil, extra rubs and gentle kissing made it easier for Prithvi to enter. Ojas knew what to expect when he was fucking others with his cock. Bottoming was new to him.

When Prithvi finished inside Ojas, he pulled out, peeling the condom off. He smacked Ojas on the ass. Ojas dived into bed and between the sheets, inviting Prthvi in.

Prithvi shrugged and said, 'Sorry, but I'd still prefer a woman!'

Lying, in what felt like a disembodied state, Ojas sputtered, 'What?'

'Ass, umm, it ... it's not my thing, really. And I like, you know, to hold boobs.' Prithvi said it all matter-of-factly, wearing his clothes.

'So … so, what was this?'

'This was what it was,' Prithvi replied, throwing Ojas's clothes at him.

'You aren't gay?' Ojas managed to ask.

'No, man,' replied Prithvi. Then he paused and asked, 'Did I say I was?'

Ojas had no memory of him ever making such a statement. But then, when do two gay men ever say 'I am gay' before flirting, talking and then fucking each other?

Ojas felt repulsed. He held on to his clothes and chided himself.

'So …' Prithvi began.

'So, what?'

'Umm … don't know if it's okay to ask … but when are you leaving?'

'As in?'

'As in, getting out of my home?' Prithvi clarified, then laughed. 'I am going for drinks with a friend, that's why.'

The impact of the punch he had felt moments earlier redoubled. He slouched. He was close to tears.

He dressed as quickly as he could and left.

All the way, from GD Block in Salt Lake to his house in Lake Town, he wept in the taxi. The driver kept asking what was wrong. He told him nothing and asked him to drive. But the driver continued asking and consoling. 'Don't be sad. Oh, this is your home? Okay, you pay me what you wish. Take care, son. Don't cry before your parents, they might be worried.'

He drove off, leaving Ojas at his doorstep.

He waited for the tears to dry.

Later, he called Divya and told her about the entire episode. She commiserated.

At his office now, Ojas thought about the episode with Prithvi while reading a blog by a gay icon. He had begun following him in 2018, when he had described his tryst with a heterosexual man at a point when neither the gay icon nor the fling could find interesting people. Day by day, his decisions and choices had confused him—to the point where he put everything aside and focused mechanically on his immediate surroundings.

Ojas closed the tab and concentrated on the dyed fabrics.

The gap between Ralph and him seemed to have widened with time. It was summer then; it was autumn now. Conversations that took place over a call on a fortnightly basis had been clipped. The last time Ralph had called, he was drunk. It was 3 a.m. Ralph had asked, 'How many guys have you fucked by now?'

'Who are you getting drunk with?' Ojas shot back.

He knew that Ralph was not in control of himself or his surroundings in an inebriated state.

'Shut the fuck up,' spat Ralph.

The yearning Ojas had felt for Ralph morphed into anger at what they had done to themselves. 'Ralph, go to sleep. It's late,' he said. Somehow, he knew that Ralph was by himself and not loafing around with random men. He was secretly relieved.

'You have taken it since … sin … ce … youuu … you left,' Ralph slurred.

Once, they tried having sex on video call. But Ojas was struck seeing Ralph. His dark circles had deepened. His body was unshaven. His clothes seemed unwashed. It broke his heart to watch Ralph this slatternly. He disconnected once Ralph had jerked off.

Early August, they met at Ralph's workplace, where Ojas had come for an official dinner. Ojas excused himself to smoke and found Ralph exactly where they had first met. They stood there. Not exchanging a word this time. As Ralph stubbed his cigarette, Ojas held his wrist and said, 'Let's go somewhere.'

Ralph followed Ojas to the car when his shift was over; Ojas had waited for him. They sipped coke while Ojas asked the driver to take the car back home without them. He returned from the pharmacy, and they checked into a cheap hotel in Southern Avenue.

Inside the room, before Ojas could say a word, Ralph went into the loo and cleaned himself. Ojas could hear water churn for half an hour. Ralph came out, sweaty but clean. He lay down for a while. It had begun to rain. The thick August rain of Kolkata. Ojas switched off the lights and let only a dim yellow bulb glow.

This time, they took off their own clothes instead of taking off each other's. No words were exchanged as Ojas lubricated Ralph with the berry lubricant he had bought. He saw Ralph's face scrunch with pain, but unlike other times, he didn't stop mid-way or ask if he wished to go slow. The condom saved him from coming too soon. The more he saw Ralph's fingers clench the sheet and his knees burrow into the mattress and his face tense with the anguish, the harder he thrust. When it was over and they had booked their separate cabs, Ojas wondered what the sex had meant. Was the love over between them?

The rain had stopped.

Ojas had not entered Ralph's flat since their confrontation. Ralph had mentioned his father's invitation for lunch a few days after he had asked Ojas to leave. Ojas had agreed to join him only if Ralph was comfortable. He said that he wanted to apologize to Sujoy as well—so far, he had been unable to; Sujoy had blocked him on WhatsApp. Ralph took a glass of rum and cola at the restaurant they were in and said, 'I think I'd rather you didn't come. I will go and make my excuses. Baba doesn't need to know about the shit I have been putting up with. Thanks. And about Sujoy … he hates you, Ojas. You've proven to him how spiteful you are. I don't think he'd care for your apology any more.'

September in Kolkata, or Calcutta—for those who feel nostalgic about a bygone era—continued oozing sweat as though it were still summer or the peak monsoons. It was also strangely stagnant, a quality that only winter could undo.

Ojas had disguised his aversion to the city before Ralph. As a teenager, he had dreamt of a life overseas, where there would be no family stopping him. He had kept his visits to the textile godowns in Bara Bazaar to a minimum because he hated the crowds, the cheap synthesis of sight, smell and noise exploding from every corner. The vision of innumerable wires above his head and people below, of an old man peeing on the sidewalk, of scrawny kids with parents, their skins tanned in the sun, made him want to run away. He was haunted by the overwhelming smell of spices, flours, dyes, sand-roasted peanuts and murri—as though he were in a city of grocery stores. And the noise! Ojas hated the incessant honking, the shopkeepers screaming into his ears to buy lipsticks for his mother or to get wedding cards designed by an in-house calligrapher. He imagined being in a city that had rolling greens that could be admired over morning strolls, and empty lanes with bougainvillea flowers cascading down windows.

It was Ralph's presence that had made Kolkata come alive for Ojas. He began appreciating the dipping lanes of Bhowanipore, and its houses with green louvered shutter windows; the tea and cigarettes stalls on the outskirts of Barrackpore, Patuli or Howrah; the crockery display in Brabourne Road; the eateries in Park Street; and Christmas at Bow Barracks with live music and styrofoam glasses of gin and cranberry juice. He remembered the lights shining in Ralph's eyes as he drew closer to Ojas surrounded by the stamping crowds.

Now, the air stirred, and Ojas remained still.

Durga Puja was in two weeks. The city had to prepare itself. Ojas sat cluelessly in his car and waited for the change to come. The city seemed to be rippling impatiently.

A sea of memories flickered past his eyes. He remembered Ralph's jubilance.

What was preventing him from going and claiming Ralph for himself?

Then again: *what was preventing Ralph?*

Ojas clutched the steering wheel firmly, resisting the urge to dial his number.

He reached home to the merry sounds of Divya talking to his family. She had come to invite them for her wedding. Before she left, she said to him, 'Ask Ralph to meet me. I want to him to attend the wedding as well.'

Ojas stood there, nodding. His mother piped in, 'Invite whom?'

'A friend,' Ojas mumbled, and looked away from her.

'Well, I hope it's a *girl* we get to see at Divya's wedding,' she giggled, and returned to her kitchen.

2

Zubina was concerned about Ralph; his restlessness was visible not only on his face but all across the flat.

When she cooked his favourite chicken, Ralph pushed it aside and said he had changed his mind. She found his clothes strewn around, languishing in an abandoned state, in every room. Lately, she had seen holes on his sheet. She warned him against smoking in bed. He considered her advice with a faint smile and then flipped on the other side of the bed without a word and continued to smoke. She rolled her eyes, muttering to herself that he had gone mad and needed to be sent to the Kidderpore Baba to be exorcised with jhaar-phoonk.

Ojas hadn't come to the flat in months. That had never happened before. Often, she wondered if she should ask Ralph about him. But she thought better of it and focused on her work.

Two days after Eid, Aadil had returned home with a pair of maroon bangles which she stored carefully; Zubina hoped to wear them at someone's wedding. She was beside herself with delight. She didn't know if love meant to perpetually be giddy with expectation; to crave more than the set hours and minutes of each day to be in the beloved's presence; to feel cared for but also experience jolts of fear—how much kindness could she expect, after all, from a man who had seen too much of the world already? Every time she felt scared, she whispered a prayer to Allah—*don't take this away from me, do not lessen your grace*. She'd remind Allah that she still feared the unanticipated, the unknown, and that she wasn't strong in the face of adversity. *Oh, God, let me have this*, she asked.

Right now Aadil was telling her about the purchases he had made to fix the hole in the roof. She listened while she chopped vegetables. He told her of the handyman he had found, who agreed to take care of matters at a nominal price. Zubina agreed to pay for the handyman and Aadil could pay for the material.

She was relieved that the roof would get fixed. That it wouldn't leak anymore. The incessant worry of her home falling apart would soon be gone.

As the clock struck seven, there was a knock, and her brother, Tausiq, and his wife, Shabnam, made an unexpected appearance.

'Bhai,' Zubina said, and adjusted the dupatta on her head. Tausiq had grown heavier than what she remembered of him as a stick of a boy. His hair sat on his head like a bowl, and his moustache nearly hid his upper lip. Unlike other times, when he'd be dressed only in a flimsy T-shirt and lungi, he now wore a brown kurta and a matching pyjama. Shabnam was glowing beside him, dressed in yellow, her face bright with make-up. From her bejewelled slippers, her pomegranate-coloured toenails poked out.

Zubina warmed the tea she had prepared in the evening and served it with biscuits. Over tea, Tausiq said, 'Aadil bhai, I have something to share … rather, an offer.'

'Oh, is that right?' said Aadil. He assumed, from past experience, that the offer would be one that would cost him but benefit his silly brother-in-law.

'So …' Tausiq was about to say, but Shabnam burst in. 'We are moving to Dilli!'

Tausiq gave her a sideways glance conveying annoyance and spoke to Aadil, who seemed confused. 'Yes, I have got a job there in a factory that will provide accommodation.'

'Arre, waah!' Zubina beamed. Only she knew how much Tausiq had wanted to move away from Kolkata.

Aadil seemed unsure. 'Okay, what's in it for me?'

Tausiq drank the tea like water, passed the empty cup to Zubina, then said, 'The person who got me the job asked if I could get another man to come with me. You see, he said that residence is given to two families in a flat, not one.'

Shabnam interrupted, 'And we don't want to be with strangers. What with our young daughter.'

'The pay is very good. In fact, they will provide for our children's education in a private English school,' added Tausiq.

Aadil sat with his mouth half-open. Such an offer seemed like the dream he had always pursued while being aware that he couldn't afford it. Zubina watched Aadil consider the matter. She knew that when he didn't like something, he'd laugh and brush it off with the wave of his hand. But this wasn't the case now. She wanted him to dismiss the idea, or to discuss it with her later before arriving at a decision.

Zubina grew apprehensive as the silence lengthened. Her thoughts went to Nazma's predicament. Her husband, Mehboob, was still jobless. Perhaps Nazma and Mehboob's family could go to Delhi. But no, they weren't all that close to Tausiq.

On the other hand, if Aadil took up Tausiq's offer, wouldn't a space in his factory open up for Mehboob? Couldn't Zubina say yes to her brother for the sake of her friend?

Suddenly, she felt very confused.

Meanwhile, Amrin and Soniya returned from their tuition classes. They barely salaam-ed their Mama and Mami. In any case, the couple was about to leave, after asking Aadil to arrive at a decision soon.

When Tausiq and his wife went, Amrin asked Zubina if their visit had anything to do with all of them going to the cinema.

Zubina shook her head, then cleared the crumbs of biscuit off the mat. Ever since Eid, Amrin had been driving her up the wall; she wanted to be taken to the cinema hall. She kept saying, 'Ammi, Neha-di went with her friends and cousins to watch *Bharat*.'

'Katrina!' Soniya gasped. 'I want to go also!' She joined the chorus with Amrin.

The two girls spent days imagining what a picture hall was like. They asked Aadil if there was a bed they could lie on, if the AC got too cold, and if the popcorn tasted like the one sold opposite their school, roasted in dry sand? He was the only member of the family who had been to the cinema with his friends when he was young.

Zubina had, in the past, clarified that she was not interested in visiting the cinema—what was the need when they had a fully functional television set with a DTH connection? She offered the same reply now.

Amrin squinted at her with frustration and said, 'You stay at home and watch the TV. Papa said he will take us soon.'

Zubina breathed quietly. She crawled under the bed to pick up a few vegetables she had arranged on a mat below. Soniya jumped on the bed, while Amrin told her, 'Yasmin said her father will take her to the cinema next month. She had to ask him for months. We have been doing it too, but now we need to be ... to be stronger ... Soniya. Are you listening?'

Amrin leapt off the bed and ended up stamping Zubina's toes. Zubina gnashed her teeth; a sharp of current of pain went through her, reminding her that her tiny, curled, sea-shell toes existed.

Amrin looked about in fright. 'Ammi, I didn't know you were under the bed. Sorry ... sorry ...'

Zubina turned to find Amrin kneeling and Soniya's upside-down face assessing her. With a push, the potatoes and onions rolled toward them.

Zubina said she was fine. She had to wash, chop and peel.

The next morning, Aadil reassured his family that he would take them to the cinema hall during Durga Puja. He would get a few days off then.

'But that's next month!' Amrin exclaimed.

'And we also have to go to the fair,' added Soniya.

'We will do both. I promise,' he said, and took a bite of the roti and karela bhaja Zubina had cooked.

Zubina had been slow all morning. She ate half a roti. She folded the dry clothes. She stacked Amrin and Soniya's stationery in separate columns by the side of the room.

'Neha-di has said she will show me the new dresses she has bought. She also asked me to help her record a TikTok video when she wears it,' Amrin stated with satisfaction.

'Are you studying, or is she calling you to talk about her clothes and TikTok?' Aadil asked. Then he nudged Zubina with an elbow. He chuckled. She smiled wanly in return.

'I am now learning preepo-g-shun. Neha-di told me that my math and science are good. Only in English and social studies I have to work hard.' At this, Amrin took out her notebook and Zubina's pile of her daughters' stationery items toppled. She showed her father the cities she had coloured on the map of India.

Zubina pursed her lips, but her obvious irritation was ignored by the rest.

Father and daughter remained invested in their private conversation as Amrin pointed to the country and its urban centres.

At Delhi, Amrin's finger stopped. 'This is the capital of India, Papa.'

Aadil asked, 'Would you want to go and live there?'

'But we live here,' Amrin said and dug her finger at Kolkata on the map.

'Yes,' Aadil replied and put his finger at the spot where Amrin's finger was. He moved her finger over the page slowly toward the north. 'But we can sit in a train and go here.' He pressed her finger on Delhi.

'New home?' Soniya asked.

'Yes, with Mama's family,' said Aadil.

Zubina held her breath while listening to the conversation. She couldn't believe that Aadil was informing his daughters before her—his wife!

Zubina dusted the walls ferociously, making the three cough. Black clouds rose. She wrapped her face with her dupatta. Each strike of the dustcloth was vehement. Aadil said, even as he coughed, 'Let me drop you two to Neha's. I could do with a walk.'

When they were gone, Zubina got down on her haunches and swept the house, not leaving any corner unattended. She removed the bedsheets caked with dust and spread a fresh one. The soiled one was dunked into a tub of brown water. Her hands hovered over the hill of dust she had gathered and she laughed to herself maniacally. 'Just big talk ...'

She scrubbed until the house was spick and span.

3

Ojas mustered energy and read a text message from a young man.

He spoke of his desire to give Ojas the best orgasm of his life. He teased Ojas by saying how much his mouth and hands liked to focus on the shaft and tip of the penis as well as the balls.

Ojas was sitting in his office. He went through the contact list on his phone and opened Ralph's reflexively, to let him know about this potential new fling. But then he stopped himself—Ralph no longer cared.

He went back to the young man's text and punched, 'Where's your place?' He paused before sending the message, but then deleted it, and wrote instead, 'Sorry, maybe next time. My partner won't like it.'

The man got excited at the mention of a partner. He texted, 'Umm, wow! OKAY BUT you can ask your partner to JOIN US. I won't mind two, haha.'

Ojas blocked him. He sat, furious. He tried poring over the list of last month's sales and purchases instead. His fury turned to sadness. He grew mournful while thinking about his life and also the way things had turned out.

He had wanted to pursue other men for himself. He had wanted to do it because he was growing older. He wanted to do it because he was anxious about throttling his desires. He had wanted to do it because he could imagine Ralph and himself settling into this life—a life where they were not bogged down by strictures or forced to desire in a certain way. Had their lives not been fluid when they had first met, when they had felt the initial spark …?

Ojas's phone beeped with another text, this time from his brother, 'Papa and Mummy are going to make you meet some people. A girl, I think.'

'What? When?'

'Now! They will be there any minute. Thought of giving you a heads-up.'

His face scrunched up in helpless irritation. He was grateful to Sarvesh for his help but hated how intrusive he tended to get. It reminded him of the time Sarvesh had asked him about his sexual identity.

Five years ago, Sarvesh had completed his tenth standard board examinations. Ojas had gone to pick him up. Ojas was not ready for his younger brother's questions.

'Are … uuh … are you gay?' That's what he had asked.

Ojas had almost lost control of the car, but he had quickly steadied his hands and legs. He considered whether he should lie or tell him the truth.

Patti Smith's 'Because the Night' played on the radio as they drove through EM Bypass.

Ojas sat there, feeling bare and exposed. Silence was important to him. It ensured his life was comfortable, peaceful rather. He chose to stay silent to stave off conflicts that knew no end.

In his office, now, Ojas felt pathetic. Guilts, regrets and frustration seemed to have piled up over the years because of his chosen silences.

Was he supposed to hide until, one fine day, he passed away? Or was he meant to explain himself to everyone?

These thoughts confused him as he saw his parents approach with a young woman dressed in a white salwar-kameez and a couple close to their own age—he assumed they were the woman's parents.

The only thing that stayed with him after the rendezvous was the shiver in his hand. Before him: a broken vase on the floor.

His parents had tried to argue with him after the prospective family had left. He had screamed at them and had finally picked up the vase on his side table with fresh sunflowers: 'I will break this if both of you don't leave. I will break this.'

His father had replied with a scorn, 'Who d'you think you are threatening?'

'Shut up,' he had yelled.

The vase collapsed.

His mother screamed, 'No, no, no …' She covered her cheeks with her hands. Her spectacles slipped down her nose.

The muscles in his father's face twitched, as he put a hand forward to warn Ojas and then withdrew it.

The ceramic vase was in splinters. Ojas stamped the sunflowers, the dewy yellow petals and the long green stems, with his tan Oxford shoes. He opened the door of his cabin to find his staff waiting outside with concern.

While leaving, his mother wept and didn't care to look at him. Her jaws shook with fear. His father regarded him with loathing and shook his head as he left.

A shame, he could almost hear his father tell him. *A shameless son!*

'I need you. Please meet me.'

Ralph saw the message as he finished work. He was preparing to return home and treat himself to a cool shower after a hectic day. A business gathering was never peaceful. This time, the kitchen had prepared a series of meals for a gathering of actors, directors and crew members working on a Bengali film. Ralph had made his classic mille-feuilles and experimented with orange madeleines and a cranberry compote to go with it. He was called for when they wished to convey their thanks; they were full of praise. The madeleines were dense—moist with crispy edges. Their citric, tangy notes blended perfectly with the tart cranberries. Hearing the compliments made Ralph's body fill with joy, but he kept a straight face and thanked them. It had been a long time since he had heard compliments.

As he left the room, his phone chimed with Ojas's text.

'Okay,' he typed. Then, after a pause, he wrote, 'Do you want to come over?'

He waited, then hastily typed, 'Or we can meet somewhere outside, I don't mind.'

Ojas replied in under a minute, 'I'd like to come over, if that's okay with you.'

Ralph booked a cab. The day had assumed an altogether strange shape. First, good things had happened at work. And then, Ojas was coming over, finally!

His body was filled with joy as he watched the city preparing for Durga Puja. Music was in the air. The dotted lights depicting flowers, animals and the goddess's face bounced off the windshields of cars and the windowpanes of the buildings.

Ralph wanted to sink into the pleasure of the moment.

He hadn't had the desire to return home like this in a long, long time. He let the happiness he felt take hold of his body.

The taxi screeched to halt before the building; Ojas and he were going to meet after months.

Ralph had changed into a pair of bright satin pyjamas that swayed as he walked around. Zubina had already cooked dinner during the early hours of the morning. There was sautéed cabbage, some leftover paturi, pulao and chapattis. It would have been enough for Ojas and Ralph if Ojas hadn't had his meal already. How could he forget the orange madeleines he had made at the hotel that day? He managed to put some away and get them home.

'Hi,' said Ojas when he entered. He was wearing a soft powder blue shirt that highlighted the small curve of his back and a pair of navy blue trousers that accentuated his thighs. As he moved to the sofa, Ralph stared at Ojas's figure. At the neck against the damp collar. At the sleeves taut around his arms.

Ralph's face grew hot with yearning.

He couldn't think why Ojas had come over, or why he seemed discombobulated. Ralph was preoccupied with the emotions that were overwhelming him on seeing Ojas walk into the flat.

Ojas removed his shoes, wore the slippers that had lain untouched all these months and took a seat as though he had never stopped visiting.

Ralph was brought back to reality when he heard Ojas ask, 'Do you have a smoke?'

Ralph fiddled with the tray on the credenza and then passed on a cigarette with a lighter.

Ojas took a deep drag.

Ralph saw the cloud of smoke float between them, then asked, 'Is everything all right?'

Ojas shrugged with a shake of his head, 'No clue.'

'Why? What has happened?'

The last time Ralph and Ojas had met had been a week ago, with Divya, over cocktails at Ozora. They had chosen outdoor seating and had sat on high chairs to see Kolkata from the twentieth floor, glittering. They had ordered Manhattans and had clicked several pictures and had then ordered a round of LIITs.

Divya handed over the invitation card to Ralph. She spoke of the venue, the expense, the amount she was pooling in. She went into intricate details about her outfit and that of her fiancé. The honeymoon to Kerala had been gifted to them by her sister and brother-in-law.

Then Ralph and Ojas talked about the waste of money that elaborate weddings were and the beauty of the more discreet ones.

Divya scoffed, 'Both of you ... don't make me feel guilty about it. You two have a private wedding in your balconies or terraces.'

After months, Ojas and Ralph shared a momentary glance with each other.

Divya cleared her throat uncomfortably, remembering what Ojas had said about a possible break-up, and changed the subject. She knew Ojas wouldn't want her to interfere and act as an adjudicator.

Divya began talking about what she going to wear in Kerala and that she might move to Bangalore with her husband if both of them got a transfer.

Ralph waited for Ojas to answer his question: what exactly had brought him here to his flat? They faced each other in the living room, the coffee table between them, with an ashtray, a red bottle of water, a pile of unread newspapers and a white notebook of motivational quotes-a-day carrying tawny fingerprints.

Ojas stubbed the cigarette in the ashtray and said, 'I screamed at my parents.'

'Oh!' Ralph considered grabbing a drink from the kitchen but Ojas kept talking.

'They crossed all limits today ...' He rubbed his hands gently against the curve of his thighs.

'What happened?'

'They got a girl to see me at my workplace. Can you believe it?'

'I can. Ojas, you haven't told them. What d'you expect them to do?'

'Okay, so it's my fault, isn't it? That's what I came here to hear.' Ojas wanted to throw something at Ralph.

'No, no, no. It's not what I mean. Tell me ... tell me what happened,' Ralph said, his tone placatory. He didn't want Ojas to leave.

Ojas balled his hand into a fist, then said, 'I was patient, initially. I let them talk to the girl's parents. And then, when they started talking about things like ... they said, I would take care of her, that I would make her my priority every waking moment, that I'd ensure she got what she wanted, that I'd buy a new flat if the house we currently lived in was not enough ... it went on ... I ... I lost it! I stood up and said that I am not ready for marriage. I said it as kindly as I could. Of course, they looked shocked, but ...'

His voice dropped. It wasn't easy for him to articulate what he had done. He opened a bottle of water.

'I didn't care,' he asserted himself, 'I said what I had to and they left. My parents dropped them off, then returned to my cabin. They asked me if I was a fool. Papa said it so loudly that the staff heard. So ... so, I began speaking loudly too.'

Ralph asked, 'What did you say?'

'I told him that he was nobody to take decisions for me. I made a living, I worked hard. And I do not wish to marry. Mummy begged me to consider the family's reputation—what would come of it if I remained unmarried? Papa said: "I waited for you to choose someone yourself but you aren't doing that. You are almost forty!"'

'I am sorry,' muttered Ralph.

'I screamed at them, told them to get the hell out of the office, and to mind their own damn business.'

'Good,' Ralph said.

'And then, I was horrible to them. I broke a vase because I was so angry, *so* angry, Ralph.'

'It's okay.'

'Where is this coming from? I have never been this angry in my life. I scared my parents! Do you know what that means? To scare your Mummy-Papa?'

Ojas wiped tears from his eyes. He had never cried in front of Ralph.

Ralph sat there, saying nothing.

Ojas sobbed quietly. He was tired. It had been a long day. He wanted to curl up and never wake up to the world after this. He wanted Ralph to come and hug him, to comfort him. The more he remembered, the more helpless he felt, and the more he raged against witnessing his parents leave his office in a broken state.

How had he become capable of such anger? He hated the fact that he could find no answer to this question.

His mind and body had grown haggard with the emotions he couldn't share; with a life he had to make sense of alone.

He knew he needed Ralph by his side. Because his presence seemed to be the only balm to his injury. Because he alone could shield him from the awful glare of the world. Ojas wished he could manage it all alone, but his trials had only led him to Ralph.

Ralph led Ojas into the bedroom. He made him sit on the bed and unfolded a pair of shorts and a T-shirt. He placed them down and unbuttoned Ojas's shirt. Ojas shut his eyes and let him. He pulled the shirt off his body and then the white vest over his head. He let the smell of his body fill his nose. It lingered. Ralph had missed it more than he was willing to admit.

Ojas wore the T-shirt.

Ralph got on his knees and his hand reached the buckle of Ojas's belt. Both of them stared down at his hand. The belt slid out. Ralph opened the buttons of Ojas's trousers and then pulled the zip down. Inside, Ojas's crotch lay cased in a grey underwear. Ralph took a deep breath on seeing the curve of his penis. Ojas raised his hip off the bed and let him take the trousers off.

Ralph placed both his hands on either side of Ojas's thighs and waited. Ojas's crotch now pulsed with life. Ralph contemplated shoving his face between his legs, of letting this ecstasy pile on to the ecstasy of the day.

Ojas sat waiting for Ralph to remove his underwear. He wondered if he should nudge Ralph towards his crotch, but he didn't want to force him into anything.

Both of them paused for a minute or two, until Ojas raised his waist, just a tiny bit, and Ralph buried his face in him.

The underwear was off. Ojas was hard inside Ralph's mouth. They seemed unable to resist each other's touch. Ojas moaned. He let past memories drain from his body as he felt the tip of his penis against Ralph's throat. Ralph's lips around his penis felt like a door to a room. He wanted to be locked this way forever.

He held Ralph's face with one hand and his hair with the other. Thoughts of the young boy's text promising him the best orgasm of his life flashed through his mind. No … no, nothing, no other mouth, no hand, could beat the orgasm he experienced with Ralph.

He attempted pulling Ralph by the hair and staring into his eyes and telling him that Ralph was his and his only.

Ralph held Ojas's butt until he was breathless.

Then he peeled himself away.

This moment that was supposed to stretch for hours, days and months, ended in a second as Ojas came over Ralph's face.

Ralph let the tears flow down his cheeks. Ojas placed his hand on his head.

The two slept.

That night, they ate dinner together, commented on the 'superb' taste of Zubina's food, and the mess in Ralph's flat.

That night, they didn't talk about why they hadn't seen each other for so long, the stubbornness and resolve that had sliced them open in half; the wound that had festered and worsened without care.

That night, Ojas began telling Ralph about the day his brother had asked him whether he was gay. Ojas recalled, 'More than the anxiety of coming out to him, I was amazed at his audacity. How could he ask such a question?'

'Really?'

'Well, we didn't share a relationship that brothers generally do. I mean, I see my father and his brothers being much closer. Sarvesh and I have this age gap, almost a decade-and-a-half … I was never there to play with him or anything. I was already passing out of school when he was getting in …'

'Right.'

'He got to know of me on Grindr though one of his friend's cousins or something. And he was rather too committed to supporting me and my identity,' Ojas smiled while reminiscing.

'Sweet.'

'Yeah, really sweet. I was terrible to him though. I shut him up. I told him something like, "I don't know what that friend of yours says or does. Not interested if he shares screenshots. Ask him to get off Grindr for god's sake…" And then I told him to forget the conversation. To end his investigation. To keep quiet before Mummy-Papa.'

'I am sure he gets it now.'

'I don't know. I feel like I killed whatever little love I shared with my family,' said Ojas, more to himself than to Ralph. 'And all because I … I don't want to fuck women but men.'

'Yeah …'

'It's as though the world needs to know how good it is to be inside a man …'

Ralph smiled, 'I can't believe it. You were talking about your family with such seriousness and then …'

That night, they laughed a little more, until the laughter seemed to spring from the neighbourhood.

That night, they slept.

That night, Ralph had soft memories of his mother. He needed no drink.

That night, Ojas didn't sleep as quickly as Ralph. He reined in the urge to check Ralph's phone—to see what Ralph had been up to all these days without him. He had never felt such desire. He wanted to study the grief he still saw on Ralph's face. He wished to understand what he had been doing with it. He chided himself for being the cause of so much sorrow. How much he had loved seeing Ralph laugh just moments ago.

He touched the nape of Ralph's neck with his lips.

There, my love, sleep.

That night, Ojas thought about his parents and his brother. He let his mind search for the pieces that would fit together to make a picture of joyous family life—a picture he had known when he was fifteen and Sarvesh was born. He had come from school and had been taken straight to the hospital. His father had kissed him with a victorious smile and had led him to his mother. His mother was crooning to the baby nestled in her arms. She asked him to come close and see the child. He looked at the tightly wrapped bundle. He saw a curled fist. How untouched the baby was. He wanted so much to protect it. His father passed a newly purchased camera to the nurse and asked her to click a 'family photo'. Ojas stood next to the baby and wrapped his hand around his mother's forefinger. His father went on the other side. 'Cheese!' the nurse said. 'Perfect family photo.' That was their first picture; it lay preserved in one of the family's many photo albums. When he was younger, he'd seek out the picture often, but for more than ten years now, he hadn't looked for it. Sarvesh presently was twenty-four, a chemistry graduate who was ready to leave home and study abroad. His parents were older and spent time talking to relatives and attending their children's weddings. They hoped for the day they'd get to organize their own son's wedding. A tear escaped the corner of his eyes. After that perfect family photo, things had come to this pass. That picture barely resembled his family's present state.

That night, Ojas edged towards Ralph, who slept on his stomach with his head turned to the left. Ojas got on top of him. Ralph groaned in his sleep and Ojas nibbled his earlobe gently. Between kissing his neck and ears, Ojas kept saying, 'I need you' and 'I miss you'.

That night, finally, both of them slept until it was late in the morning. Zubina rang the bell ten times.

4

The news of moving to another city had left Amrin and Soniya enormously excited. It was the capital of the country! They were desperate to see India Gate. Amrin had said, 'I want to go there and sing Jana Gana Mana.'

Soniya added, 'We will also meet the pesi-dent and do salaam, like this ...' She clambered on to the bed and pressed her fingers to her forehead and stood in attention.

For two days, Soniya wouldn't stop mentioning Delhi. She crafted a tale of their imminent departure, which she relayed to her friends; Amrin pointedly rejected her version. 'Nothing is confirmed, Soniya.'

'You know nothing,' Soniya dismissed her. She imagined wearing her yellow Eid dress on the train journey. She imagined that she'd buy new clothes. Pack a separate suitcase. And leave behind toys for some of her friends.

When she saw that her parents were ignoring her remarks about Delhi, Amrin decided that the matter was dead.

She took a marker and crossed dates on the calendar by her bed. She counted down the days to Durga Puja. She looked forward to visiting the cinema hall and a possible outing with Neha-di.

Now, as she entered her home with Soniya, she found her maternal uncle in conversation with her parents again. She was reminded of Delhi. She threw her bag to the floor and sat beside her Mama and Mami. They talked about the school they'd be admitted to and the facilities it would provide.

Amrin and Soniya kept asking questions.

Will there be a playground to play in?

—Yes

Will there be a zoo to visit?

—Of course.

Will our cousin Mou play with us?

—We are a family, and if she agrees, yes.

Does Dilli have cats?

—Many.

Does Mami love cats?

—Sure.

Can Mou be left behind and can a cat be adopted and taken instead?

—No, Mou is a human being.

Then why is she so boring?

—She is a serious girl.

Is there a New Market in Dilli?

—There are various places just like New Market there.

Will we be closer to the moon from Dilli?

—No, the moon is closer to America.

At some point, Aadil took over. 'When does your recruiter want to hear about the decision?'

'Next week,' answered Tausiq.

Zubina said, 'Give us time. Our roof will undergo repairs.'

'Arre,' Shabnam butted in, 'what repair, Zubina-di? You are going to sell this off and move to a flat in Dilli, na.'

Tausiq added, 'You are getting a chance, a light Allah has passed down from ...' He pointed towards the ceiling with his thick forefinger. 'You cannot think so much about this and that. I will help you sell this house off.'

Zubina said, 'No, bhai, you don't understand. This is not like the Park Circus house we had, which we simply left when … well, when …' Her voice trailed off.

'What do you mean?' asked Tausiq and said, 'I didn't leave the house like that, or Ammi…'

'And we took Ammi to our house immediately when she couldn't stay there anymore,' Shabnam added. 'I took care of her day and night, I left Mou with my mother and looked after *your* Ammi when Zeenat-di …' She blew her nose into her dupatta; tears rolled down her eyes.

Tausiq cleared his throat and turned to Aadil, 'You decide and call me soon.' To Zubina, he said gravely, 'We did the best we could after what happened. Unlike your husband, I couldn't buy a house, but I had a home where Ammi came and lived until her last breath.'

'Bhai,' Zubina tried saying something that would not come across as insensitive. 'I didn't … I didn't mean anything really.'

Shabnam dabbed her eyes and said, 'It's okay. Now she's up there, happy and peaceful by Allah's grace.' Her eyeliner and mascara were all over her cheeks. Soniya whispered to her, 'You look like a bhoot, Mami.' Shabnam frowned at her and then dabbed her face with precision.

Tausiq rose with many exaggerated 'oohs' and 'aahs'. Amrin and Soniya burst into peals of laughter. Zubina and Aadil asked their girls to be quiet and waited until the couple had left the house.

Amrin expected her father to join in their mirth, but he headed to the door, saying, 'I will be back in sometime.'

Zubina removed her dupatta and cooked the vegetables she had chopped. Amrin was bewildered to see her parents this way—almost taciturn. Soniya climbed on to the bed. She turned on the television and changed channels.

This was good. Going to Delhi. Having a flat. Studying in a private school that was fully paid for, and living with Mama-Mami.

Why did her Mami mention Zeenat-khaala? Amrin had no memory of her whatsoever.

Amrin especially couldn't understand why her parents were not as enthusiastic about Delhi as Soniya and her.

Aadil couldn't stand the mysterious quality the future suddenly seemed to have.

He went for a stroll once Tausiq and Shabnam left, past the lanes where families cooked dinner and prepared for sleep. Young boys waltzed about dressed in bold, printed T-shirts, their jeans below their waists, snug around their shins and ending above their ankles; the length and colour of their hair flustered Aadil.

He knew the neighbourhood like the back of his hand. His family had come from a village in North Bengal. He had never cared to ask where it was and if they would return. He was content being a city-boy. He made friends, some of whom were still around, some of whom had left for cities like Bombay or Delhi, a few of whom had their lives taken away by alcohol or unexpected ailments. Not one of them had left in a manner that would allow for fond farewells. One fine day, Aadil would hear that this-one had gone to Bombay or that-one had died on his way to the hospital in the middle of the night. Back then, he hadn't thought much about these vanishings. He had his sisters to care for, after all, once his father had left home along with his elder brothers—again, without saying bye.

How it happened still perplexed Aadil. One morning, when he was sixteen, Aadil had seen his mother sobbing. He had asked her why she was crying and she had told him, 'Your father has gone to Hyderabad. Atif and Amaan also decided to leave because they found good work there.'

'Left? Hyderabad?' He couldn't put it together. His brothers and father were doing fine with their jobs in the leather factory with him. He hadn't seen their bags being packed.

'Your father was unhappy here. He had been hoping to leave for a long time.'

'Okay.' That was all Aadil said. He got ready for work.

Soon, they heard that their father wanted them to leave the big house they stayed in as he couldn't afford the rent anymore. He was renting a house in Hyderabad. Aadil asked if they should pack and come to Hyderabad as well. His father said, 'Let us settle down first, son.'

'Where will we live until then?'

'Rent the smaller house that is closer to masjid. It's available, did you know? I will ask the baadiwalla to reduce the rent for you.'

Aadil, his sisters and his mother moved to the smaller house. Aadil's father didn't send money, and Aadil had to pay the rent. His conviction that all of them would join his father and brothers waned. In due course, all communication with his father and brothers stopped.

Aadil tried to contact them when he had to get his sisters married, but there was no response. Once both of them were married, he worked day and night to save money to buy the house he had been renting. He took care of that; still his father or brothers did not respond to his messages. Once, a brother called—but it was a hurried conversation and it brought the family no peace. Under pressure, Aadil got married. The next month, his mother died of a cardiac arrest at his sister's house. He did everything he could to contact them about her demise but to no avail.

It was on the day of Amrin's birth that he got a call from Hyderabad; his father had passed away. He mumbled 'okay' in response to the message. He scanned the roof of the house he had bought. He lived here with his wife and daughter. A heaviness clogged his throat. The call had come all too late.

Now, here was the moment to leave the *smaller* house.

Aadil began his journey home. A range of options weighed him down; choices fell pell-mell like rain upon him. Come to think of it, the idea wasn't at all bad. He could sell the house at a good price and then buy one somewhere in Delhi and live close to (but not in the same house as) Tausiq and Shabnam. Or he could simply put the money in a fixed deposit and save for his daughters' education and marriage. Who could tell what they would do? He had to be prepared.

He reached home and found Zubina at the stove, cooking disinterestedly.

He changed into a vest and lungi. He sat opposite her, quietly picking at the nails of his toes.

Zubina spoke, 'What are you thinking?'

His nail remained partly chipped. 'About?'

'Selling the house? Are we going to do that?'

'I don't know.'

'You can't sell the house! And how can you take such decisions all by yourself? Don't you think you ...'

'This is my house!' objected Aadil. 'I bought it myself, so I can decide what to do with it. It wasn't gifted to me by your sister or mother.'

At that Zubina sat up. 'Good. Go and sell it then. Give it to whoever shows up at the door!' She muttered that hell awaited the family.

Aadil's jaws clenched tight. His eyes studied the house, and rested on Amrin who watched them argue. Zubina cleared the clutter nosily. Soniya was absorbed in the TV show; her back was glued to the wall.

Aadil said, 'Let us eat.'

The girls arranged themselves on the mat. Aadil and Zubina sat opposite them. All four of them had plates filled with chapatti, rice, stir-fried potatoes and mashed pumpkin.

Zubina snapped, 'Eat fast, it's getting cold.'

Amrin asked, 'Are we moving to Dilli?'

Zubina continued to eat, but glanced at her husband.

Aadil shrugged. 'You two say—what do you want?'

'It would be fun!' said Amrin.

Soniya contemplated and asked, 'What if Mou steals all my doll's clothes?'

The three of them erupted in laughter.

Aadil said, 'No, no. She won't.'

Aadil and the girls spoke to each other, but Zubina ate in silence.

In bed, Aadil heard the sheets rustle, the bed creak, as Zubina lay down beside him. He swallowed the guilt that rose from the pit of his stomach. Why had he spoken to Zubina like that, as though he had already sold the house? Of course, he wanted her to take decisions, but sometimes, he wanted to be able to take firm action as well. This was *his* house, all said and done.

No, no—he chided himself for thinking that way. It was *their* house, yes.

He gently placed a hand on her waist. He felt her body shiver under his touch, as though it had been claimed by a cold wind. He moved closer and let his lips rest on the nape of her neck. He kissed it to say he was wrong, that he shouldn't have spoken to her that way, and that he would make up for it. The exact words for this declaration, he did not know. All he knew was that he was hoping to seek forgiveness and undo any damage done.

He kissed the back of her neck again and breathed into it as he fell asleep.

That night, Zubina slept facing her daughters.

Was this another departure?

First, she had left *her* home—her mother, sister and brother.

She entered a new neighbourhood with strange people, and a new house with an old woman, who would die the following month. *An ill-omen*, she thought to herself at that time.

Nazma had taken her around the circuitous lanes and introduced her as a newly-married girl; she told all the women that they had once been where Zubina was.

Zubina still remembered the sadness she felt at every introduction, the way she strained to smile, and the two- or five-rupee coins strangers would press into her hands to welcome her, as though she were begging for alms.

After that, things began to change. Sona asked her to share her bench by her stall. She offered her chicken lollipops and talked about work. The neighbourhood's old woman's daughter-in-law invited her in—her mother-in-law wished to speak with her. All the old lady did that day was nod. For an hour, Zubina examined the neighbourhood in silence. Her eyes had travelled to every corner. She understood where people lived, where they shopped, where the tailors and cobblers were, where she could buy a sachet of shampoo and a kilo of rice, and where she could get a quick facial before a wedding. When it was time to leave, both bowed gently and smiled. Zubina would have missed the old lady's smile had she not seen the corners of her lips twitch.

Zubina remembered the night-time noises of the neighbourhood—people talking, televisions playing music, dogs howling.

To leave this and go to a new place? Her heart sank at the prospect of it.

Not a second departure, not so soon.

After marriage, she had imagined that her second departure would be her final departure, to her grave, where her body would remain eternally until Allah called her to heaven. That was how she had imagined life unfolding ... but now, the future seemed to have something else in store for her.

5

At the tenth ring of the bell, Ojas shot up, wore his T-shirt and dashed to the door. It was Zubina. Her exasperation turned to amusement when she saw him. 'It's you!'

Ojas shrugged, still sleepy.

'You were gone for a long time,' said Zubina, and moved towards the kitchen which had leftover glasses and plates from last night's dinner.

'Yeah, work …' He searched for some excuse.

'Yes, yes, he told me you were too busy with your work,' she said as she started clearing the dishes. 'Has the load lessened?'

'Yeah, somewhat.'

She rinsed the saucepan and asked, 'Chai? Coffee?'

'Chai for … for both of us.' He took the bottle of water to the living room where Ralph was arranging the cushions.

Zubina moved about excitedly, making remarks about how lonely the flat had been without Ojas. She brought them the tea and said, 'Both of you, now, stay together, hold on to each other like true friends, *aalingon koro aar chummo diye …*' She stopped midway—did she just say: embrace one another and kiss and make up? Ojas stared. Zubina patted her cheeks and said that stupid things came to her tongue when she got excited. She went back to the kitchen announcing that the flat finally felt alive with Ojas around.

Ralph laughed. He could barely hide his bafflement at her last words. Ralph wondered if Ojas wanted to speak. Where were they placed? Were they supposed to be back together? He tried forcing a smile.

'She knows things,' Ojas shook his head.

'I mean … I mean, like, how? Why would she say that?' Ralph said to hide his embarrassment.

Ojas guffawed.

No sooner had Ojas retired to the room to change than the doorbell rang. Ralph saw two girls with plastic bags. The girl who was a head taller than the other inquired, 'Is Ammi here?'

'Ammi?' Ralph was confused.

'Yes, she works here,' the tall girl, who he assumed was older than the other, said in a shrill voice.

'Oh,' he understood, 'Zubina-di?'

The two girls nodded at that and shifted warily.

Ralph called Zubina. 'Come, see, who's at our door today.'

Zubina emerged from the kitchen, wiping her hands on a square towel she carried while she worked. She was surprised. At Ralph's insistence, she seated them on the sofa and went to get mango juice.

Ralph asked in Hindi, 'What are your names?'

'I am Amrin,' the elder girl said in English.

The younger one followed in English, 'I am Soniya. What is your name?'

'Me? I am Ralph.'

'You are Kiss-chain, no?' Soniya asked.

'Yes, I am a Christian. How do you know?'

Amrin nudged Soniya while Ralph conjectured, 'Your mother told you, didn't she?'

The girls nodded.

Ralph didn't know how to converse with kids. He sat there and wondered what he should ask next or if he ought to switch on a cartoon show for them to watch. This was the problem with not having siblings, especially younger siblings. He had no idea how he was to entertain a child.

Suddenly, Amrin asked, 'Have you been to Dilli?'

'Yes,' replied Ralph, grateful that she was asking the questions.

'Is it like Kolkata?'

'Very different, but all cities are the same at the end of the day.'

'Will there be more places to buy sparkly gowns?' Soniya was curious and precise.

'I guess,' Ralph shrugged, then asked, 'why do you ask?'

Zubina appeared with two glasses of thick mango juice. She said, 'What are you talking about?'

'They were asking me about Delhi,' Ralph said, handing them the juice.

'Oh,' said Zubina.

'We will go there after Durga Puja,' Amrin piped in, and took a sip.

'Oh, a trip! That's wonderful,' Ralph said and beamed at Zubina.

She played with the tray listlessly and clarified, 'No, my brother found job at a factory there for Amrin's father. So ...'

'You are going to move there?' Ralph asked.

Amrin was about to speak, but Zubina spoke over her. 'We don't know that yet. We are still thinking about what to do.'

They heard the door unlock and Ojas came into the living room. He looked around and smiled at the gathering. Ralph introduced the girls to him and said they had come to give some bags to Zubina. He told him about Zubina's family's plans to move to Delhi.

Ojas said, 'That's interesting, Zubina-di. Are you excited?'

It was then that they noticed how uncomfortable she looked when her mouth opened and closed noiselessly. The joy at seeing

Ojas had disappeared. The idea of shifting did not excite her as much as it did the girls, who jumped in their seats and yelled, 'Yes, very much. New school, new home, new everything.'

Zubina swallowed the words that emerged. To her daughters, she said, 'Okay, have the juice and don't disturb them. I will finish cooking and then we will go home.'

The girls chorused a 'yes' and she moved toward the kitchen to avoid discussing the matter further with Ralph and Ojas. The two men could see that she felt guilty—it followed her like a shadow. She was depriving her girls of something she was not ready for.

Ojas joined the kids on the sofa and asked, 'Who does Zubina-di like more?'

'Me!' Both spoke at once.

Ojas laughed.

'She just wants everything for herself!' Soniya grew indignant.

'Oh, and you always want what *I* want,' said Amrin, and swung her head away.

'But you are the older one, no?' Ojas asked Amrin.

'So? I don't need to carry her in my arms for that.'

'Yes, but you should take care of her as the big girl,' Ojas said.

'I do, but that doesn't mean she can come and do whatever I do,' Amrin said angrily.

'No, I don't …' Soniya tried to defend herself. 'You're just jealous.'

'Okay, okay, that's it,' Ralph tried to butt in.

It was then that Amrin smacked Soniya at the back of her head, so hard it sent her down to the floor.

Ralph and Ojas reached down in horror; they picked Soniya up. Zubina rushed in, hearing the sudden ruckus. She yelled as Soniya broke into tears, 'What happened?'

'She pinched me when we were seated,' Amrin said, poking the side of her waist to show where Soniya had attacked her.

Soniya wailed loudly as Zubina snatched her from Ralph. She rubbed the crown of her head to check for bruises, but there wasn't any. 'It's okay, it's okay,' she told her. Then she looked at Amrin and said, 'Let's go home and I will tell your father about this racket. Ill-mannered girl.'

'No, Ammi, I really did not …' Amrin inched close to Zubina to tell her it was all Soniya's fault. Zubina raised her hand and slapped her right there in Ralph's flat. 'Shut up.'

Ojas went to comfort Amrin, 'Zubina-di, why … they're kids.'

'These are kids? You call such animals kids?' she asked, her voice enraged. A weakness seemed to have taken hold of her ever since Delhi had entered her life's equation.

'It's okay, Zubina-di, you go inside,' Ralph said; the day had taken a bizarre turn.

Zubina now scolded Soniya, 'I hit your sister. Now wipe your tears. Come with me to the kitchen.'

Amrin sobbed and held her cheek. She glared at her mother and sister. Ralph went to his bedroom and returned with a handful of chocolates. Sujoy had given it to him from his work trip to Bangalore the previous weekend. He knelt before Amrin and put the chocolates in her hand and said, 'Here, enjoy these. Don't cry.'

He went into the kitchen and offered sweets to Soniya, too.

Ojas sat Amrin down and told her that being the older one was never fun. He told her he had a younger brother, who irritated him as well. She listened to him, wiping the tears off her cheeks. He said, 'Younger ones think the world is all about them sometimes.'

Amrin nodded, not fully understanding what he meant.

Ojas continued, 'But we older ones are the first, always. Remember that. We are the first ones our parents loved and will always love.'

'My mother hates me, I think,' replied Amrin, and broke into a sob.

'No, no, she is only angry.'

'Whatever, I don't care. I will finish my studies. I will become a teacher like my Neha-di and never be with them,' Amrin snarled.

'Of course, you will be a great teacher ... but remember, teachers who are loved don't hit.'

Amrin opened the wrapper of a chocolate and popped it in her mouth. It was then that Zubina reappeared with Soniya. 'Let's go,' she said.

Amrin ignored them and dangled her legs from the sofa.

'Get up. Your father will be home.'

Ralph said, 'Don't worry, she won't say anything to him. I have talked to her.'

When she heard this, Amrin helped herself off the sofa and trudged along with some nervousness. Her mother and sister were at the door, wearing their slippers. Amrin swivelled around to Ralph and Ojas and grinned with her chocolate coated teeth. They waved her goodbye. She saw Soniya wave to them graciously.

Bitch, she muttered.

Ralph was in a gloomy mood following Zubina's departure. In the balcony, he narrated to Ojas how Zubina's slap had reminded him of his mother.

He was in tenth grade. They had gone to a birthday party of his mother's friend's son. Ralph was dressed in brown corduroy pants and a beige jacket. His mother was glowing in a blue skirt, with a grey stole over a white full-sleeved shirt that had frills.

'Now, go on, your friends are there. I will meet mine and be with you in no time,' she said and led him to the corner of a big hall. A giant inflatable Mickey Mouse shivered under the weight of kids who threw balls at each other.

'I am not a kid, Maa. And why isn't Sujoy here? He is my friend. Not these brats,' the teenager in him announced.

'Well, my love, Sujoy's family is not Pamela's friend ...' She pushed him gently away from her.

Ralph went to a corner, took a glass of Limca, and felt bored. He saw the zoo-themed cake on the centre table and rolled his eyes at it. Sujoy would have laughed with him at such a juvenile cake. They had already advanced to learning pineapple upside down cakes and they were critical of anything cream-laden.

When the cake was cut and the music was played, his mother joined her friends on the dance floor. He wished he had stayed home with his father. She tried to get Ralph to dance. He made a face and pleaded with her that they go home. She said, 'Twenty more minutes, Ralph? *Tarpore baari jaabo.*'

Her going-home-later was to last a bit. Ralph went to the dessert counter and loaded his plate with the petit fours, a cinnamon roll, strawberry pudding, jalebis and a gulab jamun. When he tried to take a scoop of the vanilla ice cream—ignoring the staff's insistence that they could do it for him—he brought the counter down to the floor.

His mother rushed and slapped him right then. She apologized to everyone on her son's behalf.

Now, as Ralph recounted this to Ojas, he said, 'We reached home and then she pushed me in. She howled at me for being a disgusting child, shameless and whatnot. I tried to run to my room. But she held me tight and asked me to apologize. I was too angry to do that. I dodged and ended up punching her tummy.'

'What?'

'Yes, I know. That was horrible. Then she slapped me again and my father watched all of it.'

'Oh, Ralph,' Ojas said, stroking Ralph's back.

'After that we barely spoke to each other for a few days. And then she apologized to me.'

'Really?'

'Yes … she did.'

'Did you as well?'

Ralph shook his head, 'Nope, never.'

Ojas waited beside him and said nothing.

As the sun set, Ralph continued, 'I miss Sujoy and the friendship we had. We were like siblings. My only brother. He has been with me from day one. Even when I wasn't fair to him …'

'What d'you mean?' Ojas asked.

'Well … I always wanted to visit his home but he refused to take me until I literally forced him to. When I reached his address, I realized why he had been nervous. The family of four stayed in a really tiny one-bedroom flat. Sujoy saw me take in the lone bed they shared and the things piled all around. I felt so guilty … forcing him to show what he didn't want to. He was agitated and ashamed. He stopped coming to my house. One day, Maa asked me to take her to his place. I did. And our mothers talked. Maa spent some time alone with Sujoy. The next day, he was back as usual. It was the happiest moment for me. Maa saved our friendship. That was then … and now … I … I couldn't speak up for him when you … '

Sujoy, later, worked hard to change his family's life; he had found a beautiful girl and he planned to marry her. Ralph had envied that and had let the envy get in the way of their association. He wanted to turn back time.

'I don't want to lose Sujoy,' he confessed to Ojas.

Ralph could see himself get older and lonelier with time. How was ageing to be dealt with all alone? He stole a glance at Ojas and wished for time to pause. Would Ojas be there with him? For a second, he saw his father alone in the big house. Then, he saw himself living that way from the mid-thirties itself. It wore him out.

Ojas placed a hand on his waist and asked Ralph to call Sujoy. They should meet for coffee. The three of them. Ojas didn't know what more he could offer. He saw Ralph regard him with seriousness.

Ralph asked Sujoy for a meeting; he agreed.

Ojas was washed with relief as he took a left and drove straight toward Science City. He could see the pulse on his wrist beat through his skin. Happiness had cast a spell. It was not simply a state of mind or an emotion he felt deep within. It was joy that shone on his brows—they did not furrow with anger or sadness any more.

He sang The Velvet Underground's 'Pale Blue Eyes' as it played in the car. His body echoed it, if bodies are capable of doing that.

Ojas was with Ralph. He took a right after Science City and proceeded toward EM Bypass. Was he pursuing the wrong life all this while—fighting, arguing with Ralph, to make himself available to others? Was Ralph right when he said that he—Ojas—was the one at fault?

They took another turn and entered the lane where Acropolis Mall buzzed with people completing last-minute puja shopping. *Certainly not*, Ojas said to himself. He had not left Ralph and betrayed him. It was out in the *open*, always.

Over coffee, Sujoy put the copy of Sally Rooney's *Normal People* down, cleared his throat and asked, 'What's up with you two?'

Ralph and Ojas shifted uneasily on their chairs; they were seated opposite each other. They didn't know how to answer that question.

Seated between them, Sujoy asked pointedly, 'Are you two back together?' He looked at Ojas. 'I mean, things ended pretty badly the last time we met.'

'Uhh ...' Ralph was about to speak, but Ojas intervened. 'Sujoy, I am sorry for what I said back then.'

'Never mind!' Sujoy still remembered Ojas's words. 'I knew you harboured such thoughts about me.'

'No, I didn't. I don't. I ...'

'I'm over it, Ojas,' Sujoy shrugged, with a hint of rage in his eyes.

There was no point in offering a rebuttal. Ojas mumbled an apology again and regarded the paperback, in which a couple lay in a sardine tin. The book's cover made him cradle his coffee. He did not make eye contact with any of them. He knew things could never go right with Sujoy.

Ojas wondered if he admired Sujoy for being assertive—admired him to the point of being envious. And whether he put him down because he felt inadequate in his presence.

Ralph broke the silence. 'We don't know if we're together, Sujoy. We didn't come to discuss that with you. We wanted to meet you.'

'Ralph, that's weird. You were in terrible pain because of the breakup and now you are coming to meet me with him because ...?' said Sujoy, dismissing Ojas's presence.

Ralph did not want to offer explanations at that moment. He only wanted to mend his friendship with Sujoy.

'I did not ask us to part ways or ... *breakup*!' Ojas hated the word—so twenties and so juvenile. It was insulting to think in terms of a breakup when he was nearing forty. Gay or straight—people divorced at that age, for fuck's sake. Here he was sitting and using the same word he had used back when he was nineteen.

'Yes, I did … but you, you just… anyway, I don't feel like talking about this,' Ralph said. He raised his glass of cold coffee and sucked hard at the straw.

'Don't get too carried away this time … please,' Sujoy said, and rubbed Ralph's knee.

Ojas ignored the irritation growing within him. He warmed up to Sujoy when he discussed Bangalore's bookshops and pubs. He said, 'I am going there around November again with Sayantani … do you guys want to join us? We can go to Ooty or somewhere in the hills.'

Ralph laughed with bitterness. 'I can't get over the last trip we had when there was a,'—he used air quotes—'"friend" involved.'

Ojas knew what he was talking about. The hills. Their trip to Darjeeling.

Ralph said, 'You and Sayantani go. Have fun. Double-dates are a bad idea.'

Sujoy didn't wish to ask Ralph what he meant by his statement.

Ojas asked, 'By the way, how did things change for the two of you? I mean, you and Sayantani …' Ojas paused, then added, 'If you don't mind me asking.'

'No, it's okay. It wasn't easy. Sayantani was dead set on not being with me anymore,' began Sujoy.

'What changed?' Ojas asked. He tried looking Sujoy in the eye. It was difficult because Sujoy talked as though Ojas were an inconsequential wall.

'We talked basically. I told her I couldn't think of a life without her and that our families were ready for the two of us

… you know, both our families had met each other and were waiting for us to declare the dates.'

'So …?'

'So, we thought it best not to look back. We would move on, together, from whatever had happened. And, well … here we are.' Sujoy leaned closer, 'I know I've been saying this for a while … but I've finally decided how to propose. I plan to propose her in the Nilgiris. That's why we're taking this trip.'

Ralph and Ojas saw that what held them together was but a delicate thread—a gathering of silly life events. Families, marriages—so many things to protect Sujoy and Sayantani from the harshest of tragedies, from the difficulties that must arise when two people in love begin to commit to each other. Ralph and Ojas did not have any of this.

In those seconds, they realized how sequestered their lives were. How lonely their love was, having only each other to rely on. Sujoy's love was nurtured enough to withstand any kind of calamity.

Both Ralph and Ojas sighed, then wished Sujoy a beautiful marriage, children and a still larger family to keep them bound.

When they were in the car, Sujoy said, 'Thanks for today. It was nice seeing you two.'

Ojas said, 'Same.'

'Yes,' Ralph added with emphasis.

Sujoy got down at the street that led to his home. He glanced at Ralph. The car started and carried Ralph and Ojas in the direction of Ralph's flat.

Ojas cleared his throat and clicked the play button on the console. Art Garfunkel's 'Bright Eyes' began. Ojas wondered if he should stay another night or return home. When the car screeched to a halt next to Ralph's apartment building, Ojas said, 'I will go home tonight.'

'Sure, you should, actually.'

Ralph placed his palm on Ojas's hand and said, 'It will be fine. I am here.' Then he added, 'We'll spend a nice Durga Puja together.'

'Thanks,' whispered Ojas.

They sat there for a minute under the evening sky pierced by yellow streetlights. Then, Ralph exhaled and opened the door of the car. He watched the car reverse and head to the end of the lane.

Ojas amped the music to full volume and drove until he reached home. He stood at his doorstep and smoked four cigarettes. Sarvesh called and said, 'Why have you been standing outside for such a long time? Just come in.'

'Yes, yes, Sarvesh … I …' His voice was husky, as though he were carrying a burden so heavy he could hardly move. All these years of tortured love and distance from his family—it seemed to weigh down on him. His voice trembled. He wished his brother could share some of the burden he carried.

'Please come inside. They are Mummy and Papa. Not monsters,' Sarvesh said, as though to reassure him that nothing had changed; that this was family; that it was elastic—stretching, folding, twisting and scrunching and able to return to its original state. Ojas was the son, the eldest one, and Mummy and Papa were, well, Mummy and Papa—older now, that's all, after caring for their darling child.

'Okay,' Ojas said. He stared up at the sky and gnashed his teeth to hold back his tears. But they ran down his cheeks. He wondered if the tears meant anything, or if they just spoke of anxiety. Was there a thing such as anxiety tears? He would have to google it. When the tears stopped, he wiped his face with the back of his hands and rang the doorbell.

6

The despondent look on Sridevi's face when her daughter asked her with a sneer if she would help her with English homework unsettled Zubina. She gaped at the screen, unaware that a new scene had begun. Amrin and Soniya clicked their tongues and commented on how heartless the daughter was. But Zubina's eyes played the scene on loop. This was the fourth time they were watching *English Vinglish* together. Mother and daughters. They'd sit through it while finishing their chores and would be overjoyed by the end. But now, Zubina couldn't get past that scene.

She gathered vegetables from the basket and took a bowl of water and sat at her doorstep to wash them. While her daughters remained invested in the film, she replayed Sridevi's ordeal and all that that awaited her own family.

Aadil seemed to be ready to sell the house and move. She felt Sridevi's helplessness—it seeped into her own body. Her vision blurred. Her mouth tried to stifle a scream of pain. She gazed at the sky for answers. But if the answer existed, it was invisible like air. Was this the start of another kind of hell? For Zubina, hell was here as much as heaven. Of course, she believed in the heaven and hell *up there*, but down here, she had learnt that both heaven and hell could (and did) exist, in the days and nights, in passing weeks and months; amidst uncertain decisions.

Aadil returned home, wearied after work. Soniya lunged toward her father and said in a sad voice, 'She hit me today.'

'What?' Amrin was flabbergasted. She had expected her sister to forget the episode when they had promised one another on the way back from Ralph's that they would not say a word to their father. Zubina had been lost in her own thoughts when they had laced their pinkie fingers.

Amrin stomped, 'How cheap, you …' Then she spat at Soniya. 'You bitch, wait and watch.'

Soniya wailed, 'She abused me also! Gaali!'

Aadil called for her, but Amrin left the house and marched straight into the evening hubbub of the neighbourhood. He cajoled Soniya, told her to not talk to her sister for the moment and forget what happened. He'd scold her once she returned.

Zubina sat through the hullabaloo and made chapattis. She ignored Aadil as much as she could. She decided to get Amrin back when Soniya pointedly refused to.

Amrin had reached the end of the neighbourhood and headed towards the main road. She hovered around the signal. Autos stood waiting for passengers. People asked drivers to take them to Park Circus Maidan. Amrin reached for her pockets. Her face scrunched up in confusion. She needed someone trustworthy to lean on.

Zubina spotted Amrin and muttered to herself; she controlled a smile hovering around her lips. The listlessness that had taken hold of her earlier vanished. She could rescue her daughter from all mishaps. She felt better about herself and her capacity to mother.

Amrin's face lit up when she saw Zubina, then she looked perplexed. 'I hate Soniya, Ammi,' she said. 'Let's go and beat her up. She's getting out of hand.'

Zubina frowned and said, 'She is small and weak. You are a big girl, aren't you?'

'But ...'

'You hurt her today. Older sisters don't hurt their little sisters.'

'Hasn't Zeenat-khaala ever hurt you?'

Zubina paused. She stifled the discomfort that rose within her as she processed the question. She said, 'She protected me. Always.'

'Well, I would like to protect Soniya, too, but she's so cunning. You need to give her a good scolding.'

'I will!' It's all Zubina could bring herself to say, forgetting that a minute ago Amrin and she had exchanged one of those rare smiles in their eleven-year mother-daughter relationship.

The subject changed and they spoke about the oldest woman in their neighbourhood, who was down now with a fever.

At home, Soniya and Amrin did not converse. Aadil and Zubina spoke as little as they could despite Aadil's attempts at saying how tasty the matar paneer was and how soft and warm the chapatti felt. Zubina ignored his remarks and placed another chapatti on his plate.

The Puja holidays for the kids had begun. Pandals along the peripheries of the neighbourhood were in the last stages of completion.

Zubina busied herself with cleaning the area under the bed. She removed Amrin's old notebooks, nibbled on by rats; Soniya's pink backpack that was beyond rescue; Aadil's old mattress, rolled and tucked away in the farthest corner; and her own rubber slippers which could not be mended.

Soniya unlocked her father's phone and scrolled through TikTok. She watched Neha-di dance to a trending remix of *Dilbar*; the volume remained low.

Amrin stood by the door. Aadil appeared and moved Amrin out of his way. He remained inattentive as she informed him that she had fared well in her test and she deserved to be taken out for a treat.

A dull tension seemed to suffocate the household.

Amrin climbed on to the bed beside her sister and whispered, 'What happened?'

Soniya wiggled and showed her Neha-di's video. She twirled her belly to the music as her hair rose in the air. Amrin pressed the like button, and asked again, 'What happened, Soniya?'

Finally, Soniya said, scrolling through the phone, 'Mehboob Uncle—Nazma Aunty's husband—is not well.'

'What?' Amrin grew pale.

'Mmm-hmm,' she said. 'Where were you?'

'I was speaking to the old woman,' Amrin answered loudly, so her parents would hear.

Zubina asked if the old woman was well. Amrin said, 'She is. Although she doesn't speak, she only looks at everyone.'

'That's her way of enjoying everyone's company,' Aadil said.

'That's an idiotic way to enjoy company,' snapped Amrin. 'I like to roam around, chatter and relish my time with Neha-di, while discussing her Puja clothes!' She expected her family to engage with her, but everyone was too engrossed in their own set of chores to pay any attention.

Amrin left Soniya to her video entertainment and rolled over to the other side the bed.

Zubina was shoving the broom under the bed. She tried removing the scrap the girls had collected from the tailor for their dolls. Aadil sat not far away. He did not attempt stealing glances at her as he so often did. Not even a year had passed since their glorious Eid, and already, a wedge had erupted between them.

Zubina kept the broom away and sighed. Her warm breath fell on Aadil's neck. He ignored it like she was some fly buzzing about him distastefully.

Zubina glanced at her daughters. Soniya was busy with the phone and Amrin had fallen asleep. She shook Amrin. As though in a dream, Amrin said, 'I don't want to go anywhere. No Dilli. I want to be home with Neha-di.' Zubina shook her again. Amrin got up with a start.

Aadil did not react to anything and fiddled with the box of hair dye he had purchased to cover the whites that had begun to grow at an alarming rate.

Zubina began to serve dinner. She had far too much to contend with—grief, displacement, lovelessness, embarrassment, anger—to question Amrin about her outburst.

When dinner was done, Aadil's phone rang. Soniya held the phone to him and Aadil answered, 'Hello.'

'Okay … hmm … okay … yes, yes … we will be there.'

Aadil disconnected and said, 'We need to go to Nazma's house.'

Aadil followed Zubina silently, thinking of Delhi.

As a young boy, when he had heard about his father's and brothers' move to a different city, he had harboured the idea of being elsewhere too. To leave behind the old job at the factory and make a fresh start in an alien city. Even as he'd approach the end of a workday, he'd think of marching through an entirely different neighbourhood.

He wanted to experience the freshness of a new place. A place where he was foreign enough to be anything he wanted. Not his father's son who worked in a leather factory. Not a brother.

He imagined meeting a girl he did not know and having one of those furtive romances he had seen his elder brother enjoying—conversations on the phone, secret meet ups. Aadil liked the idea of it, but life, as he knew it, offered no time for such pursuits. His days barely offered room for a moment's imaginative thought.

Upon waking, he'd rush to the bathroom, stand in the queue and exchange pleasantries with the elders and friends in the neighbourhood. He'd get ready, run to work and keep working until eight at night. After that, he'd be too tired to wander anywhere, so he'd return home with the groceries his family would need. He'd eat dinner, discuss with his mother the things he needed to buy the next day. Then there was sleep to catch up on ...

He waited for things to change. But change never came.

It had been more than two decades. He had been working at the factory from the time he had been a fifteen-year-old boy. At sixteen, his mother and sisters were entirely dependent on him. Of course, his sisters helped by working as house help or caterers, but they were both much older than him, and he couldn't make claims on their money. He could also never articulate his youthful fantasies of adventure before them. Such was the gulf and his dreams remained sequestered …

At twenty, his employer gave him some money, which helped him buy the house. He worked day and night, tirelessly, at half-pay for years, so as to pay off the loan.

By thirty-eight, he had given up all hopes of being in another city. He had a wife and two girls to care for. The white hair on his head was proof. He was not in his twenties anymore.

As they drew closer to Nazma's house, Aadil thought: *I was living the life of a family man when I should have only been a twenty-something boy—free of responsibilities, free of worries. What a sin to waste one's youth! God wasn't charitable with time.*

Aadil watched Zubina run towards her friend. She was wailing. Zubina coaxed her to speak. Nazma tried, then howled yet again, 'What wrong have I done … why did I deserve this …?' She collapsed in Zubina's arms. She pleaded for an answer. 'Why didn't Allah just take my life instead? I am … I am done … living with all this …' The wailing went on. Zubina stood stock still. Sona had to help Nazma stand up.

Aadil left them there and went inside Nazma's house. He found a couple of men gathered around the chowki where Mehboob lay; his hands were on his stomach and he seemed oblivious to the world.

For Aadil, this wasn't a new scene. The moment Aadil had been told on the phone that Mehboob was dead drunk, that he was panting and crying, that he was in intolerable pain and his stomach hurt, he could predict what he'd bear witness to. He had seen too many friends in the same state. In fact, Mehboob himself had seen their common friend die of alcoholism. After the friend's death, Aadil had assumed that Mehboob would give up on drink, but he refused to. So, Aadil started pulling away from him. He couldn't bear the idea of losing one more person he valued; of confronting something as grave as the loss of a friend again.

Now, here he was, standing at Mehboob's bedside, watching his gradual descent into death.

A taxi was parked at the back of the house. The men gathered around Mehboob and carried him over to it. They asked him to keep chanting god's name and said that everything was going to be fine. Aadil whispered a prayer and held the door open. Mehboob's eyes opened; they met Aadil's. To Aadil, it felt like both of them were asking each other for forgiveness for all that had passed between them.

Aadil held Mehboob's hand and said, 'You will be fine.'

Once Mehboob was in the taxi, Zubina and Sona helped Nazma in; she was still wailing.

The taxi left.

Zubina and Aadil made their way home. They walked together. It was eleven at night.

Zubina said, 'Will he get better?'

'I think so ... if he doesn't drink, he might.'

'I can't see Nazma like this. That woman is ...' Zubina felt unable to continue.

'Hmm.' Aadil wanted to place a hand on her shoulder to comfort her. But he didn't.

'I don't know if I can leave her like this and go anywhere.'

'Huh?'

'I can't leave her like this. I can't go to another city and begin afresh ... my life here is not done.'

'But ...'

Aadil wanted to tell her to push away the thought—that through his twenties, he had hung around for others; that, now, neither his mother nor his sisters were there with him. His sisters were happy in their own homes with their kids, and his mother was dead.

'Things and people will come and go, Zubina...'

'I can't ...' repeated Zubina.

'I was only thinking it's a better opportunity ...' Aadil continued, '... for our girls.'

'There are good private schools here.'

'There will be more money there.'

Zubina couldn't argue any more. 'You go, then. I will be here. You see what it is like first.'

They had reached home. Aadil hadn't offered a response.

He knocked at the door and waited. It wasn't just Zubina, he told himself, it looked like Amrin, too, was having second thoughts about leaving. Aadil, while tinkering with the box of hair dye, had heard her.

Aadil knocked again. What would change Amrin's mind, he wondered. She had seemed so happy about the new school, the new city; he could see the young boy in him jump as his daughter laughed.

Zubina took over and knocked at the door. Again and still again. There was the sound of some rustling; feet touching the floor. The latch was released and the door opened.

Amrin waited for an explanation with puffy eyes.

'Mehboob has been taken to hospital,' Aadil said, fixing his lungi.

'So …' asked Amrin, stifling a yawn, '… we won't go to Dilli?'

Before Aadil could reply, her mother scolded her, 'What is this? What have the two things got to do with each other? Go to sleep …'

It felt to Aadil as though it wasn't just his home, but the whole neighbourhood that had gone quiet when Zubina raised her voice.

Aadil took his place on the bed. Amrin claimed hers. Finally, Zubina switched off the lights. She waited by the window, observing the neighbourhood go to sleep through the grille. Dust particles rose in a swirl outside and stung her eyes.

The fuzzy October air seemed to beckon her and tell her something—but what? She drew the curtains with force.

7

Ojas lay in bed after an unusually quiet dinner with his father.

He had returned home after meeting Ralph and Sujoy, and had hoped for a conversation. He had anticipated confrontation, a full-blown exchange at some point. He had hoped to ask his father about the girl and what had become of the family. He had wanted to let him know that their struggle felt Sisyphean, an endless battle that would never end.

Ralph had texted Ojas, 'Don't force things. Parents are unchangeable after a point.'

Ojas grunted. He wasn't forcing anything on anyone. He wasn't forcing Ralph to embrace his views. And he wasn't forcing his father to come to terms with who he was. He was only trying to let them know that he needed their reassurance.

Ojas failed to convey any of this.

Dinner with his father remained frosty and tense.

While Ojas tried to sleep, he thought of the time Ralph had moved out of his parents' home and his father's reaction to it.

It was the winter of 2017.

Ralph's house in Alipore.

Mike was panting. There was the sound of Sellotape being cut—snap-snap—and of cartons being dragged.

The Alipore house had gone silent since the day Ralph's mother had taken her last breath. That was a year ago. A faint whiff of vanilla and cinnamon still lingered in the house, even though Ralph scarcely baked in his mother's kitchen anymore.

Ojas filled a carton with running shoes and three pairs of flip-flops. He entered the yellow room, which had a study table with books on baking; the books were covered with a film of dust.

Mike followed him about. He was restless. He sniffed Ojas all over and would not let him move. Ralph had to scold Mike, after which he sprinted downstairs.

'I think Baba is unhappy,' Ralph said, and stuffed clothes inside a box.

'Your mother just passed away. Maybe he worries he will be lonely,' said Ojas. He had always lived with his family. He shuddered at the thought of hunting for another apartment in Kolkata, despite toying with the idea of moving out every now and then.

'But I want to go, Ojas. I can't be in this house anymore. It's … it's like what Sujoy said … I won't ever be able to accept Maa's death and move on if I keep seeing something of her wherever my eyes go.'

'Yes, I understand. But maybe you should also think about the parent who's still alive. I mean, your father …'

'Oh, so, you think I am being selfish?' Ralph didn't want to fight with this man he had met a year ago. Finally, he had been able to make a relationship work for more than a few months. He wanted to avoid petty conflicts. He wanted to remember how grateful he had been when Ojas decided to help him with the move to the new rented flat in Tangra.

'No, no. I am sorry. I didn't mean that …' Ojas's voice trailed off. He didn't know how to tell Ralph, without hurting him, that he *was* being selfish. Leaving his father in a big house with a young dog to take care of was nothing but selfish.

The cartons were taped and labelled with markers. Trolleys were parked by the wall. Plastic bags and pastel-coloured totes lay sprawled on the bed. Ralph said to Ojas, 'Thank you for coming and helping me through this. It means a lot.'

'You're welcome …' Ojas drew him close and kissed him lightly on the lips.

With that, Ralph and Ojas pushed each trolley down the stairs. The wheels collided against the edges of the black marble stairs that had chipped and dented over time.

Ralph's father stood by the main door, dressed in his usual grey shirt and black trousers, as though he were still working with the Income Tax Department. Ojas got the last trolley down. Ralph's father and Ojas had never exchanged a word in private. Ralph had always been there when Ojas had come for lunch or dinner over the weekends.

That afternoon, Ojas halted before Ralph's father to catch a breath, a trolley by his side. He saw the old man's face and tried to say something to him, to make it easier.

'Are you sad?' he asked.

Ralph's father replied, regarding the wheels of the trolley, 'Well, does it matter?'

'I am sure it does.'

'How exactly?'

'Uh …' Ojas fumbled, '… you're his father, and I can see it's hard to live alone.'

At that, Ralph's father laughed. 'I have no problem staying alone. I never had siblings of my own and both my parents went off to work. I can manage. I …' He ran his fingers along the old walls and said, '… I am thinking more about this house. Our home and Mike.'

Ojas saw Mike scurry past the table to get petted by the bony fingers of Ralph's father.

'Yes, I understand,' said Ojas. He stared at the mahogany dining table. It was old. On it was a stick of butter softening in a metal dish, a glass jug with red roses, and a newspaper weighed down by an ashtray that carried a reproduction of Van Gogh's 'Sunflowers'.

'You understand? What do you understand?' Ralph's father lit a cigarette and took a drag.

'That ...'

'You have stayed with your family your whole life, right? You've told me as much. And here you are, helping my only child leave the house ... and you tell me you understand?'

This conversation wasn't going the way Ojas had expected. He had hoped for a heart-to-heart. But things seemed to be taking a completely different turn.

Ralph's father continued, 'Do not speak of things you have no idea about. You're too young to make certain comments. You have not had a family of your own. Perhaps you never will.'

To Ojas, all at once, the world swirled. The jug on the mahogany table seemed to shake. Ash seemed to spill out of the ash tray. The butter seemed to turn runny and stain the newspaper. Ojas steadied himself and said, 'Does a family of my own amount to having a child and a wife? Is that what you are saying?'

Ralph's father moved away from him and opened the windows. The hinges created a racket. He didn't offer a reply.

Ojas continued, 'All this while, I thought you *understood* Ralph ... but maybe I was wrong. Maybe Ralph is right to move away.'

Ralph's father grimaced. He walked towards him awkwardly, and the cigarette inadvertently singed Ojas's arm. Ojas yelled, as Ralph's father dodged him, moving with all the strength he had in his body.

Ralph assumed his father was hurt. 'Baba?' he called from upstairs. He came running down and placed the carton he had been carrying on the table. Standing between Ojas and his father, he asked, 'What was that about?'

'Nothing,' said his father, regarding Ojas's forearm, and marched off to his room.

'Ojas?' Ralph said, hoping for an explanation.

'It's nothing, you heard,' stated Ojas, hurt and fury palpable in his eyes.

Mike gravitated towards Ojas; he again started getting in the way—sniffing Ojas's crotch and then his ass.

'Mike, no,' admonished Ralph.

Mike was not ready to listen, nudging, falling over Ojas. 'Stop, Mike ... stop,' Ralph kept saying.

'Oh, lord, Ralph, just cut out the screaming!' Ojas lost his composure.

He left in his car with the cartons that had been loaded.

In Tangra, Ojas had already started moving the cartons into the apartment with the help of the security guard and Zubina-di—she had been recommended by the landlord and had already been asked by Ralph to work in his flat. The moment she entered, she got to work. She cleaned the floor twice, prepared the bed, placed the crockery and started arranging bottles of water in the refrigerator. She asked about the meals to cook, but Ojas told her not to worry about it just yet.

By the time Ralph reached, it was time for dinner. They ordered takeaway from Kim Ling, a restaurant they would begin to frequent often in the days to come. Ralph asked, 'What happened with Baba today?'

Ojas sighed, but Ralph was adamant. So, he recounted what had happened.

Ralph said, 'Oh god, Ojas. I am so sorry. He acted as though he didn't mind my decision to move.'

Ojas picked the ball of manchurian with chopsticks, dipping it in the hot garlic sauce; he leaned forward to eat it grumpily. Ralph finished his meal early, leaving some of his dinner behind. 'I am full. I don't feel like eating any more.'

'Okay.'

When they were in bed, Ralph faced Ojas and asked, 'Am I horrible for leaving my father?'

'No, baby, you're not,' Ojas ran his hand through Ralph's hair and knotted fingers in his.

Ojas could scarcely confront his disappointment in Ralph's father. Ojas's father wore his distaste for men like Ralph and Ojas on his sleeve, but Mr Gomes ... Mr Gomes hid his disdain. It was what cowards did.

As time went on, Ralph's father grew persistent in his apologies to Ojas in private. The first time, Ojas had said to him, 'It's okay, uncle. Bygones.'

'We're good?' Ralph's father kept asking whenever they met, and Ojas always said that they were.

It mattered and then it didn't—it's how Ojas made his peace with the fall of Ralph's father in his eyes.

Ralph's silence about his father, though, remained disconcerting.

On their first day in the Tangra flat, Ojas had not considered the fault lines that develop between sons and fathers over time—he merely saw the strain between Ralph and his father as a minor hiccup in a regular relationship—but now, he saw things differently.

He was no longer able to have a conversation with his father across the dinner table about business, staff problems or the crippling state of the economy—let alone things that were more personal. There was something so specific about the kind of relationship fathers and sons, or mothers and sons, shared, he began to realize. These relationships did not slip into one another to form a composite whole. Their weave and texture remained distinct. He wished he had the words to describe what it meant for a father and son to love each other, to respect one another, to talk to each other; and how it felt to watch the warmth transform into an impenetrable coldness.

His mother, after the episode at the office, had continued conversing with him as if the incident had never happened. She'd have tea sent to his room. She'd peeled carrots and beetroots and make his favourite vegetable juice that he could carry to work. She'd arrange his breakfast. Before he'd leave, she'd talk of something ordinary—Divya's wedding, for instance, and the pending shopping. The fear on her face, when the vase shattered, was gone.

If all relationships were more or less alike, why didn't his father behave like her? Why couldn't he come to his room with a file, discuss work, or tell him about the new doctor he had found? Why weren't fathers meant to love like mothers?

Ojas's mind was full of questions to which he had no answers. By the time he woke up, he forgot about most of these puzzling thoughts; the day began as it usually did, with his father's silence.

When Ojas reached home from work, he went to his brother, Sarvesh's room. Sarvesh was on his bed with the phone in his hand.

'Have they said anything?' Ojas asked and sat beside him on the bed.

Sarvesh shook his head, 'No, but I feel you have to go and talk to them.'

'Talk about what?'

'You know what very well,' Sarvesh said to him in a matter-of-fact way.

'You don't understand.'

'What else can you do? Tell me? They hope that someday you will get a bride. Just go tell them you can't and let them know you are who you are.'

Ojas felt the urge to envelope his brother in a hug. A long warm embrace they had scarcely shared. He was overwhelmed by Sarvesh's impassioned plea. How innocent and fierce his face and voice were. So unlike the young boy he had known a few years ago. How could youth assert itself so differently for him and his brother? All these years, he had thought that every age stood for something common. Ten: a grasping child. Twenty: an excited, willing-to-experiment adult. Twenty-five: a grown-up who sought freedom and ambition.

Yet ... Ojas had never fit in.

He realized that, if tables had turned, he'd never have been able to tell his twenty-four-year-old brother to have a heart-to-heart with his parents. What made Ojas so different from Sarvesh? Growing older had revealed to Ojas the differences, rather than the similarities, between those he had shared his life with. Irreconcilable differences. And the fact that the degree to which each of them could trust differed.

He left the room.

In the living room, Ojas asked, 'Are we going out?'

His mother was fasting. She was creweling with spools of yellow, blue and green. She said, 'Why not!'

They waited for his father to respond. He cleared his throat and said, 'Why do you want to go outside? The three of you go, I am too old for this.'

Every year, Ojas recalled, they went out for one night during Durga Puja. And it was always his father who planned it. This was the first time his father was reluctant and his excuse was that he was 'too old'.

Ojas said, 'Papa, we can go for a drive at least.'

His father nodded. 'Sure, wherever you want.'

Ojas tried helping his mother in the kitchen once she stopped creweling. His mother said, 'It's okay, you go sleep. I will do it.'

'I want to do it, Mummy,' he replied.

'Here, put the milk in the fridge then. It's cool now.' She handed him the vessel.

He leaned into the refrigerator and wiped a shelf with a cloth. He placed the vessel inside. He agonized over the normalcy of their interaction. He wanted to apologize to his mother, but he didn't have the words for it.

He asked, as he poured some Diet Coke for himself, 'Mummy, do you not like me?'

'What?' his mother asked. 'Of course I like you. Why won't I?'

'I don't know. I am … I … well, I was terrible that day, wasn't I?' He took a sip of the Coke.

She shrugged, 'I don't want to talk about it. I am fasting.' She wavered, then added, 'And I am praying for you. You're my son, my first. It makes me worried seeing you this way.'

Ojas waited.

She squeezed the rag with which she had cleaned the cooktop and said, 'God will hear me, I promise. Everything will be all right.'

Ojas put the glass away and left; she made her way to her room.

She had crushed him. He felt diminished by her words. He wanted to forget this conversation. That it had ever happened. That a mother could make you feel smaller through acts of sincere love.

He went to his brother's room again and said, 'Did you see that with Papa?'

'Yes, I did,' replied Sarvesh.

'He was supposed to suggest going out, he was supposed to choose where. Remember, we used to fight with him—that we'd go where we wanted and not to the places he chose?' He opened the balcony door and went out to smoke.

Sarvesh followed him and they both sat on the plastic chairs.

Ojas took a puff and asked, 'Isn't it sad what's happening to our family? Imagine what will happen when you leave for the US! The three of us will just grow old and tired of each other.'

'I am asking you again to tell them the truth. You don't deserve this.'

'Sarvesh, can you please not repeat yourself like a stupid goat? It isn't so simple. Have you seen how they are?'

'Sure—but maybe they will hear you out and understand you. You're not a young boy they can dismiss.'

'So you think if I go and talk to them, they'll lap up the explanation? And d'you think they give a fuck about whether I am a young boy or an old man? I am still their son.'

Sarvesh didn't know how to counter that. He looked for answers in the evening sky. Is there a science to desire? He had never thought about it until now. He muttered, 'Maybe what you say will soften them ... since you're saying it to them as their son.'

Ojas stubbed the cigarette. 'If what I said made any difference, they wouldn't have come to my office with that family and that girl!' There was an anger in his voice. 'They caught me at a moment when they assumed I wouldn't be able to say "no" or walk out. They don't respect me, you know, or my boundaries. Because I am their unmarried son, they believe I have no life to claim as my own ...' He swallowed a sob that rose in his throat. 'Nor do I have ... privacy. I don't ...'

'You need to give them a chance.'

'You trust too much in life, Sarvesh,' said Ojas. 'I really don't know how I'm going to put up with them when you are gone.'

'Why don't you move out?'

'Huh?'

'Why don't you go and live with the man you are with?'

'What do you mean?'

'I think the more you hover in front of their eyes, the more they'll keep getting worried.'

'You think I should move out? That it will solve anything at all?'

Sarvesh stood up. He seemed irritated—his brother would not listen to him, but seemed intent on seeking his opinion.

'No, it won't solve things, but at least it will lessen the everyday bickering. Since you have decided not to say anything to them about yourself, it's best to stay out of their way.'

Sarvesh left Ojas. Before him lay an empty plastic chair and the vast darkness of the night.

It was the first time Ojas had spoken to his brother at length. It healed him to know that there was someone at home who listened to him. Who believed that he wasn't weird or foreign. He felt grateful to have someone to speak to besides his mother's peacock crewelwork.

In his room, Ojas talked to Ralph about his workday and then they jerked off over a video call. Ojas did not tell him what had happened at home and his discussion with his brother. He was being careful because he knew how delicate the situation was.

When Ralph said, 'I am glad you will be home tomorrow,' Ojas relaxed.

As he tried sleeping, he thought about Sarvesh asking him to move in with 'the man'.

Somewhere, there lurked within Ojas this shape-shifting creature named happiness; it breathed words of a home with Ralph.

Post douching, Ralph showered and fixed himself a cup of black coffee. Shashti, the sixth day, an 'off day' for him, after working without a moment's rest. The flat was in order. Zubina had already cleaned, cooked lunch and left before it was noon. She appeared wearied and distant. He tried to make conversation with her, but she answered in monosyllables and remained busy.

By 3 p.m., Ojas was in the flat. They hurled themselves at each other, peeling off one another's clothes.

Once they had sex, they ate Zubina's deliciously cooked malai kofta with jeera rice and deep-fried slices of brinjal on the side. In the room that smelled of the strawberry lubricant, sex and semen, they fell asleep.

Ralph dreamt of his mother—her excitement over Durga Puja and how she attended it in the neighbourhood with her friends, dressed in a crisp new saree. He saw her returning home with him. He could hear her recounting to his father everything that had happened. 'I cannot wait for the Dhunuchi Naach tomorrow,' she said, twirling around.

The next day—still in his dreams—his mother and he spun round and round. 'You cannot be doing that. Do you know how to do it?' Ralph's father told her. 'You haven't seen me,' she said, and hopped around, tucking her pallu at her waist.

Back when his mother was alive, his father never went to the puja but Ralph did with his mother. He saw her dance. Every year. She was called the Christian woman who knew the dance better than any Hindu. How much he missed her and the joys she brought to his life. Even in his dreams, he missed her.

The dream of his mother dancing shifted to other memories, distant ones, and spun into fiction—these were scenes that had never happened.

On the other side of the bed, Ojas wandered through unreal events and snapshots that he could not explain to anyone if he happened to wake. In one scene, he and his father peered over images from their family album while his mother got snacks. His mother's embroidered peacock stole glances, too. Ojas asked Sarvesh to join them but he remained uninterested. So, Ojas, Mummy and Papa took in the photographs to remind themselves about the family they were.

Suddenly, that screen flitted to another, here, Ojas was kissing Ralph. His family watched them in stupefaction. He didn't stop to explain what was going on. From the corner of his eyes, he saw his father glare at him with revulsion and then, there was a smile. A smile that almost hinted at an embrace.

And then there was another scene; *good lord, no*, Ojas screamed at the top of his voice. He had killed his father. His father was dead because Ojas had kicked him hard on the leg. They were ready to get down the stairs to go for a drive. The kick sent him rolling down the steep steps. What had he done?

Ojas woke up, breathing heavily. He was glad it was a nightmare and not reality. He grabbed a glass of water and saw Ralph still asleep. He moved closer to him and put his head on his stomach that surged and dipped like a baby's. He stayed like that until Ralph wrapped his hands around him and patted him to sleep.

In the evening, they got ready to go for a drive. Ralph wore a pair of blue chinos and a white half-sleeved shirt. Ojas changed into a maroon crew-neck T-shirt and black jeans. Ralph snapped the tag off Ojas's T-shirt and said, 'You look so hot.'

Ojas smirked; he admired himself in the mirror. 'Thanks.'

'You should wear these T-shirts more often. They make your body appear shapely,' Ralph said and sprayed perfume all over himself and applied a touch of pink lip gloss.

'If you say so. You are looking hotter than ever, too.'

'Am I?'

'The spark has returned to your face,' said Ojas, and kissed him on the forehead.

'I am past the threshold where I could hope for sparks.'

'Wait till you're a stone's throw away from forty,' Ojas said and kissed him again.

In circles, they did the same thing they had over preceding years. They passed through the much talked about Sreebhumi pandal, which had been made to resemble a palace from the Maurya Dynasty. The queue left them with no choice but to enjoy it from the outside.

Next, they made a stop at AJ Block in Salt Lake. Tucked away in a quiet, well-lit lane with two-storey bungalows, the pandal sat, primly dressed. There was no theme to attract crowds, but blue and white plaits of fabric gave the pandal's exterior a quaint beauty. Women dressed in silk sarees, men in white sherwanis, went inside, clicked pictures and offered their prayers. Ralph and Ojas followed them. The pandal was lit by a chandelier. When Ojas shut his eyes, Ralph did too, and only saw his mother dance before him with her cheery smile.

Various men clicked pictures of their wives; Ojas asked Ralph to pose before the goddess. Ralph refused demurely. Ojas tried persuading him. Ralph kept watching the goddess, draped in a heavily sequinned red saree, holding silver weapons in her hands, a ferocious lion guarding her; she was standing over the body of Mahishasura. Around her, other gods and goddesses stood in a semicircle, with gold chalchitra embroidery.

Ojas pleaded, 'You are my goddess. Pose, no.'

Ralph stood still. He didn't know what to do with his hands, so he kept them folded behind him. He remembered his childhood, when he went pandal hopping with his parents; his mother'd make him stand in front of the idol to get a picture. He'd flash a wide-toothed smile. It's the same smile he offered now as Ojas clicked.

When they ambled along the neighbourhood, Ralph told Ojas about the news he had read that day, of the Internet shutdown in Kashmir. 'Can you imagine! I was horrified.'

'I am tired of reading the news, you know. This is why I always stayed away from all political commentary.'

'Well, you're too privileged to be concerned,' said Ralph, to brush the topic away. Then he clicked pictures of Ojas against a mural carrying prints of Jamini Roy's art.

'My father wanted me to get into politics,' Ojas said. 'I remember him going crazy about party membership ... claimed it would help in business and shit.'

'I didn't know this ...'

'Well, I said no!'

'Why?' Ralph put his phone away.

'Are you out of your mind, baby?'

The way he said the word 'baby'—it made Ralph do a double take. He was about to say something. Then, he stopped himself.

Ojas looked for another pandal; he wanted to break the silence that seemed to have wedged itself between them.

Neither Ralph nor Ojas knew where they stood with each other. They did not know if they had the right to exchange words of endearment.

A breeze floated past their faces and ruffled their hair. Ojas folded his arms and felt the uncanny chill of October. This sight of Ojas walking, his arms crossed, cold, reminded Ralph of Darjeeling.

It was the particularly cold December day in 2018. Ralph and Ojas had landed at Bagdogra Airport at 9 a.m. They found a man with a placard reading: 'Mr. Garg'. He was their driver.

It was a four-day trip, not the touristy kind, because both of them had visited the hills as children with their families. It was Ralph who insisted that he wanted to go to Darjeeling with his partner. The reservations had been made—a fancy hotel overlooking the mountains; a day at the hotel spa; a walk around the tea estates; a drive through the surrounding hamlets.

Ojas said that a friend of his could join them for a bit the day before they were meant to depart.

'Who?' Ralph asked.

'Aritra … remember I told you about the friend who was doing a PhD in UK and studied tribes?'

'Oh, okay,' Ralph said, disappointed. 'He's staying at our hotel?'

'Nah, he's booked elsewhere. And he will only join us in the afternoon. He's leaving soon after. He's going for some trek.'

'Right!' Ralph wasn't comforted by Ojas's claims that Aritra would be a temporary presence.

As their car crawled up the hills, Ralph clicked several pictures and showed them to Ojas. Ojas told him that the one that captured the houses below—with the clothes on the clothesline—would be perfect to post on social media. Ralph did that, then asked, 'Are you happy?'

'Very much,' replied Ojas, watching the small houses and the eating kiosks pass them by.

'It's like I am reliving childhood memories with you,' Ralph said and held Ojas's hand.

'Same.'

At the hotel, for meals, there was a buffet spread. They entered their room, freshened up and slept, until Ralph woke Ojas up and said, 'Let's go out. The afternoon is lovely.'

Ojas cuddled Ralph and kissed his face dreamily. They kissed for some time until Ralph pleaded, 'Come, no. We should not miss the sun.'

They rose for a short walk and then went to Kunga, a Tibetan restaurant. After that, they shopped. Ralph bought a lamp and a couple of other decorative items for his living room, which he paid to have delivered directly to Kolkata. Ojas purchased tea and clothes for his family—shawls, beanies, gloves—and a skein of yarn for his mother. By the time they were done, the sun had set and they were tired of walking. They went to Glenary's and decided to have pints of beer.

Ojas's face screamed exhaustion but Ralph gleamed with joy. The live music, the beer, the spicy food in cold weather and the one he loved in front of him—it made him nostalgic.

'You know, Maa and Baba loved this place. They would always come here and drink until one of them realized it was time to leave.' Ralph's face fell. He blinked hard to avoid crying.

After dinner, when they walked, Ojas put his arm around Ralph, and asked, 'What happened?'

'Nothing. I don't know why I feel bad ...'

Ojas gently rubbed Ralph's back as they walked in the foggy darkness toward their hotel, 'It's okay. I am here with you. You are not alone.'

'I am alone ... Ojas, it will never happen again ...' his voice seemed to ring in the eerie silence of the hills. 'Maa's gone and what hurts most is that I won't be able to come here again with her.'

A group of boys were passing by, so Ojas moved his hands away from Ralph and stood back. Ralph saw Ojas, his arms crossed, shivering; he was breathing out thin puffs of air. Ralph wanted to remember Ojas this way, always. He wanted to preserve their time together—talking, walking, shopping and eating.

The next day, it was as though someone had come and pulled the rug from under his feet.

Ralph and Ojas walked around AE Block of Salt Lake, even as the crowds thinned. They decided to order chai, then eat from food stalls that sold fish fry, rolls, chow mein and biryani.

Ojas's eyes darted to the crowd sharing a joint in a corner over a plate of chicken drumsticks. He spotted Aritra in their midst.

Ojas had talked to Aritra in 2016 on Grindr. They had met a couple of times over drinks. He was in Kolkata on a sabbatical, to work on his new academic text on a tribe in Bengal. Ojas could no longer remember the name of the tribe, but he recalled the discussions they'd had after two wild orgasms. Aritra told him of his fieldwork, of the archives he had dug through, of the books he had read and his views on a culture's erasure. Ojas remained fascinated by these stories and kept in touch with him, even when Ralph hated it.

Now, Aritra saw Ojas and suggested that they meet for coffee the next day. He was to leave for London after that. Ojas agreed, unlocked his phone and asked if his number remained unchanged.

Ralph was carrying packed boxes of food and a bottle of Coke, when he found Ojas taking the number of a man who was sitting next to him.

The man said goodbye and left, without noticing Ralph.

Ralph looked at Ojas and passed on his food. They ate without speaking a word. The faint sound of laughter from the group at the momo stall made the atmosphere feel less desultory than it was. Ralph munched on his chicken roll, peeling the oily paper cover.

Ojas finished his paneer tikka and used a tissue to wipe off the stains on his fingers. Then, he said, 'Aritra was here. We've decided to catch up tomorrow. He leaves for London after Puja.'

'Right,' Ralph replied, and took a swig of the Coke.

They decided to take another stroll down an unlit lane. There was space between them now. At the end of the lane stood a man with an ice cream trolley. They got double chocolate cornettos and stood by the sidewalk, watching buildings bathed in blue and white lights.

Ralph licked his cone and tried to focus on the present. He was standing with Ojas in a dark lane beside an ice cream trolley. He was in the presence of a man who wasn't truly his.

He had never felt so alienated, despite having a man by his side. Men always provided him protection … but for the first time he felt no such thing.

Between Ojas and the ice-cream vendor, he couldn't tell who was more of a stranger.

Ralph had been searching for love. And it was nowhere.

The still air suddenly picked up speed. Ojas held Ralph by the arm and said, 'It's going to rain, I think.'

Ralph moved away from him. He looked at the disturbed canopies of the chatim trees; they were flinging their devilish aroma all around.

He went to the car with Ojas, who drove, humming Adele's 'Chasing Pavements'.

It did not rain that night. Ralph sat on his bed with his guitar and a plate of Nutella sandwich he had fixed for himself. Ojas had chosen to return to his home in Lake Town. He told Ralph that he felt guilty about abandoning his family during this time of the year.

Ralph adjusted the chords and tried playing a tune. It sounded terrible. He readjusted the chords and played again. And yet again. Until it was four in the morning. His sandwich lay unattended and the tips of his fingers were bloody.

8

Zubina's eyes felt drowsy. Yet she couldn't sleep.

She was plagued with guilt—was she being selfish; was she abandoning her family?

It was impossible to get rid of the gnawing feeling in her heart after seeing Nazma and her husband. She couldn't see Nazma suffer; she couldn't leave this place she called home when her friend was in trouble. She couldn't do it.

She was also assailed by memories of her sister—her stubbornness, her insolence, the pain she brought on all of them twelve or thirteen years ago.

Amrin rose and complained she couldn't sleep. Dogs were prowling about the neighbourhood, making a racket. She joined her mother on the mat, while Soniya and Aadil snored on the chowki.

Zubina regarded her gravely and asked, 'Why don't you want to go to Dilli?'

'Uh … I … I like being here. I have very close friends … and the old woman there doesn't want me to go.'

Zubina was perturbed when she heard about the old woman. Her daughter was growing up much too fast. 'When did you get close to her?' she asked.

Amrin hesitated, 'I … I sit with her sometimes.'

'Go to sleep,' said Zubina. 'It's getting late.'

Both of them took their respective places in the bed and stared fixedly at the ceiling that had been repaired and cleaned.

The next morning, Soniya asked if they were planning to go to the fair. Amrin was in the middle of preparing tea and Zubina was clearing potato peels off the floor.

Zubina said, 'Let your father come. He will decide. I have to go and work.'

Soniya made a face and arrived at plans independently for the evening—she made a list of the rides she wished to pay for, and the chocolate ice cream she'd get to eat afterwards.

Aadil came; he was cursing Prakash and Hamid yet again for fighting while queuing up.

'Are we going to the mela today?' Soniya asked, ignoring her father's mutterings. She had no interest in what was going on between people.

Aadil said, 'Not today. I have work. Tomorrow, we have been given an off. We will go then.'

Soniya retired to her corner with her dolls, dejected.

Amrin asked, while passing the tea, 'And what about the cinema hall?'

'I have a lot of work, Amrin. When will you understand? Even the holidays I expected aren't likely.' Aadil said.

Amrin retorted, 'Ammi and you are the same. Always work, work, work. I wish I had someone who could take me around.'

Aadil took his tea and said, 'When you grow up and earn your own money, you take us with you.'

'Never,' Amrin hollered at him and then at her mother, 'I will go with Neha-di while you all can go to Dilli.'

'Amrin …' Aadil tried.

Amrin left her tea, moved Soniya out of her way and climbed to the chowki. She sat facing the wall with the phone.

Serves him right, Zubina thought to herself.

Aadil glanced at Zubina, almost begging her to calm Amrin. But she ignored him. In any case, she had to get ready for her work.

Zubina changed into a fresh bottle green salwar kameez and covered her head with a white dupatta. She dried the water on her face with a towel and lathered it with a skin brightening cream.

The smell of chatim flowers filled Zubina's nostrils when she crossed the main road and entered the lane toward Ralph's flat. She let the sun soak through her skin and enjoyed the walk. The plastic bag containing empty lunchboxes swung in her hand as she sang a song.

She was eagerly waiting for winter. Of course, she hated to touch the cold water when she washed the dishes and mopped the floor. But she liked how odourless and dry her body felt once the harsh sun retreated. She could almost imagine the light drape of a stole, soft on her bare arms. The nihari-puri breakfast at Sona's winter stall would satiate her hunger. And the warmth of tea through the day would keep her going. How could she abandon this city at this time of the year for someplace else?

She reached Ralph's house and got to work. It was Ashtami, the eighth day of the Puja. Ralph said, 'No dinner today. Going to a colleague's place after work. Just need tea and butter toast.'

No sooner did her parents leave for work, than Amrin announced to Soniya, 'I will be back in a minute. You stay right here.'

'But where are you going?' asked Soniya, as she applied her mother's lipstick.

The door shut; Amrin avoided answering Soniya's invasive questions. She strutted past the old woman who sat with a cat on her lap. She asked Amrin, 'Where are you off to?'

'Far away from you,' Amrin hollered and rolled her eyes.

She was on her way to her tutor's house.

She couldn't understand why everyone wanted to know where she was going. Nobody asked when she was going to the bazar or to school. 'Nobody is allowed secrets in this neighbourhood,' she mumbled to herself. She continued to walk until she was at Neha-di's door. She knocked and it opened to reveal Neha-di herself, holding a pair of jeans in her hands and a black full-sleeved top, with words that read: 'Well Dressed and Obsessed'. She was going to the mela today, she said, and she'd make a TikTok video later with her friend's help.

Amrin waited for a bit, but Neha-di seemed busy. She said that she was only passing by and that she was waiting for the new TikTok video. She paused. No invitation came her way.

It broke her heart.

Finally, she left.

On the way back, the old lady asked, 'You're back, aren't you?'

'I will go away. One day,' replied Amrin.

The cat's loud mew frightened Amrin. The old lady said, 'She won't kill you … why does your mouth look so small and sunk?'

'It's … it's not,' Amrin stuttered.

'It reminds me of this …' She pointed to Amrin's crotch and laughed hysterically. Amrin cowered with shame and ran. She bit her lower lip till it singed.

At home, Soniya had not only smeared her mother's lipstick all over her lips but had also managed to slip into Zubina's white salwar kameez, the one she had worn during their Eid-shopping. Amrin shrieked at her, 'What are you doing?'

Soniya catwalked around the house with a brown tote bag in her hands. The white salwar kameez swept the floor. She said with a hiss, 'What's your problem?'

'Oh, the whole world is trying to steal my joy,' Amrin thought. 'The djinn is on the loose, determined to make me unhappy.

And that old woman. May she die!' She bent and scooped half a glass of rice to wash, then boil for lunch.

Amrin and Soniya had a meal and watched a Bollywood crime drama intently for an hour. Soniya was still in her mother's clothes. She paraded about the house playing various roles—she was a lawyer, then a lead actress from a TV serial they watched regularly at 8 p.m., then the owner of a big business where she went about ordering imaginary people because she was bored.

Amrin was far too occupied with thoughts of her tutor's plans to pay attention to her sister's theatrics.

It was 6 p.m. She opened the almirah and chose a maroon kurta and blue jeans. Soniya was under the bed. She was now fighting men who had kidnapped her, apparently. Amrin raised the pile of clothes on the last shelf of the almirah and scooped out the money she had saved. She counted and re-counted it. One hundred and fifty rupees. She stashed this away in her pocket and announced, 'I will get some chocolates for us and return in no time.'

'Sure,' came Soniya's muffled response, as she imagined herself getting abducted for being the most beautiful woman in the world.

Amrin closed the door and trooped towards the street where autos lined up. The maroon and golden pandal in the neighbourhood was alive with music, and visitors sauntered about dreamily. She marched in and hoped that her mother or father would not bump into her anywhere. Then she left.

When she reached the end of the road, her face grew hot with anxiety. There were too many vehicles. People seemed to be out and laying claim to the entire city. She was never on the main road alone, not at this hour, at least. Her mother always forbade her, saying, 'All kinds of rascals are waiting to jump and rape you.' Rape? Amrin had wondered what that meant exactly. Her mother had waved her hands about and said,

'They will force themselves on you!' She detested her mother's vagueness.

She was about to make a U-turn and return to the safety of her house, when an auto with two other passengers halted beside her, 'Park Circus?'

Amrin got in without a word.

In the auto, Amrin held on to the metal rod on the side tightly, while the other sweaty palm cupped a knee. The act of venturing someplace without informing her parents was the most foolhardy thing she had ever done, decided Amrin. Her parents would be worried to death and search for her, and what if she got lost? At the same time, she told herself, wasn't it *their* mistake for prioritizing work over her? Anyway, the plan was simply to see Neha-di's friends; then she'd leave.

After a twenty-five-minute ride—on a quieter day, it would have taken her no more than ten minutes to get here—she got off the auto. She paid the driver and entered the Park Circus Maidan. Amrin was overjoyed the moment she set foot inside. Stalls of food everywhere; women and men offering block-print mehendi; a gaudy procession heading towards the enormous pandal; children lining up for rides; music and announcements from the speakers.

It made her forget her parents, and inhale the scent of freedom. Here she was, outdoors, all by herself. She had made this journey and landed at the right place. She was now even willing to forgive the old woman. She was going mad, poor thing. For a minute, as Amrin took in the surroundings, it didn't matter to her if she met her tutor. She had mislaid the purpose that had brought her to this place.

Zubina returned to find Soniya in her clothes. She was dancing maniacally. Zubina ordered her to change, which Soniya ignored as she spun some more. Zubina asked her where her sister was, to which Soniya replied, over gasps, 'She … said she … will be back … went to buy cho … colates.'

Zubina rolled her hair into a loose bun, and applied powder to her face to dry her perspiration. She dodged Soniya's flailing arms and said, 'I am going to Nazma's house. If Papa comes, tell him there's some tea, he can warm it and have.'

At Nazma's, the house stank of sweat and sickness. The tubelight had conked off, so an emergency lamp was on. Nazma's children greeted Zubina, but Nazma broke into tears at once. Zubina sat beside her and asked, 'What has the doctor said?'

'They will do operation. Lee-bhar is damaged,' she wept.

'Nazma, it will be fine. He will return home.'

'I have no money to manage anything. Nothing,' cried Nazma. 'All has been spent, and I haven't been able to keep the shop open between hospital visits.'

'How much do you need?'

'Remember those ten-ten rupees we were depositing? Sona took me to the lady, may god bless her. She gave me hundred rupees, saying it was a part of the emergency money we could get. I've have fed my children with that for the last two days.'

'Here,' Zubina said, drawing a hundred rupee note from her purse and pressing it in Nazma's palm. 'Take this. It will help you manage for a few more days.'

Nazma took the money and wept inconsolably in Zubina's arms. Zubina wiped the tears off her face. She thought of her mother and the pain she had endured day in day out, after she got married. She thought of Nazma's pain. She thought of people she knew only vaguely, who had died of oral cancer without ever having smoked or chewed tobacco; she recalled how pained they were to see that all the care they had taken to lead exemplary lives had come to naught; that the smokers in their homes were surviving, even thriving, while they collapsed. Zubina's mother, Nazma, those distant acquaintances who were dead or dying—they were all living the consequences of someone else's sin.

A couples of minutes passed, then Nazma raised her head; her snot had wet Zubina's shoulder. Zubina expected her to take a cloth and wipe it off; instead, Nazma opened a packet of tobacco and tucked a small ball by her gums. Zubina cleaned the snot with an old paper and said, 'Okay, then. Amrin's father will be home soon.'

As she stepped outdoors, it felt to her like she was entering a new, air-conditioned home. The air was clear. She waved a salaam at the old woman, who beckoned her and asked, 'Was that your girl who talked about dying today?'

Zubina was shaken. 'No,' she said, 'why would she say that?'

'Oh, then it must be someone else,' the old woman said. She petted the white cat who often sat on the tin roof of Sona's stall but was now on her lap. The cat had clawed her, and her hand had light red bruises. She said, 'Her mouth looked so small. She could see an end coming, it seemed.'

Zubina found her comments bizarre. She decided to ask Amrin what went on between the old woman and her.

At home, Soniya had gone to sleep wearing all the makeup and Zubina's clothes. Amrin was still to return. This was not normal, Zubina decided. She dialled Aadil's number, but he did not take her call. She peeped through the curtains and asked the neighbour if she had spotted Amrin. The lady said that she had seen her going out around 6 p.m., 'dressed very well'. When asked if there was something wrong, Zubina said, 'No, no.'

Something was wrong. It was 7.30 p.m. Amrin couldn't possibly have been shopping for chocolates for more than an hour. Maybe she had gone to a friend's house. Or, yes, she must have gone to the factory and persuaded Aadil to take her somewhere. They will be home soon.

From the machine in which the sugar swirled into a big pillow of cotton candy, to the large chandelier in the pandal—in less than twenty minutes, Amrin knew what the fair held after taking a full tour. The gold jewellery adorning the gigantic goddess enthralled her. The djinn surely couldn't overthrow such beings.

A guard came to move her away and let in the crowd behind her pass. She couldn't believe that being by herself meant she could be anywhere she liked without her father calling, her mother warning her or her sister throwing a tantrum. She let the air carry her past the stalls that sold stationery, toys and makeup sets. She moved to the food counters and gaped at the large crescent-shaped momos being dunked in orange-red chutney. Licking a mango popsicle, she watched a Ferris wheels go round, with girls and boys howling as they ascended sky-high. It made her head spin.

She noticed a young man getting a skull inked on his wrist. She walked to the mat on which the man, applying the ink from a pen-like machine, sat. She stamped her feet to announce her presence and asked, 'How much?'

'What tattoo do you want?' the artist asked, completely absorbed in his craft, even as the young man winced.

'Small,' she said.

The man paused and looked at her. 'What the hell is small?' Then he added, 'Where are your parents?'

Amrin stepped back. She drew the outline of a heart on her wrist with her finger, and then said, 'Dil shape.'

'That will be eighty for a small heart. Only for you.'

Amrin swivelled and went to a corner, where a family of three was asleep. She counted the money that was left. One hundred and twenty rupees. She would definitely be able to make it back home, even after the tattoo.

She marched to the artist and waited her turn. It was then that she noticed a group of boys and girls enter the gates. Among them, right in between, hand-in-hand with a tall, lanky boy, was Neha-di. She was in the 'Well Dressed and Obsessed' top and a pair of light blue jeans. Her lips were bright red and her hair had been pinned back, with strands curling in the front like tendrils.

Amrin jostled past people. She rushed past a child playing in dirt. She almost dashed into the balloon hanging from a tall wooden staff. She got her face smacked by a lady's purse.

At last, she reached the group she had her eye on.

'Isn't Amrin with you?' Zubina asked Aadil the second she saw him at the door. He scanned his surroundings, as though Amrin were hiding somewhere in the vicinity, and said, 'No, not that I can tell. I have been at work.'

'Why did you not take my call?'

Aadil checked his phone and said, 'Maybe this thing was silent.'

Eight in the evening. Zubina paced about the house trying to imagine where Amrin could have gone. Soniya jumped on the bed, grabbing both sticks of chocolate her father had got for his daughters.

After drinking some water, Aadil said, 'She must have gone to the pandal, where else? She will return.'

'She has been out since six o' clock!' Zubina exclaimed.

'Oh. Maybe she went to chat with Neha.'

'You know nothing. Neha has been out with her friends. Her mother is also away. The house is locked.'

Aadil looked exasperated. It had been a tiring day. He had been waiting to return home and lie on the bed. Clearly, resting was not an option. He said, sighing deeply, 'I will go and check.'

Zubina asked Soniya, 'Did Amrin say where exactly she was going? Did she tell you if she was meeting anyone?'

Soniya pouted, 'No, I told you, she was going to get chocolates.' The stick of chocolate she had been licking had started melting in her hands and was now dripping down the white kameez. Zubina screamed, 'What have you done?'

She grabbed Soniya and tried yanking the clothes off her. Soniya cried at the top of her voice. Zubina kept insisting that she get out of her kameez. Soniya thrashed about, almost hitting Zubina's face with her arms.

That's when there was a knock. Zubina let go of her daughter. Soniya lurched back with a thud.

Sona, Zubina's friend, entered. 'What happened?' she asked.

'I don't know where Amrin is!' Zubina said.

'She must be out with her friends. Aadil-bhai told me to see you once,' said Sona, 'so I came.'

Soniya started wailing loudly in a corner.

'End this drama, or I will beat you,' Zubina told Soniya sternly. Her daughter immediately stopped crying, but muttered she wished to die.

'Zubina! You must be so worried!' Sona sat her down and poured her a glass of water.

Zubina hadn't felt this way in a long, long time. So many things in one day. Not since the time Amrin was four and Soniya had been born, had she felt this overwhelmed.

Zubina was feeding four-year old Amrin, when a call came for her on Aadil's phone. There had been low network coverage all day, and Aadil had to rush outdoors to a stronger coverage area; he returned, scratching his head. 'Your sister,' he said.

That was all.

Zubina felt her hand quiver.

After Zubina had left her Park Circus home, it had transitioned into a guest house for Tausiq and Zeenat, who came as and when they pleased.

Once, at midnight, when Tausiq and Zeenat entered within ten minutes of each other, their mother screamed, 'What's going on with the two of you? Who comes at such odd hours?'

Alcohol reeked from their bodies. It filled the room with an unbearable stench. Bangla, whiskey, bidi and cigarettes.

The two of them dismissed her. 'Go sleep, sleep. Don't start all this drama now. We need to wake up and go to work.'

When the mother protested, Tausiq threatened her, 'Do you want us to go and die? Is that what you want? Say it and we will kill ourselves.'

The lone woman was terrified. She withdrew to a corner.

A week or two after her sister's botched phone call, Zubina heard from her mother; she narrated the entire drunken midnight episode.

Zubina felt a wave of sorrow sweep over her.

The next time her mother called, it was to tell her of Tausiq.

Tausiq had returned home and announced that he was going to Saudi Arabia to work. Zubina's mother was overjoyed. But Zeenat was displeased—Tausiq could tell. He screamed at Zeenat, 'You aren't happy, are you? Jealous bitch.' He spat abuses at her and left the house.

'Did you see that?' Zeenat glowered. 'This … this is what my siblings call me. Both Tausiq and Zubina think the worst of me.'

'Don't mind them, please,' the mother said weakly. 'They are young. What do they know of the world? Let it go, I beg of you.' She paused and then asked, 'But why would they say that to you?'

Zeenat laughed, 'You think they're right, don't you? That your daughter is a shameless slut?'

'No, not at all, not at all,' her mother protested. But Zeenat wasn't listening to anything she had to say. She took a stash of bidis, struck a matchstick, stepped outside and said, 'I want to die, I really do.'

When her mother had told her of Zeenat's outcry, Zubina, who was a new mother then, felt unable to move a muscle.

Zubina's heart always fell when she heard the word 'die'—she felt it when her sister threatened to immolate herself; she felt it again when the old woman spoke of death; and she felt it when her younger daughter wished she wasn't alive.

Sona comforted her.

Could Amrin be ...?

Not Amrin, not the child she had protected. Zubina had wedged herself between her family in Park Circus and her family here like an impenetrable wall, to keep her Amrin secure when she was born. Not even air could pass between the two households.

Another half an hour passed; Amrin did not show up.

Soniya had gone to the bed and was now pretending to be Neha-di. She ordered her students in whispers.

The group Amrin had been eyeing was about to walk past her, but Amrin's stare caught them off-guard. They paused.

Amrin wondered if Neha-di had seen her, but it seemed she was engrossed in a conversation with her boyfriend.

So, Amrin said, 'Neha-di!'

Her tutor turned, startled. 'Amrin? Is that you?'

Amrin managed a smile and waved.

Her tutor left her boyfriend and the larger group, 'What are you doing here?'

Amrin had answers ready. 'I am here with my family.'

'Oh, that's nice. Go on and enjoy yourself then.' Something about the word 'family' made the tutor wary. She scanned the pandal; she didn't want Zubina reporting to her mother that she was out with her boyfriend. She returned to the group and waved at Amrin. It was a closed cohort again, and they proceeded towards the stalls in the mela. One of the girls had suggested a spot for them to make a TikTok video.

Amrin looked on. Was this all? Would Neha-di not introduce her to her friends? Amrin was pained. She had dropped her dreams of Delhi for Neha-di. She had refused to discuss the capital because she couldn't imagine Neha-di's life going on without her immediate presence.

Amrin strode toward the tattoo artist.

She had expected to be introduced to Neha-di's boyfriend. She had learnt jokes she could regale her with and had come with gossip from the neighbourhood to entertain her. Surely, she would take keen interest in knowing that Sana-di, her TikTok rival from the neighbourhood, had been laughed at by her friends because she had copied Neha-di's style and dance moves. Surely, she'd burst into peals of laughter when they heard about Prakash-bhai, who had been roughed up by his parents in front of everyone for having an affair with a Muslim girl he planned to marry. Ah, what a funny scene that was! He had fallen in love with Hamid-bhai's sister! The girl had cried and had protected Prakash-bhai; she had clambered on top of him like a shield. And Hamid-bhai had shielded her in turn. He ended up getting most of the kicks and slaps.

Such stories! And her tutor simply had walked away.

The images of Neha-di taking her along with the group, treating her to food, looking out for her in the crowds like an older sister, protecting her from 'rascals' like a concerned mother—they fell into pieces, became one with the dust that leapt off the ground as she strode on.

Amrin reached the tattoo artist. His previous customer was gone. The artist was cleaning the tip of his needle. She plopped down on the mat and said, '*Chota dil*'. She thrust her right wrist forward. Little heart. Please.

For Amrin's first birthday, Zubina had called her family to her new home.

Zeenat, Tausiq and her mother were present at Zubina's house for dinner. They cut a small cake and shared it. Zubina saved a slice for Nazma and Sona, and fed everyone mutton korma and paratha. Amrin was passed around.

Zubina could sense Aadil's sadness. His mother had recently died, and his sisters had refused to participate in a celebration so soon after a family demise. Amrin remained with her father as the others ate and offered advice on child-rearing.

That evening, Zubina was brimming over with joy; the exhaustion that came with working in the homes of others and parenting seemed to dissipate and make way for laughter.

When it was time to leave, Zeenat pressed two five-hundred-rupee notes in Zubina's hand and patted it with love. Zubina balked. She shook her head. Her mother held back her shock. Aadil was changing Amrin's nappy in the corner, and was unaware of the proceedings, but Tausiq snarled, 'Don't take it! We know where it comes from.'

At that, Zeenat flared and slapped his flabby cheeks, 'I have had enough of you and your jibes.'

Her mother cried as he was about to pounce on Zeenat, 'No, no.'

Aadil witnessed the kerfuffle. The only emotion Zubina felt then was shame. Not anger or pity or sadness, but utter shame that her family was exposing itself to her husband and little child; that it was spreading filth in this house, too.

Zubina took Zeenat outside. She pocketed the money, wiped Zeenat's tear-splotched face, held her by the elbows and said, 'You go home. I will ask Bhai to manage Ammi.' The sisters hugged.

Zubina went indoors, packed some food for her mother and then escorted Tausiq and her out, saying, 'Take care ... I will visit soon ...'

She was filled with relief when they left.

That was the last time her family came over.

For days after Amrin's first birthday party, she could not face Aadil. She was filled with embarrassment. At any mention of Amrin's birthday, Zubina winced.

Sona stepped out of Zubina's house, then returned with a plate of food covered with a newspaper. She placed this on the mat and said, 'I had prepared this earlier today. Eat.'

Soniya settled down in a corner and watched the television screen with rapt attention. Zubina's white salwar kameez was smeared with chocolate marks, lipstick stains and dirt.

Zubina told Sona that she needed to visit the washroom. She opened the almirah, took out a scrap of cloth she used as sanitary napkin and headed to the loo, grim and broken.

It was dark inside the cubbyhole that was called a washroom. She had forgotten to switch on the light. She started to change her napkin, then paused, trembling. Tears sprang to her eyes.

At last, the tears.

It felt to her like she had held them back for far too long.

Where are you, Amrin? Come home, my little girl.

She could hear the tears call for her child, as she changed her napkin and cleaned her hands. She wanted the heavy darkness outside to consume her right there.

She continued weeping because she couldn't in front of others. She had to hide her pain like she hid her shame and guilt.

Her brother had not made it to Saudi Arabia because he had fallen in love with a girl named Shabnam weeks before he was to submit his visa documents.

Zeenat remained unaffected by the news, while Zubina felt happy. The wedding was conducted in a quiet manner at the bride's residence. What Zubina remembered of the ceremony were the plates heaped with food—all very delicious.

The family should have known peace after this. But it was difficult for the household to adjust with a new member. Tausiq and Zeenat had arguments recurrently.

Three months later, Tausiq rented a house elsewhere. He had secured a job as a waiter in a restaurant. Tausiq and Shabnam left the house to Zeenat and the mother. The mother communicated with Zubina regularly over the phone which Zeenat had gifted to her. Zubina sensed the grief and loneliness in her mother's voice, but she could do nothing to rescue her.

One summer, when Amrin was two-and-a-half, her mother told her, 'Zeenat got a man last night. He dropped her off, had water and left.'

'Did you ask her who it was?'

'I did. She shut me up, saying it was someone from that NGO workplace.'

'She's lying … it must be that damned lover of hers.'

Her mother whimpered, 'They stank of daaru. I am so used to the smell now. Earlier, I would vomit … but these days …' Her voice trailed off and Zubina disconnected the phone saying she had to get back to work.

There was no work right then. She just couldn't bear to get angry and tell her mother what she had seen back when she was seventeen. It pained her.

To this day, she remembered her disconnecting the phone on her mother; the way she neglected her grief. It weighed her down so heavily.

Zubina's worries about Amrin and her guilt at the way she had once responded to her mother's concern became an amorphous ball of grief.

Zubina could barely move an inch and face the world beyond the dingy washroom. Someone was at the door, banging it again and again. She would have to wash the soiled napkin the next day.

Amrin paid for the tattoo and ambled along with her arm straight. The crowd had multiplied and she couldn't keep her eyes fixed on anything. She thought she saw Ojas enter the pandal. She tried to follow the back of his head, but her eyes landed on the bobbing head of a familiar man. It was Yasmin's father. There, at his side, was Yasmin, in makeup, a cerulean blue gingham frock and a choker snug around her neck. Amrin avoided her, lest her father ask questions about her family's whereabouts.

She spotted Neha-di and her friends get off the Ferris wheel. Neha-di was laughing. She made fun of one of her friends for crying while on the ride. Her boyfriend was on a call. Amrin toyed with the idea of an escape, but she saw Neha-di walk towards her.

'I got a tattoo,' Amrin shouted, and extended her arm to Neha-di.

'Amrin! What is this?'

'A tattoo,' she repeated, with a blush and a flicker in her eyes.

'I can very well see that. What have you done to your arm? How could Zubina-apa let you do this?'

Amrin had expected a pat on the back and compliments. Neha-di held her by the wrist and shook her arm, 'Amrin, this is going to remain forever.'

Forever? A whole life? For Amrin, the idea was strange; she only knew about the now, today, and the next festival that awaited her.

Neha-di let her hand drop and left Amrin to herself.

Amrin marched into the pandal because she didn't know where else to go. Yasmin's father had picked his daughter in his arms to show her the goddess. Yasmin clapped with joy.

An intense longing for home overtook Amrin. She missed her father—the person who indulged her to no end. He had promised her an outing and Amrin had defied him by going on her own. He had told her that she'd make a lot of money one day and take the entire family to the cinema. Far from working towards that end, she had become selfish. Cruel. Amrin chastised herself. She thought of her mother—the only woman who illuminated her world when everything felt dark. Her mother would never speak to her like Neha-di had right now or that silly old woman had at one point. She was hard to please, yes, but she also reminded her that she was a big girl who had responsibilities. She made Amrin feel important. Zeenat-khaala must have been such a great example to Ammi, she thought. Her sister—how much she wanted to protect her; instead, she had left her at home. All alone and sad with no one to play with. She had abandoned her family to come here. She was mortified.

Amrin wove through the crowds with her tattooed arm, and headed back to the main gate. There were tears in her eyes. She felt no better than the broken doll she owned, lying under a heap of scrap. Tears streamed down her cheeks as she stood at the busy thoroughfare of the Park Circus crossing. The vehicles were honking loudly and the crowds were turning boisterous. She needed to get home.

Aadil felt a sense of enervation. He had been running all evening. He had ransacked the whole neighbourhood, had asked every possible person, but no one else had seen Amrin except for the one neighbour who had watched her leave.

Most families were out to celebrate, and their houses remained locked. Aadil knocked at a few doors assuming that his daughter had got locked inside, but there was no response. Zubina's calls were persistent and he disconnected his phone each time with the same 'no' and irritation.

It was half-past nine. *Where on earth are you, Amrin?* He could feel the younger Aadil roar in his chest—the way he had when his father had disappeared with his brothers.

The younger Aadil had spent days hoping for the return of his father and brothers. Then, a stray hope had roused in him. He had found the energy to wait and be patient—to stop thinking of them, and to start focusing on work, and to hold on to the dream of leaving the city if one of his brothers or his father returned.

The dream came to an end the day his mother told him that his brother, Amaan, had called. Both his sisters were married by then. He was alone with his mother in their little home. Ever since he was a child, he had been used to seeing her in deep conversation with herself—head shakes, nods, smiles and brows raised in worry. But that day, she was louder than usual and refused to stop even when Aadil told her it was time to sleep.

He asked her, 'What has happened to you?'

She remained expressionless and said, 'Your brother, Atif, got married.'

'What?'

'They did not call me—the mother who gave birth to the groom,' she said and continued muttering to herself.

Aadil felt like a ballon that was floating, directionless. The stray hope that had once sprung up in him vanished into the sky. Everything he desired was beyond his reach.

The next morning, he decided that his mother needed someone to be with her—a replacement for two lost sons and a husband and daughters who had moved on.

He had to marry. It came as a compulsion, not a choice.

Amrin's disappearance made Aadil confront a past he had wished to bury. He imagined answers to her whereabouts lay in his own chequered history. He tried to push away all thoughts. A pile of rubbish—that is what memories amounted to.

He reached the main road. He exhaled and waited as the city zoomed past him. At one end of the road, a line of autos had come to a halt. The passengers were getting down.

Aadil's eyes fell on a tiny girl, almost like his daughter. The girl paid the driver and stood opposite him, separated by the kerb, a flyover and a deluge of people. What a strong little girl, Aadil thought. The lights glowed red, and the girl began crossing the road, until she was right in front him.

'Papa!'

It was his daughter, after all.

Amrin had *found* her father.

She clasped his hand and took him home.

9

At a colleague's flat in Newtown, on Ashtami evening, Ralph chugged his third drink—pineapple juice spiked with vodka. Everyone lounged around and smoked; the speakers in the house came to life with J.Lo. Sujoy and an intern arranged plates on the floor and served sizzling chicken tikkas with green chutney.

The music grew louder and the chicken tikkas and pork momos were replaced by plates of spaghetti in marinara sauce. After Ralph finished eating pasta, the intern handed him his guitar. He asked him to play; they had recently discovered, from his Instagram, that he was good with the guitar. Ralph refused, but finally conceded to his favourite intern Debjani's request. He strummed mechanically; others identified the song and started singing, '*Kyun aaj kal neend kam khawab zyaada hai …*'

When the plates were moved to the washbasin in the kitchen, the penultimate drinks were made. There were no mixers this time, only a finger of vodka that was to be drunk in a single swig and that burned the throat.

Ralph fell back and stretched himself on the floor. He looked at the ceiling as his head throbbed.

Suddenly, he felt a hand brush his thigh. He opened his eyes. The intern smiled at him and said, 'Daddy.' Ralph smiled back dreamily. The intern leaned closer to Ralph's ear and asked, 'Do you want to go inside?'

Ralph kept his eyes shut, unable to follow his thoughts. He didn't respond. He seemed to have fallen asleep.

The intern shook Ralph, and Ralph careened into a strange kind of wakefulness. He stood up. The intern led him to a room. Sujoy was dancing with various colleagues and winked at Ralph as the door closed behind him.

The intern placed his hand on Ralph's thigh and pushed him towards the bed. Ralph fell in a daze. The intern unbuckled Ralph's belt and fingered the zip of his jeans, murmuring how badly he wanted to suck daddy off. Ralph blinked at the swirling ceiling, aware only of movement. Someone's hand was on top of his crotch.

Ojas flitted by across the ceiling. Ralph was on his knees, mouthing words, as Ojas placed his hand on the crown of Ralph's head. He let himself be petted and caressed by Ojas's big hands. He unzipped Ojas's stiff trousers. Ralph heard himself beg for love.

The intern entered Ralph's line of vision. He asked, 'Why are you crying?'

He wiped a tear off Ralph's face.

Ralph pushed him away, 'No!' He realized he wasn't erect. 'I am sorry,' he said, hitched his jeans up and left the room.

Ralph opened the door of the apartment and ran down the stairs.

What was he thinking, inviting a young man inside a room and then discarding him as though he were nobody? He swiped his phone to find a cab. It was 1 a.m. There were no taxis close. A ghostly silence blanketed him in the darkness. Only stray dogs howled, keeping their nightly watch. The word 'daddy' reverberated in his head and he hated the sound of it. Gone were the days when he could assume he was young; when he could call the older men he desired 'daddy'. Now *he* was the older man. He had never imagined that the tables would turn on him so soon.

Ralph stumbled into the main road where cars sped away like lightning. Except for the faint music coming from a pandal in the distance, the surroundings were eerily quiet and desolate.

Nine cabs cancelled; finally, the tenth one didn't. Ralph waited patiently.

Suddenly, he spotted Sujoy heading toward him. He looked bewildered. 'You left? Is there anything wrong?' he asked.

'Nothing, I don't feel like being there anymore.'

'Okay,' Sujoy said. 'Should I come with you?'

'No, I'll be fine.'

Without a word, Sujoy hugged Ralph. Ralph held on to Sujoy; if he could, he would've screamed in pain. Sujoy whispered in his ears, 'Leave him … you're so unhappy, Ralph.'

Ralph did not reply. He continued embracing Sujoy. His friend. His family. Tears pricked his eyes. He let them fall down his cheeks, wetting Sujoy's shirt that he held with a tight fist. Sujoy rubbed his back, 'It's okay … it's okay. I'm here …' Ralph kept sobbing. He wanted to tell Sujoy everything he hadn't in the past few months, but he couldn't find the words. Sujoy kept saying, 'It'll be over … I'm here.'

Finally, Ralph pulled himself away. A car screeched to a halt next to him. He wanted to speak, but now was not the moment. *Perhaps next time*, Ralph thought, as he entered the cab while Sujoy held the door open.

The driver eyed Ralph with suspicion from the mirror. Ralph didn't give a damn that the driver believed that Sujoy and he were a couple. All he could feel was sorrow—it was like blood, it coursed through his body.

Memories of the Darjeeling trip came rushing to his mind.

The second day in Darjeeling, Ralph and Ojas woke up to a misty December morning. As the sun began to rise, the thick fog enveloping the Kanchenjunga cleared up. They called for tea and sat by the window and watched the sea-blue colour of the sky and the towering trees. Ojas recounted memories of Darjeeling to Ralph. Ralph remembered the preceding night's sex with Ojas on the warm mattress. He heard Ojas share his love for sunrises and sunsets in the hills. The talk paused as they drank their tea and then went to the hotel's restaurant for breakfast. Aritra was supposed to see them around 11 a.m. There was time for that. Ralph asked Ojas if he'd like to go to the nearby church. Ojas agreed.

Mall Road was thronging with people. Tourists were standing by the railings, getting pictures clicked with the mountains in the background. Locals were seated, watching some dance performance by children. Ralph and Ojas passed an 'I ♥ Darjeeling' hoarding, around which people hovered. They reached St Andrew's Church, its white façade glinting in natural light, atop the curve of the hill. They took the stairs and entered the church, where people had finished their Sunday service and were filing out. A few turned to look at Ralph and Ojas for a moment, but then ignored them; the locals were used to tourists everywhere. Ojas saw Ralph go to the priest and talk in whispers. He returned, saying, 'We can sit for a while. I spoke to him.'

'Sure,' Ojas replied.

The church now knew pin-drop silence. Ralph and Ojas took their seats in a dark brown pew; even the priest had left. Ralph joined his hands and prayed. Ojas followed suit. After making a few wishes for his family's good health and a steady relationship with Ralph, he realized he had nothing else to ask or say. He sat back and observed the cross. He ignored the laughter and murmurs outside.

Ralph prayed and whispered, 'Amen'. He told Ojas how much his father liked visiting the neighbourhood church and praying. Sometimes, his mother would berate him for spending far too long meditating on god; nonetheless, she'd wait for her husband with Ralph. 'I could sit here for hours and not get restless,' Ralph said with his hand placed in front of him.

Ojas rubbed Ralph's hands. 'We can come here whenever you want.'

Ralph leaned into Ojas. A mix of scents—musk, patchouli and chamomile—filled the church.

Aritra called Ojas when they were taking a stroll by the flower patch outside the church. Ojas finished the call and said, 'He's at his hotel. Should we go?'

The hotel was not far from theirs, but the hike across the Mall Road was tiring. The crowds had somehow increased, and it felt like everyone was getting in everyone else's way.

In the hotel's lobby, Ojas's friend introduced himself to Ralph. 'Hi, I'm Aritra.'

'Ralph,' he replied, sizing him up.

'Yes, yes, heard a lot about you,' Aritra said, and gave a side hug to Ojas.

'Okay, that's new,' smiled Ralph.

The three of them planned to go straight to Glenary's because Aritra was dying for a cup of coffee. Upon entering, Ralph filled his basket with three croissants, chocolate chip cookies and blueberry muffins. He waited at the counter and paid. Ojas and Aritra managed to find a table on the deck overlooking the hills. Here, they spoke about Aritra's upcoming forty-five-kilometre trek to Sandakphu.

'Basically, it's with a bunch of strangers. I am doing it because I feel fit for a change and I don't think I'll be up for this a year later,' he said, as he ate his croissant.

'Yes, that's when you will sit in England and write books,' Ojas chuckled.

'That's the plan.'

Ralph put two packets of sugar into his cappuccino. 'How many of you are going?'

'No clue. But I will get to know soon enough,' Aritra said, and offered Ralph a tissue to wipe the foam off his lips. 'There is a WhatsApp group with sixty people, but I don't know who's who.'

'Thanks,' said Ralph, taking the tissue, 'It must be snowing up there,' Ralph dried his lips. He found his face getting warmer.

'Oh, yes!' Aritra said, excited. 'It is! In fact,' he said to Ojas, 'I am planning on doing a little fieldwork there during my trek.'

Ojas laughed. 'You're going on a trek ... forget work for a change.'

Aritra went on to share his experiences with gay men in London. Ralph realized that Aritra was not bad company. When they were done, they took Aritra to Mall Road, and helped him buy whatever he needed. Aritra only picked a novel, *Hot Milk*, from the bookstore and said, 'I can't buy too many things. Who is going to carry it and trek!' At 2.30 p.m., they parted because Aritra needed to rest.

In their room, Ralph said to Ojas, 'He is nice only.'

'I told you. He is good company.'

'He's so tall.'

'Yes, he hates it. He keeps saying that he wishes he were a few inches shorter and had more fat around his ass.'

Ralph laughed. They kissed each other longingly. Ralph shut his eyes and saw the salt-and-pepper curls, hardened jaw and prominent chin of Aritra flash through his mind. They began taking off each other's clothes, but Ralph suddenly withdrew. 'Wait. I am tired.' All he could see were a large pair of hands, offering him tissue at Glenary's.

Ojas kissed Ralph on the forehead. 'Sure.'

When they were in bed, Ojas asked, almost teasingly, 'Are you attracted to him?'

'What?' Ralph said, playing with a strand of Ojas's chest hair. 'No.'

'Come on, tell me, it's okay!' Ojas held Ralph's hands.

Ralph bit his lips, 'What if I was?'

'Umm, I would totally understand it. He is an attractive man!' Ojas began loosening his grip on Ralph's hands.

'What do you mean?' Ralph asked.

'You know what I mean,' Ojas shrugged and pressed his very erect cock against Ralph's thighs. He felt for Ralph's crotch. He was equally hard in his boxers. 'Looks like baby wants it.'

'No,' Ralph said.

Then, they began kissing. Ojas went down on Ralph and Ralph felt as though he were unshackled. He was permitted to think of whoever he desired. He imagined undressing Aritra's large body; his tongue licking his brown nipples; Aritra's long fingers coiled around his throat.

Ralph felt Ojas's mouth on him and imagined Aritra's lips around every part of his body. Before he knew it, he had orgasmed.

In the evening, Ojas, Ralph and Aritra went to a pub and shared drinks, but they realized it was too noisy to talk. Ojas suggested they go somewhere else. Ralph was ready, but Aritra, who was on Grindr, said that there was a cute guy near the pub he wanted to meet. Half an hour later, Aritra had tired of flirting with the man and decided to leave the pub with them.

They reached Ojas and Ralph's room and sat by the open window. The nighttime view was surreal, with tiny flashes of lights blinking on the hills. They looked like shimmering waterfalls. Ojas popped open a bottle of red wine that he had purchased at Mall Road. They drank the wine from water cups. Aritra asked for a cigarette, but the pack in the room was empty. He was about to go down and buy a pack downstairs, but he had had too much to drink. He was unsteady on his feet. Ralph held him so he wouldn't fall. Ojas volunteered to buy the cigarettes.

Ralph and Aritra were in the room alone. They did not talk. Ralph's hand rested on Aritra's hairy arm. Aritra turned to Ralph and said, 'Thank you for letting me join in. I had a great time with the two of you.'

Ralph said, 'That's good to hear. I …well, I feel similarly.'

'It gets so lonely in London, being away from home. I … I had gone there thinking I'd immediately get a partner because there'd be more … more men available?' He laughed. 'But it's shit.'

'I am sorry.'

'Nah, it's okay. When I went abroad, initially, the desire to find love was so strong that I didn't at all mind leaving home. By the time my PhD was over, I pined to return … to seek my friends and my people.'

'But …'

'I've come to terms with the fact that there's no love. So, my family and friendships protect me.'

'Aritra …'

'They make me happy.' Aritra looked into Ralph's eyes with absolute sincerity.

Ralph nodded and said nothing.

Aritra yawned, 'Where's Ojas? Wasn't the shop next to the hotel? Sorry … I think I blabbered. I may be drunk.'

Aritra's hand pulled away, his body straightened; the hairy fold of his stomach was revealed. It was either that, or the drink swimming in Ralph's body, or Ojas's absence—Ralph bent and kissed Aritra on his cheeks. He felt sorry for Aritra—that's what he told himself. He wanted to offer him physical reassurance.

Aritra kissed Ralph back on his lips. His mouth carried the smell of drink, and it made Ralph want to pull away, but instead, he kissed him back.

Suddenly, the bell rang. Ralph jumped back, and ran to open the door.

'I had to walk down to the shop two roads away,' Ojas said, panting.

Ralph moved across the room carrying the full weight of guilt. Aritra flipped open the cigarette packet, finished a smoke, then left.

The next day, he'd be gone by 6 a.m. Ralph believed that they wouldn't be seeing each other again.

He begged Aritra with his eyes to stay. Yet, a part of him wanted Aritra to go—he couldn't deal with what he had done.

Ojas lay in bed and skimmed through photos on his phone. Ralph milled around the room, confused. Aritra had behaved as though the kiss hadn't happened. He probably wouldn't reveal anything to Ojas. Was it best for him—Ralph—to forget about his time with Aritra, too?

He folded and stacked his clothes, then Ojas's. He rearranged the chairs. He put the glasses away.

Would Ojas leave him?

Halfway through cleaning the table with a tissue, Ralph felt queasy. He had spent all this time acquainting himself with another person's habits, quirks and idiosyncrasies; and he had been stupid enough to risk toppling over everything he had built.

Would he ever find a man like Ojas again?

He left the tissue on the table and slid next to Ojas. He said, 'Aritra and I kissed.'

Hiding was not an option. He would never be able to face Ojas if he kept matters concealed.

Ojas's hand froze; he examined Ralph's mouth. 'When I was gone?'

Ralph nodded.

Ojas had nothing to say. He stared at his phone again.

Ralph said, 'I am sorry I shouldn't have done it. I am sorry. I am sorry.'

'It's okay. I don't want to talk about it.'

Ralph had expected Ojas to fly into a rage, throw a fit, make a scene. Yet …

'What is it, Ojas? Are you hiding something from me?'

'What?'

'Is there something I should know? How can you be so calm when I tell you I have kissed another man?'

'I am not okay with it but … I also don't know how to react because … I think …' Ojas tensed, then tried saying casually, 'I think I would have done it, too, if I were alone with Aritra in this room.'

'Oh my god! Are you fucking serious?' Ralph was beside himself with rage.

'What's so shocking? It is what it is. Let's face it … after what happened in the afternoon.'

'You're telling me you would have kissed another man if I happened to be away?'

'Well, if we're talking specifically about Aritra … yes. And we were drunk, after all …'

'Ojas, do you even hear yourself? Do you see how you sound?'

'I don't care how I sound … I did not *actually* kiss him, did I?'

Ralph couldn't fight this fact. He had no moral ground to stand on. He couldn't accuse Ojas of being a philanderer if he had himself philandered that evening. He left the bed and lit a cigarette. Curls of smoke hovered before his eyes.

He did not know right then that this trip would overturn his relationship with Ojas. He did not know that Ojas's casual dismissal of the kiss he had shared with Aritra was not a sign of Ojas being willing to let go and leap into the future. Rather, it became the point where Ojas got stuck—he could not pull away—and eventually, he pleaded for an arrangement that allowed him to relive the moment again and yet again, on his terms. He could kiss, hold and fuck other men.

This could not have occurred to Ralph in Darjeeling. So much of the future lay shrouded in thick mist.

Ralph and Ojas took off their clothes and lay on the warm mattress, not facing each other. They fell asleep without exchanging a kiss, or saying goodnight, or switching off the lights.

A new life awaited them.

The half-soiled tissue remained on the table, exactly where Ralph had left it. The trip was over for the two of them that night.

The morning after Ashtami, Ojas sat at the breakfast table with his family. His mother was adding finishing touches to her crewelwork. Ojas asked why his father had not joined them for breakfast. She showed him her work and said, 'He's tired. His knees ache.' Ojas tried focusing on what she was displaying. It was a body of a peacock, neat lines in glinting royal blue. It stood on a suspended tree branch. It held on to it as though it were holding on to life. The neck was long, almost twisting … and then there were two heads—instead of one—with hooked yellow beaks touching each other. Ojas's finger ran along the bamboo hoop that held the fabric taut and then traced some of the threadwork. He took in the two beaks, almost indistinguishable from one another. It was impossible to tell who the feathers belonged to—this bird or that. To Ojas, it felt like the love of the birds was suffocating, stifling.

'Beautiful,' he murmured to his mother.

The peacock remained on his mind as he checked his phone to see if Ralph had messaged. He saw a text left by a man in his late twenties—'When are we meeting, you handsome sweetie?'—who he had considered sleeping with during his separation from Ralph.

A grin flitted across Ojas's face for a moment, but then he went back to looking worried. He opened the chatbox with Aritra and saw his own picture. He was sipping coffee and Aritra had captured the moment sneakily.

Coffee with Aritra had been short and pleasant. Aritra talked about his new job at the University of Sussex; racist remarks he had overheard from white colleagues; and the students' love for his course on tribal studies. Ojas listened to him with full attention but Aritra had to meet a date. They wrapped up their meeting sooner than expected. While Aritra was booking his cab, he asked Ojas, 'How's it going with Ralph?'

Ojas paused and then replied, 'We're fine. Small fights here and there but, you know, it's the usual.'

'Sometimes, I wish I had stayed here.'

'Why?'

'If not with you, I'd have settled down with someone *like* you.' Aritra waved at the cab approaching them. 'It almost hurts to see so much love between two people. Especially two gay men.'

When he was gone, Ojas mulled over Aritra's words. He could feel Ralph standing next to him with his hand around his waist. Both of them—Ralph and Ojas—were the envy of others. Ralph was his and he was Ralph's. What more could either of them ask of life?

The past few months without Ralph had been nothing but hell. He didn't care for young men praising his 'dad bod', his 'skin brighter than the best pride march in the world', his 'smile so sweet one could go without dessert for a year'.

He missed Ralph's eye-roll when he'd read such saccharine comments. He missed hearing him say, 'This is cheap'. How they would laugh! They'd put their phones away and make love. After a long time, Ojas could see his life aligning with one person, one man only. And that man was Ralph.

He was about to dial Ralph's number and ask him to meet him. But he was reminded of his get-together with his colleagues in Newtown.

So, he called Sarvesh and asked him to get everyone ready. They would go for a drive.

Ojas and his family drove around the city. Ojas remained by his father's side as they pandal-hopped. His father talked to Sarvesh about Durga Puja visits when he was young, about the increasing pollution and population problems of the city, and about how the festival kept art alive. Ojas tried eavesdropping. Now and again, his father would direct a sentence at him—for this, he was glad; at least his father had started speaking to him.

Throughout the evening, Ralph was on Ojas's mind. His Ralph. He prayed for the two of them.

At night, once they had returned home, Ojas entered his father's bedroom. His father sat up on the bed and put the television on mute. He was watching news on Kashmir; the anchor was going ballistic, praising the prime minister for his able leadership and for removing terrorism from the region. Ojas asked, 'Are you fine?'

'Just a little pain here,' his father pointed to his right knee.

Ojas placed his hand on the knee. How weak his father had become, he thought.

'I have called a doctor for an appointment. He practises in Salt Lake,' his father said.

'When should I take you?'

'Why will you go? Mummy and I can go.'

'No,' Ojas said, 'I will take you.'

'If you insist'

'Papa ...' Ojas paused. 'I ... I won't marry.'

His father glanced at him and then shifted his gaze to the television screen. 'Okay. We only think you should have someone to look after you when you get older.'

'You all are here.'

'We won't be here forever.'

'I will be fine ...'

'Okay, if you say so,' his father replied, reluctant to continue the conversation.

Ojas stood up to leave the room, but his father's question startled him, 'Why is it that you don't want to marry?'

This was the moment to pour out his heart; to reveal what he had kept to himself for so many years; to tear down weeks of silence.

Ojas said, 'I like the life I have ... I like it enough to not want anything else.'

His father gazed at him. 'I ... I worry for you. Why are you like this?'

'How am I, Papa?'

'You never speak to me clearly. Ojas, marrying someone is the most beautiful thing.'

'Papa, I ...'

'I see you and think: Why does he want to choose loneliness? My good boy ... what went wrong?'

Ojas fixed him with a glare. 'Nothing has gone wrong, Papa. And I am not lonely.'

'I hope not, son.'

Ojas left the room.

He saw it clearer than ever—the absolute truth would destroy more than it would heal. The family would alter irrevocably. He wasn't ready for what would follow if he spoke in absolute terms.

His mother asked him, 'Should I get the peacocks framed and put it up in your room?'

He regarded the older peacock crewelwork. Still striking. And then the new set. 'Sure, whatever you want.'

He left for Ralph's flat, saying that he wouldn't be home that day.

It was Navami, the ninth day.

At Ralph's, Zubina was leaving when he entered. She went off without a word, without even saying, 'It's you!' Ralph was in bed, looking idly at his phone; Ojas walked in.

'How was your get-together?' Ojas asked.

'I drank too much. How was yours?'

'Pleasant. Aritra had to go for a date, so, we were there for only an hour.'

'Okay.'

'I took my family out after that, which was fun,' Ojas said and touched Ralph's cheek.

'Was it?'

'In a way.'

'How?' Ralph asked.

'Just … they fuss over me so much. Though to be honest, I've only begun to resent such care,' replied Ojas.

'Sometimes, Ojas, I think it all starts there,' Ralph stated as Ojas lay beside him. 'Nothing will work if things there aren't fixed there, you know.'

'Stop talking like Sujoy, Ralph,' scoffed Ojas. 'It's like him to read one of those books and speak this way.'

'I don't need Sujoy or his books to tell you certain truths.'

Ojas drew close. 'Ralph, listen, my family is not like yours. It's very, very different.'

Ralph put his phone away and shut his eyes. They were quiet in the silence of the afternoon; they could hear the chirping of the birds.

Ojas slid closer to him.

They tried falling asleep together, but Ralph began speaking, 'How much will you make me pay for that one error, Ojas? And for how long? The kiss with Aritra was a mistake. It was a big, big mistake. I am so sorry about it. I didn't even like it.'

'I am not punishing you, Ralph,' Ojas said. 'This isn't about him. This is about us ...'

'No, it isn't. It is about that night in Darjeeling. I know it is.'

'That's ...'

'That's all there is. And for fuck's sake, I can't let this continue any longer. You asked me to give things a shot. I did. And it's not working for me.'

Ojas tried making sense of Ralph's words. Ralph rose and burst into tears. Ojas held his face in his hands and said, 'I am here. I am here, baby. Please don't cry.' He pressed his forehead against Ralph's. He could feel Ralph's breath on his nose, even as he said, 'I want to protect us, always.'

Ralph raged at him. 'You're just selfish ... so selfish and self-centred. You never once thought what I wanted.'

With that Ralph grabbed him by the collar, glared at him through his teary eyes and then let go. He sat by the dressing table and wept inconsolably.

Ojas looked out of the window. A few seconds later, he said plainly, 'If you are suggesting we part, I won't let that happen. We will be together. And the way you desire. Just you and I.'

Ojas left the room, stubbing his toe against the chair blocking his way. He went to the balcony and breathed in the afternoon air.

It was Aritra's words from the previous day that reverberated in his mind. That … and his father's fear that he'd lead a lonely life. No, he wanted to tell his father. He wasn't lonely and he'd never be. Surely, what he shared with Ralph was love?

Ralph emerged. He had put himself together. He wrapped his hand around Ojas's waist and let his head rest on his shoulder.

The pain in Ojas's toe felt sharper and spread across his body. He wanted to sit because it hurt to stand any longer.

Was this love or was it an attempt to stave off loneliness? Ojas exhaled and felt as though an answer blew from his lips and got carried away by the breeze.

He thought of the peacocks, their slender necks in a knot.

10

2012. Zubina had given birth to her second daughter. Tausiq, then twenty-two, and his wife were planning a child. He had now been employed for more than a year at a garment factory. Twenty-nine-year-old Zeenat was on the lookout for a house with two rooms, for her mother and her. The old house was falling apart. She did not return home drunk anymore. She took her mother to the doctor when required, and helped cook meals for the two of them. Everything seemed stable. It felt as though the children had finally grown up.

But their lives changed after the winter of that year.

It was a chilly afternoon in Kolkata; the city had witnessed a sudden dip in temperature. Zubina's mother had finished her afternoon round of prayers and sat bundled up in a thick maroon shawl. She found Zeenat packing clothes in a new bag. It did not her take long as she didn't have much to wear—a few sarees with petticoats and blouses, a cardigan, a couple of salwar kameezes, undergarments and toiletries. She wore the abaya over her salwar kameez and asked if she looked fine.

'Mashallah, you look ten times more beautiful in this,' said her mother.

'Do I?' Zeenat asked, then wrapped a shawl around her body. 'Here!' She handed her mother three hundred-rupee notes. 'Keep it in case you need it.'

Nervously, her mother asked, 'Where are you going?'

Zeenat's face shone. 'I am going to Shantiniketan. Only for two days. I have asked Bhai to look out for you. His family will get you food,' she said and looked at her mother with love.

Her mother asked, 'Who are you going with?'

The intimacy they had shared seemed to have snapped. Zeenat went silent. Then, as though she couldn't keep it to herself any longer, she said, 'There's a man who I love, Ammi. I have been with him for more than seven years now. This is the first time he's taking me somewhere.'

'Seven years! Why don't you marry him?'

'Well,' Zeenat hesitated and sighed. She tried hiding the sadness in her eyes, 'He's ... uh, he's married.'

'Oh ... he can't leave her and marry you?' She tried to suppress the urge to admonish her daughter. Sleeping with another woman's man, the shame!

'It's ... it's not so easy. I mean, we are thinking ... but ... anyway, I need to get going.'

With that, she was off in the black abaya, with her bag, like she was a princess. A motorbike sputtered noisily and halted in the lane. She was supposed to hop on and reach Howrah Station, where her lover waited. The driver of the motorbike worked for her lover. She greeted him and sat facing left, holding on to the bag tightly.

The mid-afternoon journey from Park Circus to Howrah Station was not without its hiccups. Too many signals. Trams were at a standstill because cars were fighting for space on the tracks. Zeenat remembered the tram rides she took between Gariahat and Esplanade as a teenager during Durga Puja. There were such few trams now. Now and again, the roads were barricaded on account of the construction of a flyover or a metro line. The bike crossed Rabindra Setu and continued at full speed. Zeenat saw the river Ganga below, glistening under the rays of the sun. The fog had melted. People stood to admire the view.

When it was time for the bike to turn left and reach the station, she felt a strong jerk; she found herself falling head-first on to the road. The driver had lost control. He had tried to swerve and apply the brakes but had revved instead, throwing them both off their seats.

The police came. They found Zeenat's phone ringing; it was Daanish. He was informed about the accident. Instead of going there, he called Tausiq. Daanish disappeared from the scene while Zeenat and the driver were taken to the hospital. They had minor injuries. The driver had fractured an elbow and got a wound on his ankle. Zeenat had broken her lower jaw and grazed her shoulder. Tausiq and his wife were at her side. She told them the truth and felt deep embarrassment. Tausiq said, 'He didn't even come to save you. He vanished. So much for your love, Apa.'

Zubina's heart stopped when Aadil passed on the news of Zeenat's accident; Zubina had been feeding four-year-old Amrin. She was supposed to visit her sister in the hospital the next day, but Soniya was down with a bad cough and she had to run to the doctor. Soniya's maladies persisted for two weeks; by then Zeenat was home.

The next day, along with her two daughters, she reached the house in Park Circus. Her mother was in tears.

'What's the matter?' Zubina asked. She put the baby down and gave Amrin dolls to play with in a corner.

'She's gone,' her mother said, wiping a tear from her cheek.

'What do you mean?'

'She has run away. She said she won't come home again and gave me this.' She showed the folded notes of money.

Zubina gave her water and prepared tea for the two of them. Her mother spoke to Amrin and swaddled Soniya. For a moment, they simply enjoyed each other's company over hot tea.

Suddenly, Tausiq appeared and handed the phone to Zubina, 'You talk.'

'Hello?'

'Zubina, my bachcha!' It was Zeenat.

'Where are you?'

'I have left Kolkata. I have moved to another city. I have a job. He helped me get it. Shoulder is recovering.'

'What are you talking about? You ran away with him?' Zubina couldn't believe it.

'No, no, we can't be together. And ...' she sighed. 'I was tired of being there. I needed to leave. To get out of that rut. But you ...'

Zubina disconnected, 'That randi! Forget her. Just forget her. She will suffer for this.' Tausiq took his phone. Her mother started recounting the many trials she had confronted since Zubina's departure.

In the days to come, Zeenat tried calling many times. Zubina made Amrin write the number down on a piece of paper and took it to the shop to get it blocked. Life assumed a normal pace. Her mother was taken in by her brother. When she passed away, nobody informed Zeenat, but she got to know anyway and sent money to her brother.

Now, Zeenat was in Jamshedpur, working and earning for herself. They did not know if she was married or had a child. It had been years since the three siblings had spoken to each other. When Zubina and Tausiq met, they avoided any mention of an older sister still living somewhere far away. For them, she was dead.

Zubina had dozed off, her head against the wall, while Sona fed Soniya. There was a knock. Zubina woke up with a jerk.

'Come inside!' exclaimed Zubina.

Amrin took anxious steps inside, followed by her father. Sona said, 'There she is. Amrin, where were you?'

When Amrin explained that she had gone to the mela with Yasmin's family because she was bored at home, Zubina had a strong urge to explode with fury. But she stopped herself. She realized that chastising her daughter would do no good. She would only end up repeating the mistakes she had made with her sister.

Zubina distracted herself and asked Amrin about the tiny black heart on her arm. Amrin hesitated and told her it was a tattoo. Soniya (still in her mother's clothes) sulked when she saw it, then made her father promise that he'd help her get one as well.

As Amrin spoke, Zubina wondered if she remembered her aunt. If she missed her when she had stopped calling or dropping by. She wouldn't remember her, of course. Zubina herself had done little to keep her memory alive.

Zubina served the food that Sona had got. She did not reveal how distraught she had been. Amrin settled back into her home; it was as though she had never left it.

The fervour over the puja was over. The girls returned from their tuition classes, exclaiming that they performed well in the test they had taken. Amrin had scored 16/20 and Soniya 10/15. Amrin was overjoyed and showed off her tenses and prepositions. She re-read the sentences she had made using words like 'building', 'friend', 'city', 'girl' and 'home' to her parents, who understood nothing but smiled in appreciation. Only one spelling mistake here and there, but she was able to write sentences, put words together to make sense in English. Soniya rolled her eyes at her elder sister's attention-seeking behaviour and pleaded with her father (yet again) for a tattoo.

Aadil announced, 'Let's go to a cinema hall today.'

Amrin jumped, dropping the sheet of paper with her score, 'Really?'

'What do you say?' Aadil asked Zubina.

Zubina said, 'You go ahead with them. I must clean the house.'

'Ammi' said Amrin, 'come, no. I know I was bad for going away without telling you. I promise I won't do it again. I will always return home on time. I won't leave you ever, Ammi! I am your big girl.'

Tears stung Zubina's eyes. She cleared her throat, 'The house has gathered too much filth. I need to clean.'

Amrin wondered if admitting the truth—that she had gone to see Neha-di and had met with disappointment—would soften her mother. She wanted to tell her how humiliated she had felt; how, the next time she met Neha-di, she hadn't even mentioned the evening; how, all told, she still admired her tutor.

'Start getting ready,' Aadil said, while Zubina continued working. He didn't know what he could do to make her feel better. He wanted her to come to the cinema hall because he wanted to hold her hand—her beautiful hand— in a dark room, while the daughters watched the screen. He missed holding her. His wife. He wanted his Zubina back.

They left in an hour. Zubina breathed a sigh of relief. She took the broom, attached it to a long stick with a firm knot and poked through cobwebs on the ceiling.

Her sister spoke to her through Amrin. Zeenat had managed to plant herself inside Zubina's daughter. Only this time, she claimed she'd never leave and that everything would be fine.

Zubina threw soiled clothes into a bucket—Aadil's crumpled lungi, Amrin's denims, panties with yellow and pink gladioli, Soniya's gingham frock. She sprinkled detergent over them and watched foam rise to the surface.

Mistakes are made by people. Was love Zeenat's mistake? Forbidden love? The thought made her think of Ralph and Ojas. The coldness she had seen growing between them—not like the coldness now between Aadil and her.

Tausiq had been waiting patiently for Aadil's decision. She couldn't bring herself to speak to either Tausiq or Aadil about Delhi.

Zubina let the clothes soak while she did the dishes. She scrubbed them with such vigour that the tips of her fingers hurt.

By the time Aadil returned with the girls, she was done. She didn't wait to hear how their experience was. Aadil was keen to say something, but Zubina snuck out saying she had to rush to work. She let them savour their conversation.

The dogs in the neighbourhood were sound asleep. The cat on Sona's tin roof yawned and stretched. The stall was shut, as was Nazma's shop and house. Sona had gone to her home in Howrah, and Nazma to the hospital. Zubina went past the tailor, who was clearing the scrap outside the workshop. The neighbourhood's old woman squinted at Zubina. She was running her hands through her wispy hair tied with a green rubber band. Zubina drew close and waited for her to speak. She did not want to disrespect her. The old woman asked Zubina to place the spectacles on her nose. Zubina wiped the frames and did as she was told. The old woman regarded her and said, 'Why are you standing there like a doll? Husband hurt you?'

Zubina bit her lips, 'No.'

'Your face looks just like your daughter's. Small and dried up!'

Zubina shook her head and left, saying, 'Salaam.'

LATE AUTUMN

2019

1

Ralph had strung rice lights across his windows. Ojas counted the bottles of wine, cans of beer, packets of cigarettes and kept the porcelain ashtray on the coffee table.

Zubina had coated the chicken and soya cutlets with egg batter and breadcrumbs. She put them in the freezer. She left after taking one long look at the flat she had cleaned for Ralph's party.

'Thank you, Zubina-di,' Ralph said at the door, and offered her money.

She took it and said, 'Enjoy. There will be a lot of work for me tomorrow, it seems.'

Ralph went back to inspecting the house. Ojas told him, 'I'll take care of things. Why don't you change?'

'It's crazy. I have organized so many parties … yet I feel so nervous about my own.'

'I am here, no?' Ojas kissed him.

Ralph swooned as he felt the touch of his lips.

A week ago, when he had embraced Ojas on Navami, he had felt the coldness of his arms. He had wondered if telling Ojas about the Ashtami evening at his colleague's apartment was the right thing to do. A part of him believed there was nothing to lose by confessing. Yet, a part of him also felt that the interaction had been too inconsequential to dwell on—there hadn't even been a kiss. Ojas continued being standoffish, and Ralph didn't push for a conversation. He considered saying something but changed his mind. Ojas had spent most of the evening rubbing his own foot. He didn't say what pained him. Ralph had tried to touch his foot to comfort it, but Ojas complained, 'Not there, please. I hurt it.'

Now, Ralph let himself be kissed. His hand latched on to Ojas's erect penis pushing against his grey sweatpants. Quietly, they went into the bedroom and threw their clothes off. Ralph said, 'I haven't douched.'

Ojas kissed his neck and made Ralph bend over, 'It's okay, baby. I have seen it all.'

They made love and then moved to the bathroom. They showered together and got ready to receive their guests. It was five in the evening.

Ralph's father, Mike, and Sujoy came together. Sujoy apologized, 'Sorry, Ralph. Sayantani couldn't make it. She had work.'

Ralph served a glass of Chardonnay to Sujoy, and red wine to his father. He placed a charcuterie board on the table, with salted crackers, walnuts, grapes, slivers of cheddar, a bowl of cream cheese, a wheel of aged gouda, slices of chicken salami and ham, pickled olive, cucumber and thick cuts of roasted paneer. Mike lapped up the water from his bowl and jounced around the flat, sniffing at Ralph and Ojas. Ojas played with him, offering him a treat. Ralph switched on the evening lights, warm and yellow. He walked to the balcony, from where they could see a hundred windows glowing pink, blue and red. Diwali and Kali Puja were almost here.

He returned to the dining table. Everyone was talking about Sujoy's impending proposal, when the doorbell rang. Ralph went to the door and came face-to-face with a spitting image of a twenty-four-year-old Ojas.

'Hi,' said the young voice, startling Ralph.

'Hello, Sarvesh. Come in!' Ralph ushered him in. He had seen pictures of Sarvesh in the past but had not thought that he'd bear such close resemblance to Ojas. Ralph berated himself for his awkward reaction and offered him a can of beer.

The topics of conversation moved from food to housing in Kolkata and the businesses collapsing in the city, to people wishing to shift elsewhere. Ojas looked at his brother who saw no hope in the city and wished to move out. Ralph's father clicked his tongue and shook his head, as he dipped a cracker in the cream cheese. He said, 'All my life I have spent here while I travelled to other cities in India. And I will tell you, no city is as welcoming and warm as ours.'

'Come on, baba,' Ralph said, 'I remember you said the same thing about Delhi once.'

'Maybe,' his father said, 'but people there are too boka-boka for me. I like it here.'

Sarvesh maintained, 'I think there are better opportunities outside. And we grow by discovering new places. I want to see the world.'

The four men nodded. Ojas shrugged, 'Young people, you know.'

The bell rang again. This time it was Divya in a black halter-neck top and white denims. 'I am so sorry for being this late, my loves.' She entered the flat. She squealed with joy to see the lights. She gave Ralph a bottle of wine she had bought. She sat between Ojas and Sarvesh.

The party moved to the balcony, where there was a pleasant breeze. They lit their cigarettes. Sarvesh and Ralph remained inside sipping their beer.

'Since when have both of you been together?' Sarvesh began.

'Ojas hasn't told you?' Ralph asked.

'No, he never tells me anything. I wish he did though!' Sarvesh's shoulders slouched.

'Since 2017. We will complete two years soon,' answered Ralph, looking at Ojas. Ojas was chatting with Divya and Sujoy. His father smoked in a corner.

'Nice. I wish he told Papa-Mummy about it. I know they won't be happy, still …'

'I know,' Ralph replied. 'Well, at least *you* know now. So that's a first step.'

'Yes, and I think you should come over to our house some time and meet Mummy-Papa.'

'You're inviting me to meet your parents? Even Ojas hasn't suggested that yet!'

'Wait, you haven't been to our house?'

'Uhh … yeah, once, when you all were away.'

'God,' Sarvesh exhaled, turning to look at his brother. 'What a way to keep a secret.'

Ojas was now looking toward Ralph.

'I didn't know my brother …' Sarvesh whispered, observing Ralph and Ojas smile at each other, '… could be so loving.'

'He can be loving and heartless in equal measure,' Ralph said solemnly.

Both of them kept talking, until Mike showed up and tried sniffing Sarvesh. Sarvesh froze. Ralph held Mike by the leash and took him away. Ojas had behaved the same way when he had first met Mike—scared stiff and freezing. The family, it seemed, wasn't used to pets.

Since everyone was now hungry, Ralph heated oil in an iron kadhai and fried the soya cutlets first, then the chicken. The food vanished in no time. Extra wine and beer were served. Ralph warmed bowls of chicken bhuna, mochar ghonto, aloo posto, shukto, mutton kosha and gobindobhog rice. His hands worked at an unexpected pace as he rolled thin discs of luchi lathered with oil on the countertop. The discs went into the kadhai and acquired crisp golden hues. Sujoy asked Ojas to take a seat while he served. Ojas insisted he would help, but finally gave up when Sujoy said sternly, 'Listen to me for once, won't you?'

In the kitchen, Sujoy asked Ralph, 'Are you content?'

'As in?'

'With Ojas, I mean. You seem to be back together … but are you content with the decision?'

'He is a good man. He cares about what makes me happy,' Ralph said, kneading some dough.

'Yes, I guess he does …' muttered Sujoy, then forced a smile. 'I wish I saw what you did … in him, I mean.'

Ralph resumed frying the discs. He ignored Sujoy, who left the kitchen with the bowl of luchi. Sujoy still hadn't forgiven Ojas; perhaps he never would.

Everyone complimented the food—the perfection with which the rice was cooked, the finely seasoned shukto, the balance of sweet and spice in the chicken bhuna. Divya almost cried while licking her fingers smeared with the mutton's dry gravy. 'It's just so good, Ralph,' she said.

'His mother loved making it on Sundays,' Ralph's father added, his voice sad.

Silence followed, but Ralph was quick to break it. 'So, are we still hungry for my coconut macaroons and chocolate mousse?'

The table chorused, 'Of course.'

Ralph brought in a tray of macaroons coated with shredded coconut. In another tray, he planned to bring in garnished chocolate mousse, with a twig of mint and powdered sugar.

Ojas helped him with the mousse in the kitchen and said, 'My favourite.'

'Yes,' replied Ralph, sprinkling sugar. It looked like snowfall.

'Will you marry me?' Ojas asked and placed the mousse on the tray.

'Can we marry?' Ralph asked and added a mint leaf to the mousse.

'Forget what the world allows. Tell me, will you?'

Ralph's eyes lit up. 'Yes, yes, and yes!' Ralph wanted nothing more. He wanted Ojas all to himself. 'Yes, Ojas, I will marry you!'

Ojas kissed him on the cheek and carried the tray.

He refused the nagging memory of the pain in his toes earlier. Love doesn't come easy, Ojas had begun to tell himself lately. Sacrifices have to be made.

In his twenties, Ojas hadn't cared for such sacrifices. Now, at the threshold of forty, he knew that all good things demanded a certain kind of letting go. It was a tough pill to swallow. But he was willing to swallow it to see the glow on Ralph's face—a beautiful face he wanted to smother with kisses. He had begun to remind himself of Ralph's little kindnesses.

Now, Ralph asked Ojas to sit with him for a while. The rage which had left Ralph shaken was replaced with gentleness. He was happy sharing an hour of silence with Ojas, and he was equally happy being with Ojas in the company of others. Ralph planned to prepare a feast every Saturday and call it their date night. He had started having sex with Ojas more often. Ralph bought clothes for him, saying, 'I know what looks good on you better than you do.'

Ojas reminded himself of all of this. He was grateful. He knew Ralph was making an effort. He tried to remove the fear within him that kept asserting itself. Ralph wanted this. And if he—Ojas—asked for anything different, he'd risk losing everything. He'd lose the calm Ralph and he had arrived at with such difficulty.

No, Ojas chided himself, he wanted this, too. A life with Ralph. The only man whose smile made him feel absolute happiness.

Over desserts, at Sujoy's request, Ralph brought his guitar out. He began strumming a tune and the guests swayed their bodies to it. When he was tired, he passed on the guitar to Divya. She swung her head and shut her eyes as she played it. Ojas watched her admiringly.

As the evening progressed, Ralph wondered if contentment meant the company of other people. Mike, who had earlier scared Sarvesh, was now sitting by his side enjoying Sarvesh's belly rub. Sujoy was helping Ralph's father get to the loo; later, he was letting him stretch his tired legs on his lap; he was offering him a last glass of the wine. Divya was fretting over her wedding; she brightened up at the mention of her fiancé's picky habits; how many things they had seen together as twenty-year-olds! Somewhere, in the kitchen of his Alipore house, Ralph's mother was still waiting for Ralph to come and rework the bundt and its lemon glaze that they hadn't perfected the last time. Even this flat, which could not get over its sorrow, was mellowing, as an autumnal breeze wafted in. Ralph was going to marry Ojas soon, and wake up each day deciding to love him, marry him all over again. If contentment was this, what complaints did Ralph have?

2

In Zubina's eyes, Ralph and Ojas had grown rather friendly. Zubina was glad to see that whatever it was that had divided them was now no longer an impediment. She managed to smile at them. She ignored the rising feeling that told her that they were more than friends. Friends did not behave this way. She had enough friends to be sure of this.

Zubina finished her work for the day and said, 'I think the two of you should marry each other.'

Both of them were engrossed selecting clothes for Divya's wedding. They paused when they heard her.

She began giggling. 'Imagine if such a world were possible! How would life go on?' She giggled some more. 'The world would end if men began marrying each other.' She was now hysterical with laughter. Their apartment echoed with it.

She noticed Ralph and Ojas looking glum, and stopped herself. She had meant it as a joke, but they had taken her all too seriously.

Ojas was about to speak, but she saw Ralph's hand go over his thigh to stop him. She swallowed hard. She waited for them to tell her of the true nature of their friendship; then she'd get sacked from her job.

But Ralph simply led her to the door once her work was done. He watched her wear the slippers. He waited until she was in the elevator and said, 'Tomorrow, come early, I have somewhere to be in the evening.'

With that, he closed the door.

She left and sighed with relief. She thanked Allah for saving her from bitter truths. She did not want to lose her job. Ralph paid her the highest of all her employers, was generous with food and was easy with days off and bonuses.

Zubina marched into the November air and pushed away all thoughts of the two men together. But images of them seemed to trail behind her. And they melded with images of her and Aadil.

'No, no, no,' she shook her head, and took a lingering look at the building where Ralph and Ojas stayed.

She visited Nazma. She found her moving meekly around her ailing husband, who was sprawled on the chowki next to their children. Nazma said, 'My sister is helping me keep my shop open.'

'I saw that,' Zubina said, and handed her a box. 'I cooked arbi today.'

Zubina said her goodbyes and walked towards her house. She stopped by the old woman, who complained about the white cat who had betrayed her and run off to the tin roof. The old woman then asked, 'Is your girl back?'

'Yes, she is.'

'Oh, I prayed when I heard she was gone. I thought she had killed herself.'

Zubina opened her mouth to tell her off, then simply made a face at her and marched off to her address.

At home, mechanically, she sorted her clothes and extracted a crumpled sheet of paper from a tin box. The box held some of the jewellery she had worn for her wedding.

Amrin and Soniya were at their evening tuition classes. Aadil wouldn't return anytime soon. She punched in the number written in four-year old Amrin's shaky handwriting.

Her thumb hovered over the call button.

That Ashtami night, when Amrin slept in the crook of her arm, Zubina didn't sleep. She remained wide awake with her eyes closed. Images of Zeenat's confident face when she admitted her love for Daanish, her laughter in the mirror when she bought Zubina jewellery at Bara Bazar, her caring touch when she said 'bachcha' that last time—everything returned as memory. No chronology, no sequence, only a rush of images like rail lines that intersected, joined and moved away from one another, taking her along.

All along, she knew Zeenat lied. She had lied when she said she had grown weary of being home at Park Circus. She had lied afterwards, too. The second her sister's voice reached her on that call, Zubina had heard the deep sigh of failure.

Shame. An emotion that could never assert itself fully in Zeenat.

In her sleep, for the first time in years, Zubina apologized to Zeenat. She sought forgiveness and forgave for the unbridgeable gaps in their relationship and for the pain that bound them both together. Zeenat's face appeared for a moment before her. Zubina found herself moving closer to her.

It was morning by the time she had a restful sleep.

When she woke up, she couldn't remember what it was that had troubled her. Perhaps, she was tired of her family, Zubina thought. Furiously, she deleted Zeenat's number from her call list and put the piece of paper back into the tin box.

Aadil was home. She shut the almirah and started making tea. He said, 'Your brother called again.'

'And?'

'He is leaving for Dilli next week. I told him we aren't going anywhere. We will stay here.'

As the tea came to a boil, Zubina saw her brother finally make a journey to somewhere beyond the city.

Zubina served tea to Aadil and to herself. Aadil asked her, 'What's happened to you?'

'We need a bigger mirror for our home,' she said. 'I can't see myself fully.'

Aadil smiled, 'Is that all? I thought you were sad.'

'Nonsense,' she waved it off, and admired the lines across his face. 'Bhai is getting a good job and our roof is repaired. What's there to be sad?'

'I will get the mirror made,' he said and took a sip of the tea. He couldn't take his eyes off Zubina's face. The things she hid there ...

'Do you feel bad about not going to Dilli?' Zubina asked after a minute.

Aadil gazed at the curtain that fluttered by the doorway. He was reluctant to offer an answer. He finally said, 'Maybe.'

Zubina looked into his eyes apologetically. So many people to apologize to ...

But before she could say anything, Amrin and Soniya came in exclaiming that they had to get ready for a mini-party at Neha-di's house. Neha-di was a graduate and her juniors in college had awarded her: she was the best TikToker of the neighbourhood!

The girls swirled with joy, toppling over the silence in the house.

ACKNOWLEDGEMENTS

My thanks to:

Kanishka Gupta: the agent, who trusted the story and saw the novelist in me.

Dharini Bhaskar: the editor and writer who saw the 'heart' in the book and made it beat more fiercely.

Sohini Basak and Shiva Govind: who read the novel and made me read it with their sharp editorial eye in its early stages.

The team at HarperCollins India: for their continued support, and Veer Misra, particularly, for the cover.

Amit Chaudhuri, Daisy Rockwell, Aruni Kashyap and Hansda Sowvendra Shekhar: for being the early readers of this book. They gave me their time and words. I feel fortunate.

Zaid Al Baset: who read the very first draft and told me to never stop writing it.

My friends: for always listening when I've had to complain and for letting me celebrate the little joys of life with them.

My family: for ensuring I was loved through the years.

'Loved and Missed' on Ralph's mother's grave was taken from Susie Boyt's 2021 novel with the same title.

Lastly, to the authors and their books that I have read over the years. I write because I read; that is the only way I know how to write.

ABOUT THE AUTHOR

Rahul Singh is an academic and a writer based in Kolkata. He works on cities—their infrastructure, planning and governance. Besides this, he writes about books for leading Indian dailies. His short stories have been published in various literary magazines and journals including Sahitya Akademi's *Indian Literature*, *Foglifter* and *Economic and Political Weekly*. Rahul is presently an assistant professor of sociology at St. Xavier's College (Autonomous), Kolkata. *Unfolding* is his debut novel.

HarperCollins *Publishers* India

At HarperCollins India, we believe in telling the best stories and finding the widest readership for our books in every format possible. We started publishing in 1992; a great deal has changed since then, but what has remained constant is the passion with which our authors write their books, the love with which readers receive them, and the sheer joy and excitement that we as publishers feel in being a part of the publishing process.

Over the years, we've had the pleasure of publishing some of the finest writing from the subcontinent and around the world, including several award-winning titles and some of the biggest bestsellers in India's publishing history. But nothing has meant more to us than the fact that millions of people have read the books we published, and that somewhere, a book of ours might have made a difference.

As we look to the future, we go back to that one word—a word which has been a driving force for us all these years.

Read.

Harper Collins · Harper Sport · HARPER FICTION · HARPER NON-FICTION · हार्पर हिन्दी

HARPER LEARNING · HARPER VANTAGE · HCCB HARPERCOLLINS CHILDREN'S BOOKS · 4th · HARPER PERENNIAL

HARPER DESIGN · BOOKTOPUS · HARPER BUSINESS